THE FOUR HORSEMEN

I hope you enjoy

Michael C. W

THE FOUR HORSEMEN

Michael G Williams

iUniverse, Inc.
New York Lincoln Shanghai

The Four Horsemen

iUniverse books may be ordered through booksellers or by contacting:

iUniverse
2021 Pine Lake Road, Suite 100
Lincoln, NE 68512
www.iuniverse.com
1-800-Authors (1-800-288-4677)

ISBN-13: 978-0-595-34488-8 (pbk)
ISBN-13: 978-0-595-79246-7 (ebk)
ISBN-10: 0-595-34488-7 (pbk)
ISBN-10: 0-595-79246-4 (ebk)

Printed in the United States of America

For Savannah and Miller

Acknowledgments

The author would like to thank all those, family and friends alike, who have helped with the development of this book. A special thanks to Dana Herbert and Dr. Mike Richards for their valuable guidance. There are many others without whom this novel would never have been completed and I would like to express my deepest gratitude to each of them as well. To my beautiful wife for believing in me. To my children for their inspiration and imagination. To my parents for teaching me to reach for the stars, even when I might fall. To Patsy Cross, my other mother, for planting the seeds. And to each of you who purchase this book, I would like to offer my humble thanks with the most sincere hope that you enjoy the fruit of my efforts.

"Laws are like spiders' webs: If some poor week creature come up against them, it is caught; but a big one can break through and get away."

—**Solon,** *Athenian Statesman*

PROLOGUE

▼

Jeff Patten was awakened suddenly by a jolt, accompanied by the ominous sound of grinding metal. His eyes quickly sprang open, and he instinctively looked to his side at the large aluminum suitcase that he'd insisted on carrying into the cabin. It was right where he'd left it, but, at that moment, it gave him little comfort.

What now? he thought as the plane lurched violently and started to slowly roll onto its side. He looked out the small window next to his head and saw a long stream of smoke and flames trailing behind the starboard engine. As he stared out the window in disbelief, he could feel the vibrations of the sinister looking storm clouds rumbling all around him. He was gripped with fear, and felt as if the dark clouds surrounding the small twin-engine aircraft were squeezing the breath out of his lungs. An intensely bright flash of lightning streaked through the sky, barely missing them.

We must have been hit by the lightning, he thought to himself.

He looked back down at the suitcase that, the day before, had contained several million dollars. But things hadn't gone as he'd planned, and now the money was safely hidden away and wouldn't be delivered until someone gave him a satisfactory explanation about what was going on and why he'd been lied to. Unfortunately, at that moment, it was looking as though he might never have the chance to get the answers to his questions.

His attention was suddenly refocused when the door to the cockpit swung open. The copilot, feverishly trying to control the plane's descent, looked back over his shoulder and screamed at the top of his lungs. "We're going down! Brace yourself."

Jeff could hear the frantic calls of the pilot yelling into the radio. "Mayday! Mayday! This is Charlie, Victor, Tango, Nine, Nine, Zebra! We've got an engine on fire! We're going down! We're going down! Mayday! Mayday…"

He looked around at the empty cabin that was starting to fill with smoke and wondered how in the hell he'd gotten himself into this, or—more to the point— why. Why hadn't he listened to his wife?

He'd had one of those feelings—that something was wrong—before he'd agreed to make this trip. Who in his right mind would agree to fly across the country to pick up a million dollars in cash for someone he'd never even met face to face?

This certainly wasn't the type of work he was accustomed to, and there were many questions he wished he'd asked, but he was being well paid—in advance— and he needed the money. After all, it was just supposed to be one night. All he had to do was fly to Denver, pick up the money, and fly back home. What could go wrong?

He was a lawyer and should have known better, and it was looking as though his mistake was going to cost him his life. He wondered if anyone would find where he'd hidden the money. Surely someone would find the clues he'd left. He just hoped they would be able to figure them out.

As full-blown panic began to set in, he thought of his wife and daughter. What would they do if he didn't survive? Who would take care of them? His daughter's sixteenth birthday was next month, and he and his wife, Sarah, planned on getting her a car of her own. He thought of his daughter's smile and of his and Sarah's last loving embrace and wondered if he would have a chance to see either of them again.

PART I

CHAPTER 1

———————▼———————

Jeff Patten was a lawyer in his hometown of Chattanooga, Tennessee. After graduating from law school at the University of Tennessee in 1959, he'd moved back home to practice business law with one of the big local firms. It was now 1972, and Jeff had his own law practice.

He'd spent his first six years in the legal profession as an associate, working long hours in the business transactions and real estate departments at Cates & Stanley, one of the most prominent law firms in Chattanooga. After that, he'd been made a partner and continued working at there for another six years. Even though the pay got better, it eventually lost its luster. He'd grown weary of law firm politics and, after much debate and soul-searching, decided to leave the firm and go out on his own.

He'd been out on his own for more than a year. The first few months had been difficult, with many hours spent developing marketing strategies and waiting for the phone to ring. But the business was finally starting to pick up, and the financial situation was improving.

He had a small suite, which—compared to his former office—offered modest accommodations, consisting of a reception area, a file room, and two offices that lined the back wall, taking up half of the space. The offices were separated from each other and from the rest of the suite by plate glass walls that did very little in the way of providing privacy. It was a lot like working in a fishbowl, he often thought, but the rent was cheap, and for now it was all he needed.

He'd been sitting at his desk in his somewhat worn—but still very comfortable—leather chair, working on a contract for one of his real estate clients. He was deep in thought when the sound of the phone ringing in the reception area grabbed his attention. After two rings, he heard the familiar voice of his devoted secretary, Stella Allman.

Stella had been assigned to Jeff on his first day with Cates & Stanley, and she'd been his secretary ever since. When he'd made up his mind to leave, she was the first person at the firm he'd told. He was a little shocked—but very happy—when she'd asked to come along with him.

"Good morning. Patten Law Firm," came Stella's familiar voice as she answered the phone. She was silent for a moment, obviously listening to the caller on the other end, then buzzed Jeff on the intercom.

"Yes, Stella," he said.

"Mr. Patten. It's Mr. Gray on the line. Shall I put him through?"

"Yes Stella…Go ahead."

Mr. Buddy Gray was one of Jeff's new clients and the reason that Jeff had gotten involved in his current predicament. He had recently hired Jeff to set up a corporation in Tennessee that was supposed to get into the real estate development business.

He wasn't quite sure how Mr. Gray had found him. They had talked several times over the phone and he'd said that Jeff had done some work for him in the past when he worked at Cates & Stanley. Jeff didn't remember ever doing work for him, but he had worked with quite a few clients over the past twelve years, and he didn't remember all of them.

"Hello?" Jeff said as he picked up the receiver and put it to his ear.

"Jeff," came his client's familiar, deep voice.

"Yes sir," he replied. "What can I do for you today?"

"Did you get the check I sent last week?"

The check he was referring to was for fifteen thousand dollars and had the word *Retainer* typed in the memo line. Jeff was not likely to forget it because he had done very little work for Mr. Gray up to that point, and fifteen thousand dollars was enough to pay for quite a bit more.

"Yes. Stella mentioned it, and I'm pretty sure that she's already deposited it." Jeff knew good and well that the check had come in, that it had been deposited, and that it had cleared, but he didn't want his client to think that getting big checks was something out of the ordinary.

"Good. Listen, Jeff. I think we're about to start this thing up very soon," said Mr. Gray. "We're talking with some investors and getting the money together to buy some property out near Memphis, which brings me to why I'm calling you."

"What can I do for you?" he asked.

"I'm going to be traveling for the next few days, and I need you to fly to Denver for us and meet with an investor. You can use your retainer to cover any travel expenses."

"Denver, Colorado?" Jeff asked with a puzzled tone in his voice. Was this guy kidding? He wasn't opposed to the idea of an all-expense-paid trip to Colorado. He had spent a good bit of his childhood summers at their family cabin in Gilpin County, about an hour outside Denver. It had been in the family since the early '20s, and his mother still owned the old place, but he hadn't been out there in many years. Since his father's death, his mother hadn't been to the cabin either, but she wouldn't think of selling it.

A family that lived down the road had been watching over the property, and it was occasionally used for vacations by family and friends, but no one had been there—as far as he knew—for a couple of years. Maybe he would rent a car and drive up there to check up on the place and see what kind of shape it was in.

"When will I be leaving?" Jeff asked.

"Today if you can. If you can't make it out there today, then as soon as possible. I was hoping that you would be available for dinner around 8:30 this evening."

"Tonight?" Jeff asked in a bewildered tone.

"If that's possible. Tell me how soon you can leave, and there will be a ticket waiting for you at the Chattanooga airport. It'll be one-way, though. The man you're meeting is arranging a charter to fly you back home tomorrow morning."

A private plane? Jeff thought to himself. This was turning out to be quite a day, and he hadn't even had his second cup of coffee. "I'll need to make some calls and rearrange some meetings, but it shouldn't be a problem to get out there today."

"Excellent! Then you can do it?"

"Yes. Let's see...," he said as he looked up at the clock. "It's just about ten o'clock now. I'll need to run by the house to get a few things together, but I can be at the airport before noon."

"A car will be waiting for you at the Denver airport. It'll take you to the Brown Palace Hotel. It's downtown, and I think you'll love it. I'll get my secretary to reserve a room for you. All you'll need to do is show up and check in."

"The Brown Palace. That is a nice place," Jeff said. "I remember staying there once with my father when I was a kid."

"And who will I be meeting with?" Jeff asked.

"You're having dinner at the Ship's Tavern Lounge this evening. It's a little café downstairs in the lobby. I was going to try to set it up for 6:30 Colorado time. They're two hours behind you. That ought to give you plenty of time to get there and get settled in. You'll be meeting with Tony Darras. He'll have a table reserved in your name. I'll call him after we hang up and let him know you're coming."

"Thanks. I'll be there," Jeff said, trying not to show too much excitement. "That's 6:30 Colorado time, right? I don't want to get that messed up."

"Yeah...that's right, 6:30 Colorado time."

"And...what exactly am I meeting Mr. Darras for?" Jeff asked. "You said he was an investor."

"Yes, he'll be making a pretty large cash investment, and to be honest, Jeff, your role is mainly as a courier. I know it's not very glamorous, but we need someone that we can trust and who can answer any questions he may have about the company. You're familiar with the company structure, and hell...you know as much as I do about the real estate business. I've got some other investors I've got to tend to, or else I'd go see him myself."

"A cash investment?" Jeff asked inquisitively.

"That's right."

"So I'm supposed to just meet Mr. Darras tonight and then fly home tomorrow with the money?"

"You got it, and that's all there is to it. That's why we're paying you the big bucks."

"Sounds fine to me," Jeff said, chuckling. "How large of an investment are we talking about?"

"One million dollars," Mr. Gray said casually. "And given that, we thought it would be safer if you came home on a private plane."

"I would tend to agree" Jeff said, trying to sound as casual as his client.

The conversation should have stopped at that point, with Jeff kindly and diplomatically rejecting his client's query. His instincts told him that there was something not right about Mr. Gray's request. Who in their right mind would ask someone else to pick up that kind of money for them? Especially someone they didn't know that well. He understood that Mr. Gray couldn't go out there immediately, but this was a lot of money they were talking about. Why didn't he just wait a couple of days and fly out there himself?

It always amazed him how complete strangers could put so much trust in a person just because he or she had gone to law school and passed a bar exam.

He knew that the assignment was strange, and something in the back of his head told him not to do it, but then he thought about the fifteen thousand dollars of retainer money he had been given. How could he pass up the opportunity to make what he thought would be easy money? It sounded so simple. Just fly to Denver, get the money, and come home the next day, billing his client for taking a vacation. What could go wrong?

"Good then. You have a good time and enjoy yourself. I'll be coming through Chattanooga in a couple of days to pick up the money. I'll call you when I'm on my way."

"I look forward to finally meeting you face to face, Buddy." They said their goodbyes, and Jeff slowly placed the receiver back in its cradle. He leaned forward across his desk and pressed the intercom button. "Stella…," he said, "will you get Sarah on the phone? Oh, and don't forget, she's visiting her mother's house this week with Patricia. You should have the number."

"Yes, sir," she replied. "Right away."

After a brief moment, the intercom buzzed again. "Mr. Patten," came Stella's voice through the speaker. She had always called him Mr. Patten, even though she was older than he and they had worked together for so many years, but he had never really gotten used to it.

"I've got your wife on the line."

"Thank you, Stella. Put her through, please."

"Here she is."

"Hey, sweetheart," Jeff said into the speakerphone. "How's everything at your mother's?"

"Just fine. Am I on the speaker?"

"Yes, I'll pick up."

Sarah hated to talk on the speakerphone and didn't say anything until she was sure that he had picked the phone up. "What's going on with you?" she asked knowingly. "Stella said you are going to Colorado." It was no secret to Jeff that Stella had a bad habit of overhearing his telephone conversations. The glass wall dividing his office from the reception area didn't offer much in the way of privacy.

"Well, yeah…One of my clients needs me to fly out there for a meeting," Jeff replied. "But it's only for one night. I'll be flying back home sometime tomorrow evening."

"Is it the client that sent you the check? The one you were talking about the other day?"

"That's right."

"He wants you to go to Colorado for him?" she asked in a suspicious tone. "Just like that? On a moment's notice? I thought you said that you thought it was strange that he had sent you that much money. What does he need you to do?"

"Well, he's got some investors lined up, and I'm going out there to meet with one of them. He wants me to pick up some money and bring it back here to Chattanooga."

He knew he shouldn't be disclosing that information, even to his wife, but it wasn't every day that he took off to go out of town at a moment's notice, and he wanted her to feel as comfortable as possible about it.

"Why are you going? Why doesn't he do it himself?"

"Well, he said he's got other obligations and can't make it out there himself. I didn't ask what he was doing." Jeff wished now that he had asked him what could possibly be more important. He was already struggling with his decision to go, but he knew his family could use the money and had already made up his mind. She wasn't making him feel any better about it.

"Are you certain that's all this is about? It sounds kind of suspicious to me." Sarah generally had great intuition. He knew that he should be listening to her, but his excitement and curiosity had already gotten the better of him.

"Well, I guess I'm not exactly certain. I really don't know anything more than what he's told me. But I don't know of anything criminal going on, and there's certainly nothing illegal about carrying money around. All I really know for sure is that we need the money right now. I'm getting paid my regular rate for every hour I spend out there. That's one hundred fifty dollars an hour for twenty-four hours. We can't afford to pass that up right now. He's already sent me a big check; all that he's asking me to do is to have dinner with someone. I'm just supposed to meet the investor at the hotel and answer any questions he's got about the deal. Then he's supposed to give me the money and I'll fly back here with it tomorrow morning. It's that simple."

"And what will you do with the money when you get home?"

"My client is supposed to come through here in the next few days to meet me and get the money. I'm sure it will be all right." He tried to use the most reassuring voice he could muster and didn't dare tell her the amount of money he was supposed to be traveling with. He'd really have to hear about it then. "I'll be flying home on a private plane they've chartered."

"Well," she said hesitantly, "if you think it's all right, then I guess you should go, but I think the whole thing sounds suspicious."

"I'll admit, it sounds a little weird, but I'm sure it'll be fine. Listen, honey, I'll call you tonight after dinner and as soon as I get home tomorrow."

"As soon as you get home?"

"As soon as I land."

"Well, I guess you should enjoy yourself then."

"I will, sweetheart," he said, again in his most reassuring voice. "And don't worry; it's just for one night. I'll be home tomorrow."

"All right. I love you," she said.

"I love you too." He was glad she hadn't asked how much money he was supposed to get. Had she known, she would have truly been suspicious.

After hanging up the phone, he walked over to the file cabinet in the back corner of his office, pulled out his client's file, put on his jacket, and headed out the door into the reception area.

As he walked by Stella's desk, he turned to her and began to speak, but before he could get a word out she said, "I know…I'll take care of everything. You just have fun in Colorado. And be careful, Jeff. I'm with Sarah. I have a strange feeling about this one."

"Don't worry. I'll be careful," he said, smiling. "You sound just like my wife. Try to keep everything in order while I'm gone."

"I will," she said, staring smugly at him. Jeff knew perfectly well that Stella could handle things while he was gone, so he left it at that and walked out the door.

CHAPTER 2

▼

After leaving his office, Jeff stopped by the house to gather some clothes, called a taxi to take him to the airport, and grabbed the keys to the cabin in the off chance that he would find the time to stop by. It would be a shame for him to go all the way out there without at least going by to check things out.

He boarded a 12:30 flight from Chattanooga to Atlanta, and after a brief layover, he was on his way to Denver. He spent his time on the plane reviewing the files he'd brought and thinking about how little he actually knew about his new client. The more he thought about it, the stranger it seemed that Mr. Gray would trust him with that kind of money.

While he didn't know his client that well personally, Jeff had taken a personal interest in his client's business and had studied it in some detail. He was so interested that he had collected some money from his friends and family that he planned to invest in one of the properties his client was buying.

Jeff's plane arrived in Denver that evening a little after five o'clock local time. He'd gained two hours on the way out there and that left him with plenty of time to check into the hotel and freshen up before dinner.

After picking up his suitcase at the baggage claim, he walked out through the revolving glass door onto a large sidewalk bustling with people. He looked up and down the street and saw a short, muscular-looking driver standing next to a cab and holding a sign with his name on it. He walked up to the man, smiled, and said, "I'm Jeff Patten."

"Jeff Patten from Chattanooga?" the cabby asked, eyeing Jeff suspiciously and slowly opening the door to the backseat. Jeff had a feeling that at some point in the past this cabby had picked up the wrong person from the airport.

"That's me."

The driver reached out, took Jeff's suitcase, and loaded it into the trunk. He turned and stepped back onto the sidewalk and opened the door, allowing Jeff to slide past him into the backseat. "I'm going to the Brown Palace Hotel," Jeff said to the driver as he slid into the taxi.

"Yes sir…That's at Seventeenth and Tremont," the cabby said, shutting the door behind him.

"Yeah," said Jeff, "I guess that's it. You'd know better than I would."

"Oh…is this your first time in Denver?" the cabby asked as he climbed into the driver's seat and started the engine.

"No…no…I've been here before. In fact, I stayed at the Brown Palace, but it's been a long time." As they drove off from the airport, Jeff thought about his last trip to Denver with his father. He was fifteen years old, and they had stayed at the Brown Palace on one of their summer trips to the cabin. They had stayed there only one night, and he didn't remember too much about it other than the fact that you could stand in the center of the lobby and see all the way up to the glass ceiling several stories above.

Later that same year, his father became ill and was diagnosed with tuberculosis. Despite all the medical treatment he received, his symptoms got progressively worse, and he died just before Jeff turned sixteen. He had passed away on a Sunday, and Jeff remembered the day all too well. It had been sunny and warm, much like today. He shrugged the thoughts of his father from his mind and focused on his immediate surroundings again. "How far is it from here?" he asked the driver.

"Oh…'bout twenty-five to thirty minutes, I'd say," the cabby said, rubbing his chin as if he was thinking really hard about it. "It really depends on the traffic."

Jeff looked up at the rearview mirror and nodded.

The driver pointed out pretty much anything and everything that could've been of interest. Jeff sat quietly in the backseat listening to the cabby, staring out the windows, and enjoying the view. The Rocky Mountains filled the sky ahead of the cab, and Jeff could see that the taller peaks still had white caps of snow on them from the previous winter.

The traffic was heavy, and it took a little longer than the cabby had said, but, after forty-five minutes, they finally arrived at the hotel.

Jeff stepped out of the cab onto the sidewalk at the edge of Denver's financial district. He looked around at the buildings where those like him toiled away the day in their offices. The hotel was just as he remembered from his childhood. His memory of the place and his last trip with his father once again came flooding back into his consciousness.

The hotel was a triangular building made of sandstone and red granite, standing nine stories tall. It was a very impressive structure, but had obviously been around for a while and, like most of the surrounding buildings, the exterior could have used a good cleaning. Jeff set his bag gently on the ground and reached into his pocket to grab his wallet.

"That's okay, sir," the cab driver said, waving off Jeff's attempt to hand him the money he had just pulled out. "Your fare's already been paid."

"What about a tip?"

"I appreciate that, sir, but it's already been taken care of. Just enjoy your stay and have a safe trip home."

"Thanks," he replied as the driver got back into the cab and pulled away from the curb, heading on down the street.

Jeff turned and walked to the front door of the hotel. He had not been disappointed with the accommodations his client had arranged so far and couldn't wait to get into the hotel to see his room.

The doorman was standing on the sidewalk as he approached the doors. He was an older-looking gentleman who smiled as Jeff walked inside. As he entered the lobby, a young man in a bellhop's uniform walked over to him and reached out to take his suitcase.

"Let me get that bag for you, sir."

"No thanks," Jeff said. "It's just one bag. I can take care of it."

"Are you sure, sir? Let me get that for you."

"All right. If you insist," Jeff said, handing his bag over.

"If you will, please step this way and follow me to the front desk."

He followed the bellhop across the lobby and walked up to the large mahogany front desk.

"Excuse me," the bellhop said to the man standing behind the counter.

"I have a reservation for this evening," Jeff interjected. "The name's Jeff Patten."

The desk attendant looked up from the guest register that was sitting on a pedestal in front of him and said in a friendly voice, "Yes sir, Mr. Patten. Welcome to the Brown Palace Hotel." He spun the large, leather-bound book around in front of Jeff. "If you could please sign in here, sir," he said, pointing at an empty line toward the bottom of the page. "I'll see about your reservation." Jeff picked up a fountain pen that was lying on the counter next to the book and signed his name.

After thumbing through another large book, the attendant looked up at Jeff and said, "Yes sir, Mr. Patten, you will be in suite 420 this evening."

A suite…, Jeff thought blithely. *Now this is the kind of client I like.*

The desk attendant turned and walked back to the wall of cubbyholes directly behind him. Some of the slots contained letters and small packages and others were empty. Most of the empty ones had a large brass key hanging from a small hook next to them. He reached toward the slot marked *420* and removed the key from its hook.

"Take the elevator to the fourth floor," he said, handing the key to Jeff and pointing across the lobby to the glass elevators. "When the doors open, take a right. Your door will be about halfway 'round the atrium on the left. You can just follow the bellman if you like."

Jeff nodded his head in acknowledgment and took the key from the man's hand. He leaned over and started to pick up his suitcase.

"Clark will get your luggage for you, sir," the desk attendant said, motioning for the bellhop to pick up the bag. "Enjoy your stay, Mr. Patten, and please let us know if there is anything we can do for you."

Jeff nodded at the man again and headed toward the elevator. He left his bag sitting in front of the desk for the bellman and moved slowly through the lobby looking around and taking in all of the sights. He stopped for a minute to listen to the music from a grand player piano that sat in the center of a small lounge area.

He made his way to the elevator with the bellhop following closely behind and pushed the "four" button. It started with a lurch and quickly ascended. He turned and looked through the glass walls as the elevator rose through the air. When the door opened, he followed the bellman to his room.

He slid his key in and opened the door, walking in ahead of the bellman. "Just put my suitcase over there by the door, please." He turned to see the bellman standing next to his suitcase and looking eagerly in his direction. "Oh yeah," he said, reaching into his front pocket and fishing out a couple of dollars. "Thanks for the help." He offered the money to the bellman, who quickly reached out and snatched it from his hand, smiled, and walked out of the room, gently closing the door behind him.

*   *   *   *

Jeff looked around and found himself in a nicely decorated room. There were actually two rooms in the suite. He was in the sitting room, and to his right was the bedroom with a large four-poster bed. On either side of the bed were small matching nightstands with Tiffany lamps. The large windows gave an incredible view of the mountains in the distance.

He stood in the sitting room by the window, staring out at the snowcapped peaks and thinking about how strange it was that, just that morning, he had been sitting in his office, and now he was in a suite, at a fancy hotel, halfway across the country, getting ready to have dinner with a man that would be giving him a million dollars in cash. And tomorrow, he would be flying home in his own privately chartered plane. *I love my job,* he thought with a grin.

After standing at the window for a few minutes, Jeff looked at his watch. It was a little after six o'clock local time, and he needed to get ready to meet Mr. Darras. He walked over to the door where the bellhop had set his suitcase and carried it into the bedroom.

He opened his suitcase, removed his files, and set them on the bed in front of him. He pulled out the suit that he had brought to wear to dinner, and, as he expected, it was pretty wrinkled. His wife, Sarah, who was supposed to be gone for only a week, had taken all of their garment bags to her mother's, and he'd had to fold up his suit and put it into his suitcase. *Why does a woman feel the need to carry five times more clothes than she could possibly use?* he wondered as he got dressed. After putting on his suit, he checked himself quickly in the full-length mirror that sat in the corner of the bedroom, picked up the files, and stepped out into the hallway.

He leaned over the brass rail outside his room and looked down on the lobby. The people below milled around on the ornate marble floors. Some carried luggage, others rested on the plush furniture that was placed in an orderly fashion throughout the lobby. In the center of the room was a huge Oriental rug and the piano he'd listened to earlier. Beautiful black onyx columns rose from the floor to the ceiling on all sides, and the last sunlight of the day filtered through the glass ceiling at an angle, softly illuminating the top few floors across the atrium.

He stood there at the railing for a minute or two, watching the sunlight slowly creep up the opposite side of the atrium as the sun made its way behind the distant Rocky Mountains. The lower floors, which were beyond the reach of the fading sunlight, were covered by an ever-growing shadow. As he watched the shadow slowly inch its way up the wall across from him, he was overcome by an unfamiliar sensation. He shuddered at the strange feeling that he was watching the shadow of death itself creeping over him. *Not a good omen,* he thought, slowly turning and walking down the hallway toward the elevator.

Jeff got on the elevator and pushed the button to take him down to the lobby. *I guess I'll sit at the bar for a few minutes,* he thought. He had about thirty minutes to kill and thought a drink might help him relax after spending most of his day traveling.

The elevator descended quickly, and he stepped out onto the polished marble floor. Directly across from him was a fireplace large enough for him to walk into without bending over. He strolled through the lobby and made his way over to the concierge's desk. "Could you point me to the Ship's Tavern Lounge please?" he asked.

"Certainly, sir," came the young man's smiling reply. "It's just through those doors." As he spoke, he pointed to an open set of French doors across the room. Just above the doors was an antique wooden sign with the words "Ship's Tavern" engraved on it.

"Thanks," Jeff said. He walked through the doors and made his way to the bar on the far side of the large room he had just entered. He could immediately see where the Ship's Tavern had gotten its name. It looked like what he imagined to be the typical nineteenth-century New England warf side pub. The walls were covered in dark wooden panels on which were hung several paintings of large sailing ships. There was also an eclectic collection of ships' steering wheels, brass portholes, flags, and other nautical items hanging from the walls.

When he got across the room, he put his file down on the bar and took a seat on one of the red leather stools.

"Can I get you something?" the bartender asked with a warm smile on his face.

"Yes, sir. I'll have a vodka tonic, please."

"Of course, sir. Coming right up." He swiftly mixed Jeff's drink and slid it across the bar. "Anything else sir?"

"No thanks. That'll do it for now," Jeff said. "Can I charge that to room 420?"

"Yes, sir," the bartender said, quickly writing out a ticket and handing it to Jeff. "Sign here please, sir."

After signing the ticket and handing it back to the bartender, he sat staring into his drink and watching the ice cubes spin around the glass as he stirred it with his index finger. He was becoming uneasy and soon found himself thinking about the questions he wished he'd asked his client before getting on the plane. He wondered why the money was being brought to him at this hotel in Denver and not directly to his client. And why cash? Why not just wire the money through a bank or give him a certified check for the money?

Had the money come from something illegal? Had he gotten himself tangled up in some kind of insurance scam? He started to wonder, for the first time, if he might actually be in some danger. Whatever the answers to his questions might be, it seemed a little late to be asking them now.

He tried to clear his head of paranoid thoughts by looking at the file sitting in front of him. He opened it and quickly flipped through its contents, thinking it would be a good idea to do so one last time before meeting with Mr. Darras. It didn't contain much: a draft of a corporate charter he had prepared for Mr. Gray, as well as, a survey drawing and a site plan of some commercial property his client had developed in Florida. He'd asked for more information about the various real estate parcel he'd discussed with his client over the phone, and Mr. Gray was supposed to get something to him, but he'd never gotten a response.

What he got instead was a large check and an unexpected trip out west. *Thank God the trip is only for one night!* He'd have had a nervous breakdown if he had to think about what he was doing any longer than that.

*   *   *   *

After fifteen minutes of sitting at the bar, nursing his drink, and wondering what he had gotten himself into, he heard a deep voice from behind saying his name. He sat up straight on the stool and turned his head to see a man with thick, curly black hair and a dark gray suit standing behind him.

"Are you Jeff Patten?" the man asked.

"Yes," Jeff replied, extending his hand toward the somewhat intimidating figure. "Are you Mr. Darras?"

"No, sir," he replied somberly without offering his own hand. "Mr. Darras is right over there." As he spoke, he motioned toward a booth in the back corner. It was occupied by a man who looked from his receding hairline to be in his early forties.

From across the room, Jeff could see that the top few buttons of Mr. Darras's shirt were left open, revealing a thick gold chain and some kind of golden amulet nestled in his exposed chest hair. They made eye contact, and he waved Jeff over to him.

Jeff stood up from his bar stool and started toward the booth, with the man who had approached him at the bar following closely behind. He couldn't help but think that he recognized Mr. Darras as a character from some old mobster movie.

And who is the guy following me? he wondered. It was probably a bodyguard, and after thinking about it, Jeff decided that if he were walking around with that kind of money, he would have one too.

As he walked up to the booth, Jeff sensed something strange from Mr. Darras. He was wearing a smile, but there was something not right about him. He couldn't quite describe what he was feeling, but it was palpable and disconcerting. When he got to the booth, he leaned forward with his hand stretched out to meet Mr. Darras'.

"Hello there Jeff," Mr. Darras said as their hands met. "Buddy's said some good things about you. It's a real pleasure." He had a remarkably firm grip, and Jeff did his best to match the man's strength.

"Hello Mr. Darras," Jeff replied. "I guess I'm at a little disadvantage here," he said as they released each other's hands. "Mr. Gray didn't tell me very much about you." He felt pretty sure that there was a reason that he didn't know much about either Tony Darras or his client, but this would be a good opportunity to try to get more information.

"That's all right, my friend. Have a seat. And call me Tony." He pointed to the other side of the booth, and Jeff quickly slid in. As he sat down, he noticed the man who had approached him at the bar sitting with another, similarly dressed man at the table closest to their booth.

"It's a pleasure to meet you, Tony," Jeff said, glancing nervously over his shoulder.

Tony looked across the table at Jeff, obviously studying him. "Oh," he said, noticing that Jeff was eyeing his companions. "Don't mind them. They're just here to make sure there's no trouble. It's not every day that I carry around this kind of cash."

"I understand," Jeff replied.

"So how was your flight?" Tony asked, changing the subject.

"It was fine, I guess. There weren't any problems or anything, but flying always wears me out."

"I'm sure your flight home tomorrow will be more comfortable," Tony said, smiling. "You'll have the whole plane to yourself…other than the pilots, that is. But they shouldn't get in your way too much."

"That's very generous of you, Tony. Chartering the plane for me, I mean. I'm sure it wasn't cheap." Tony started to reply but was interrupted by the waiter approaching the table.

"Can I get you gentlemen anything?" the waiter asked. "Something to drink…an appetizer perhaps?"

"You need anything? You want another drink?" Tony asked. "What was that you were drinking at the bar? How 'bout another one of those?"

"Sure," Jeff said, looking up at the waiter. "Vodka tonic please."

The waiter nodded his head and looked over at Tony. "And for you, sir?"

"That's a man after my own heart," Tony said. "Make that two."

"And how about an appetizer?" the waiter asked.

"No. No appetizers tonight. We're just going to have some dinner, unless you want something, Jeff. They got those little snails…what do you call 'em?"

"Escargot," Jeff replied. "But no. I'm fine. I'll just wait for dinner."

"You sure you don't want anything? I'm buying."

"No thanks, Tony."

"Would you gentlemen like to look at the menu?" the waiter asked, setting a large, leather-bound menu on the table in front of each of them.

"Yeah, sure," Tony said. "We'll take a look at those. Thanks."

"I'll give you a few minutes to look over the menus while I get your drinks for you."

"Thanks," Jeff said, looking up at him with a smile. The waiter nodded again and walked toward the bar. When he was gone, Tony pushed his menu to the side and looked back at Jeff. "Where were we now?"

"I was just telling you how much I appreciate the use of the plane tomorrow," Jeff answered.

"Oh…think nothing of it, my friend. It's the least I can do for someone carrying that much of my money across the country," Tony replied with a big smile on his face. "And how do you like your room?" he asked, once again changing the subject.

Jeff couldn't tell whether he was just making small talk to keep the conversation going or whether he was deliberately avoiding any discussion of the money.

"Oh, it's great," Jeff answered. "I've got an incredible view of the mountains."

"That's good. It'd be a shame to come all the way out here to Colorado and not have a good view of the mountains."

"That's the truth," Jeff said, nodding his head in agreement. He looked down at his menu for a minute and then looked back up. Just about everything looked good. "So how do you know Buddy Gray?" he asked.

The question seemed to catch Tony off guard, but he quickly regained his composure and answered as if he hadn't missed a beat. "Oh…Buddy and me. Yeah…well, he and I go way back," he said somewhat nervously. "We've been doing business together for years."

"What kind of business, if you don't mind me asking? I know that real estate development is a fairly new venture for him, but he seems to know what he's doing."

Tony seemed to be a little nervous now that Jeff was asking the questions. Jeff couldn't put his finger on it, but it seemed as though there was something not quite right going on, and with the way Tony acted when confronted with Jeff's simple questions, it was becoming more and more clear that he was intentionally being kept in the dark.

"No. I don't mind. Not at all," he said. But it was clear to Jeff that he did mind. Jeff got the feeling that he was stalling, trying to come up with an answer. "Mostly importing and exporting," he finally said. "You know, a little of this and a little of that. Wherever we can make a little money."

"That sounds like a good strategy," Jeff said smiling, not knowing what else to say. It was hardly the answer he was looking for, but it was apparently all he was going to get. He wanted to know something specific—something he could try to verify once he got back home—but Tony was already nervous and obviously didn't like answering questions. He hadn't exactly gotten a wealth of information about his client, and he felt uncomfortable pushing it, so he decided to back off.

The conversation went on for a while, occasionally interrupted by the waiter, who returned to drop off their drinks and then again to take their dinner orders. When the waiter came to take their orders, Jeff still hadn't figured out what he wanted to eat. Tony recommended the filet mignon and ordered himself one, so Jeff told the waiter to "make it two."

Throughout the evening, Jeff did most of the talking and Tony mostly listened, interjecting every now and then as if to show that he was paying attention. Jeff tried several times to ask if he had any questions about the company he was investing in, but Tony just told him that he trusted Buddy Gray and "if he's putting his money in this deal, then I'm gonna put mine in with it."

"It sounds like you trust Mr. Gray," Jeff said. "But if you have any questions about the company structure, I'll be glad to discuss it with you. That's why he asked me to come out here and meet with you." Tony asked a few questions, but it seemed to Jeff that he was asking them just to satisfy him. He was obviously more interested in his steak and potato than he was in their conversation. From someone putting up this kind of money, Jeff expected a little less apathy.

When they were finished eating, they pushed their plates toward the edge of the table, and Tony looked at Jeff with a serious expression on his face and said, "Well, I guess it's time to give you what you came for."

Jeff, who had loosened up considerably after the two drinks he'd had with dinner, started feeling nervous again. He wanted to ask why they were using this much cash. Why wasn't Tony delivering it himself? And why didn't they just wire the money from Tony's bank account? All sorts of questions had been racing through his head since he'd spoken with his client that morning. He was nervous about taking the money from Tony, but, on the other hand, he wasn't doing anything illegal, and he was being well paid. He was suspicious, and rightfully so, but he didn't want to upset Tony or his client; he wasn't about to accuse either of them of doing anything wrong without any facts to back it up. He would just take the money, go upstairs to his room, and stay there until it was time to go back to the airport tomorrow morning. After all, it was probably all in his head.

"So, you have it here with you?" he asked.

"I sure do," Tony replied. "It's right here under the table." He reached down below the table and lifted a large aluminum briefcase up onto the seat next to him. He patted the case lightly and looked at Jeff with a sinister smile. "Here it is."

Jeff looked at the case and didn't know what to say. He was excited, but more than anything, he was nervous, and he started wishing that he had held off on the filet at dinner and just stuck with the drinks.

"Let's walk out to the lobby," Tony said.

"All right," Jeff replied.

"You take good care of this for me, Jeff. It's a lot of money, and I'd hate for anything to happen to it." Tony's mood was suddenly very serious and he looked at Jeff with piercing eyes.

"Don't worry. I'll guard it with my life," Jeff replied, hoping to put Tony at ease. "I'm going straight to my room after we're finished here, and I'll be there till tomorrow morning."

"Good...good..." Tony said. "And get a good night's sleep, Jeff," he added as the smile he'd been wearing earlier returned to his face. "I'm gonna send a driver tomorrow around 9:30 in the morning to pick you up. Your plane is supposed to leave around 10:30. I figure that ought to give you plenty of time to get to the airport and get loaded up. The pilot is a friend of mine. I use him all the time, so don't worry, you'll be in good hands."

"That's great," Jeff said sincerely. "And I really do appreciate all the hospitality."

"Oh, think nothing of it, my friend. I appreciate you delivering this to Buddy for me." Tony stood up, reached into his pocket, and pulled out a large wad of bills held together in a gold money clip. He slid the bills out of the clip, peeled a hundred off the outside, and tossed it down on the table. He peeled back five more bills until he got to a fifty and then tossed it down on the table too. "That ought a take care of it," he said as he put the money back in its clip and stuffed it into his pocket.

"That should more than cover it," Jeff said, nodding in agreement. "I appreciate the dinner, Tony. It's been a real pleasure."

"Same here."

"I hope we get the chance to do it again," Jeff said politely, but at that moment, all he really wanted was to get back to his room. The thought of going through what had turned out to be such a nerve-racking experience a second time was the last thing on his mind.

They started walking toward the large French doors that led out to the hotel's lobby. Tony was carrying the case, and Jeff walked behind him, unable to avert his gaze.

Tony's bodyguards, who had sat patiently while Jeff and Tony ate their dinner, had already stood up from their table and were waiting for them just outside the doors. When Tony and Jeff walked out through the doors, the men fell in behind them, and the four of them walked together into the lobby.

When they got close to the elevators, Tony stopped, turned, and lifted the briefcase in Jeff's direction. "Here you go," he said. "And remember, Jeff, there's a lot of money in here, so watch your back."

He probably couldn't have thought of a worse thing to say to Jeff if he'd tried. Jeff did his best not to think about having to watch his back as he reached out to take the case from Tony's hand. He had to flex the muscles in his arm when Tony took his hand away and he felt the full weight of the case.

"Heavy, isn't it?" Tony asked with a smirk on his face.

"It sure is," Jeff replied. He was surprised by just how heavy it was.

"Small bills," Tony said, chuckling.

"Should I give you a call when I get back to let you know I made it?"

"No...don't worry about that. Buddy will call me to let me know that you made it all right. You just get a good night's sleep and have a safe trip home tomorrow."

Jeff put his free hand out and shook Tony's. "So I don't need to call you or anything?" he asked, confirming what Tony had just told him.

"No, I'll talk to Buddy tomorrow. If he trusts you, I trust you. Just be careful and everything will be fine."

"Well...I guess this is it then, Tony. It sure was a pleasure meeting you."

"Same here," Tony replied. "I'll see you to the elevators."

"Thanks," Jeff said as he turned and walked toward the elevator doors. He was now very conscious of the case he held at his side. Although he knew it was just his imagination, it seemed to Jeff that everyone in the lobby was looking right at him.

He said a last goodbye to Tony and walked into the elevator. When the doors closed behind him, he felt a rush of relief. He was now in possession of the money and on the way back to his room. As the elevator rose, he looked down at the lobby to see if he could see Tony or either of his bodyguards. They were nowhere to be seen.

When the doors opened again, he cautiously poked his head out into the hallway and looked from side to side. He didn't see anyone and headed straight for his room. When he got to his door, he quickly went inside and set the case down on the bed, looking at it for a moment and imagining its contents. He walked over to the television set and turned it on, then walked back to the bed and sat down.

He tried not to think about the money, but it wasn't long before his curiosity started to get the better of him. He'd never seen that kind of money in one place before and was anxious to have a look. Looking the case over carefully for the first time, Jeff noticed the combination locks next to keyholes on each of the latches that held the case shut, and as he pulled on the latches, he quickly discovered that they were locked. *Oh well...,* he thought. *They wouldn't be stupid enough to leave it unlocked.* He lay back on the bed with his head on the pillow and tried to focus again on the television. He hoped that it would take his mind off the money, but it didn't. He tried flipping through the channels but just couldn't stop thinking about the case at his side.

After staring at the latches for a minute, he decided to have a go at the combination locks. He turned the dials so that the combination on each latch was set to *0-0-0.* He knew it was a long shot and didn't expect it to work, and it didn't come as a shock when his tug at the latches produced no result. *Maybe I could pick it,* he thought, remembering his younger days when, through a lot of trial and error, he had taught himself to pick simple locks. He'd read a spy novel as a young boy and became determined to teach himself to pick a lock. It took him several months to become proficient, and this would be his first real opportunity to use his self-taught skill. All he needed now was a paper clip or a bobby pin. He stood up and walked to the desk where he'd set the file he'd brought, pulling one of the paper clips out.

He tried several times but wasn't able to line up the pins inside the lock mechanism. He wouldn't give up, though, and after nearly thirty minutes of fumbling with the paper clip, both latches were open. His hands were trembling as he opened the case and saw that it was indeed full of money. It appeared that the case was full of one-hundred-dollar bills, wrapped in ten-thousand-dollar bundles. It didn't take long for him to realize that he was looking at much more than a million dollars.

He pulled out the bundles and set them on the bed in hundred-thousand-dollar piles, carefully flipping through every fourth or fifth bundle to make sure that they were all hundred-dollar bills. When he had completely emptied the case he had eight hundred bundles, which amounted to eight million dollars. No wonder it was so heavy.

What the hell is going on? he thought out loud as he counted the last few stacks. They were clearly up to something, and whether he liked it or not, he was now knee-deep in it too. Obviously, they were lying to him. Why had they told him there was one million dollars when there was actually eight million, and what else were they hiding? Whatever it was, he wasn't happy about being involved without his knowledge. He should have listened to his wife. Why would they be sending eight million dollars in cash across the country, and why was Jeff the one carrying it?

He paced around the room, wondering what he should do next. Should he just carry the money back home as he was instructed and act as if he didn't know anything was amiss? Should he try to call his client and tell him that he wasn't going to carry it until he knew what was actually going on? For all he knew, this money was a payoff for a murder or the proceeds from some other illegal venture. Whatever it was, he decided that he wasn't going to be a part of it. If they wanted their money, they would have to explain to him exactly what was going on, and if they couldn't, or wouldn't, then he would be happy to turn the money over to the police, and Mr. Gray and Tony could get it back from them. If they weren't doing anything illegal, then they shouldn't have any problems, but he wasn't about to carry their cash across the country until he knew why he had been lied to. He had too much to lose by getting implicated as a conspirator in some illegal scheme.

What would he do with the money, he wondered, until he had a chance to talk to Mr. Gray? He needed to put it somewhere safe, where no one would find it, and if he was going to do something, he needed to do it immediately. They were expecting him to get on the plane tomorrow morning. He picked up the phone and called down to the front desk. "This is Jeff Patten in room 420. Can you get me a taxi?"

"Yes sir. I'll be happy to," the voice on the other end of the phone responded.

"Great. I'll be down in a minute." He had to go immediately if he was going to pull his plan off. He would be cutting it close, but, if he hurried, he could be back in time to catch his ride to the airport.

He moved quickly around the room getting his stuff back together so that he wouldn't have to mess with it when he got back to the hotel.

When he was finished packing, he walked over and sat down on the bed. The money was still lying in a pile next to the open case. He quickly put the money back into the case, not worrying about how neatly it was arranged, closed the lid, and pushed the latches until he heard them click shut. He gave one last look around the room, picked up the briefcase, and walked out.

CHAPTER 3

▼

Jeff looked down at his watch. It was now 10:45, and he was standing alone on the tarmac waiting for someone to come out of the hangar to meet him. He hadn't slept at all last night and was eager to get on the plane and stretch out. He had gotten back to his hotel just in time to run upstairs, get his bags, and check out before Tony's car arrived to take him to the airport.

He talked with the driver some on the way to the airport, trying very hard not to act nervous or suspicious, but the driver didn't seem to be interested. He had been dropped off with his luggage outside a private hangar where the driver told him to wait, and he had been waiting outside the hangar for a half hour when, finally, a man approached from behind and spoke to him.

"Mr. Patten," the man said unexpectedly. Jeff had been expecting the hangar door to open and was a little surprised when the voice came from the other direction.

"Yes," he said in a surprised voice, turning around to see a tall, thin man approaching him. The guy was every bit of six feet tall and had thick, curly black hair and a big bushy mustache.

"Sorry I'm late," he said as he took off his sunglasses and looked at Jeff. "I'm John Davis, your pilot, and I'll be flying you to Chattanooga." When he got close, he reached out to shake Jeff's hand.

"Good to meet you, John," Jeff said, offering his own hand and trying not to appear too annoyed about having to wait. "I'm Jeff Patten." They shook hands, and after reaching down to pick up his bags, Jeff followed the pilot to a small door leading into the hangar. When they reached the door, the pilot knocked loudly and turned back to Jeff. "We'll be ready to go shortly."

"Thanks," Jeff said as the door to the hangar opened.

The pilot stood outside the hangar for a few seconds talking to the person who had come to the door to let them in and then turned his head toward Jeff. "Come on inside," he said as he stepped through the door. Jeff followed closely behind, carrying Tony's suitcase in his right hand. It was heavier than the suitcase full of clothes he carried in his left, but it didn't feel as heavy as it had the night before.

"That's our ride," the pilot said, smiling and pointing to a white twin-engine propeller plane sitting directly in front of them. "She's a beautiful aircraft, isn't she?" he asked rhetorically. "I'll need to check a few things before we get started, but we should be on the runway in the next thirty minutes or so. If you'll wait here for a minute, I'll have them go ahead and roll the plane out of the bay, and you can get situated."

"All right," Jeff replied, setting his luggage on the ground.

"You need help with those?" the pilot asked, gesturing toward the two cases sitting at Jeff's feet. "I'll have one of the men load them on the plane for you."

"Yes, thank you…," Jeff replied hesitantly. He looked down at Tony's suitcase and then pointed to it. "I'll carry this with me in the cabin if that's okay."

"Suit yourself," the pilot said, waving at one of the hangar attendants who was standing on the other side of the hangar by one of the planes. When he got the man's attention, he called him by name and waved him over. They spoke a few words to each other, and then he came over to help Jeff load his suitcase into the back of the plane.

After everything had been stowed securely in the plane and the preflight check had been completed, the hangar crew hitched the plane to a small towing vehicle and pulled it out of the hangar and onto the tarmac. Jeff followed outside, giving the plane plenty of room to maneuver.

Once they had the plane outside, they stopped and a short set of stairs was wheeled up to the door. The crewman who had helped load Jeff's luggage climbed up the stairs, opened the door to the passenger cabin, and motioned for Jeff to come aboard. Jeff climbed up the stairs and had to bend his head slightly as he stepped through the door.

He'd never been in a private plane before and was pretty impressed when he finally got on board and looked around. There were four rows of plush leather seats. Each row had two seats and was split by an aisle running down the middle of the cabin. At the rear of the plane was a bathroom, and there was a door separating the cockpit from the cabin.

"Make yourself comfortable and have a good flight. The pilot will be with you soon," said the crewman as he started to walk away from the plane and back toward the hangar.

"Thanks," Jeff replied to the crewman as he walked away. He walked to the first row of seats and sat down, setting the briefcase underneath the seat next to him. He made himself comfortable, and after ten minutes or so, the pilot came through the door and looked at Jeff who, by that time, had almost fallen asleep.

"We're just waiting on the copilot," he said, stooping over to squeeze his tall frame through the door. "He should be right behind me."

"Whenever you're ready," Jeff said, yawning.

"Shouldn't be more than a few minutes, and we'll be ready to go. Just make yourself comfortable and enjoy the ride." He obviously noticed that Jeff was tired, because, as he was headed up to the cockpit, he turned around and said, "Those seats recline if you want to nap, and there's pillows and blankets in the compartment above your head."

"Thanks," Jeff said as the pilot climbed into the cockpit. He left the door open behind him for the copilot, who entered a few minutes later, said a quick hello to Jeff (who again had almost dozed off), and then climbed up into the cockpit and sat down in his chair.

The pilots talked to each other for another few minutes, and then Jeff heard the sound of the engines being fired up. The copilot turned to look back into the cabin and said, "We're about ready to go. We're asking the tower for clearance now. Stay in your seat while we taxi and during takeoff. Once we get in the air, you can move around if you need to, but you'll need to stay in your seat as much as possible."

Jeff nodded in acknowledgment to the copilot, who then shut the door between them. *I'm on my way home at last,* he said to himself as the plane taxied to the runway. The plane turned to line up with the runway and came to a complete stop. A moment later, he felt the plane start to quickly accelerate, pinning his head against the seat. He looked out the window watching the ground shrink away below and took a long, last look at the mountains as the plane turned east. Five minutes later, he was asleep.

*   *   *   *

Jeff was startled out of his nap by a sharp grinding noise followed almost immediately by the loud crack of thunder. He knew better, but it felt as though it had come from inside the plane. Scared and confused, he looked out the window again just in time to see a brilliant flash of white light. The plane shook violently and began rolling on its side. He stared in amazement at the flames trailing behind the wing.

The door to the cockpit swung open, and the copilot, who was struggling with the controls, looked over his shoulder at Jeff. "We're going down!" he yelled. "Brace yourself!"

As the fear gripped him, he noticed that they had rolled nearly ninety degrees and were still rolling. He looked out the window again and could see that they were quickly approaching the tops of the trees. He couldn't believe what was going on around him, and was fairly certain that this was the end.

He thought of his family first, but his last thought—before hearing the wings being ripped from the fuselage as they met the tree line—was about the money. He hoped that someone could follow the clues he had left. Would anyone ever find it? What would his client do when he found out the money wasn't on the plane?

CHAPTER 4

▼

It was storming badly outside, but Lieutenant Greg Jackson didn't mind. He had the evening off, and was content to stay in the barracks and read the new book he had bought the day before. It wasn't as if there was anything else to do. He had been stationed at Arnold Air Force Base, just outside of Tullahoma, Tennessee, for the last six weeks and during that time had become quite an avid reader.

The barracks were quiet that evening. There were a few other soldiers in the rec room, playing Ping-Pong and cards, but most of the usual occupants had the pleasure that night of recon training in the woods around the base. The mosquitoes in that part of the country were as bad as Greg had ever seen, including the two years he spent living on a base in the swampy Louisiana backcountry, and it had been raining very hard for several hours. It all made for a horrible day to be doing recon training. He was glad to be inside, even if it was in the barracks.

He heard the door swing open and looked up from his book to see who was coming in. When he saw it was Major Townsend, he quickly sat his book on the footlocker at the end of his bed and got to his feet. Greg had not had the opportunity to observe the major in action, but his reputation preceded him.

"At ease, soldier," the major said sharply.

"Yes, sir," Greg replied, relaxing a little bit.

"How many men do we have in the barracks tonight?"

"Not many, sir. Most of the men are recon training, but there are about ten of us still here, I think."

"Round 'em up and meet me at hangar three with a sidearm and your rain gear in ten minutes."

"Yes, sir. Are we going somewhere, major?" Greg asked.

"I'll explain later. Just round up the men that are here and meet me at the hangar in ten minutes."

"Yes, sir."

The major turned and walked back out to his waiting jeep and drove off. Greg quickly put on his fatigues and rounded up the other men that were in the barracks. None of them were happy about interrupting their down time to go out into the rain, but Greg explained that the instructions came directly from Major Townsend and were not subject to discussion. They quickly got their gear together, put on their ponchos, and headed over to hangar three.

When they arrived at the hangar, the major was standing next to his jeep talking to a colonel that Greg had never seen before. They were leaning over the hood of the jeep studying a map that they had spread out in front of them. When the major saw Greg and the others come in, he motioned for Greg, who was the ranking member of the group, to come over. Greg walked quickly over to the major's jeep.

"Lieutenant, this is Colonel Marshall."

"Good evening, sir," he said, throwing up another sharp salute.

"At ease, soldier," the colonel said as he turned back to the map in front of them. "You see this mountain?" he asked, pointing to a large wooded area about thirty miles from the base.

"Yes, sir."

"A plane went down on that mountain a few hours ago, and we've got to find it."

"One of ours, sir?" Greg asked in a concerned tone.

"No, this was a small civilian aircraft."

"Shouldn't that be handled by the civilian authorities, sir?"

"No, soldier," the colonel said forcefully. "It should be handled by us. Any more questions?"

"No sir." Greg was taken aback by the harshness with which the colonel had replied.

"Good. I want you to put men here, here, and here," he said, pointing on the map to roads that circled the mountain where the plane had crashed. "I want checkpoints set up at the bottom of this mountain on these roads, and I don't want anyone to go up or come down without my express permission. And I mean nobody! Is that clear?"

"Yes, sir!" he replied forcefully.

"It looks like we have about twenty men here. I want a perimeter set up around the entire mountain. Anyone found should be detained and immediately brought to me."

"Yes, sir," Greg said, sounding confused.

"We don't have a problem here, do we lieutenant?" Major Townsend chimed in.

"No, sir. Like the colonel said, we've only got about twenty men here. Any perimeter line is going to be spread pretty thin. We could round up some more men, sir."

"There's no time for that, and we want to minimize the number of personnel involved in this operation. Now, get your men together."

"Yes, sir," Greg said, turning and walking back to the group of soldiers standing inside the hangar. About half of them had come from his barracks and the other half were from another barracks whose soldiers were also doing recon training. They loaded up in three jeeps and a big deuce-and-a-half troop truck, pulled in behind the colonel's vehicle, and headed to the mountain he had pointed to on the map.

The weather improved as they drove, and by the time they got close, the rain had stopped and the clouds were starting to thin out and give way to the star-filled sky. After an hour spent driving through the country along dirt and gravel roads, they reached the base of the mountain, where the colonel's car came to a stop and its occupants got out.

Greg's jeep pulled to the side of the road next to the colonel's and stopped. They were at the intersection of two disused logging roads that had probably been cut by timber companies at some point in the past to harvest the trees from the mountain. He got out and walked over to the colonel, who had spread the map back out over the hood of his vehicle and was standing over it with a flashlight talking to another lieutenant that Greg didn't recognize. "I want two men on this road and two on these other roads. I want these intersections blocked," the colonel said, pointing to the map as Greg approached.

"Yes, sir," the other lieutenant replied.

"And form a perimeter between the checkpoints. This map shows a road that circles the base of the mountain. I want a man every five hundred yards along that road. No one goes in, no one goes out, unless I talk to them first. Got that, lieutenant?" This time he was looking right at Greg.

"Yes, sir."

"My team will locate and secure the crash site. We'll radio you when we've found it. Maintain radio silence until then. If you find anyone, hold them until you hear from me."

"Yes, sir."

"I want to be clear, lieutenant. No one goes up that mountain unless I say so, and you are to maintain radio silence, except in an emergency, until you hear from me!"

"Understood, sir…radio silence," Greg said, feeling a little annoyed at the repeated instructions. He was not happy that he had been dragged out into the rain, at night, to hunt some civilian crash site that shouldn't even be the responsibility of the Air Force. They had civilian authorities to handle these matters. But he had orders (from a colonel, no less), and it was not his prerogative to question them.

He saluted the colonel once again and walked back to the vehicles that had lined up behind them. He relayed the orders to the men and they set off down the road, stopping every five hundred yards or so to drop someone off. About three-quarters of the way around the base of the mountain, Greg told his driver to park their jeep and sent the truck with the remaining men to complete the perimeter. Then he got out and walked to the front of the jeep.

When the truck carrying the rest of the men was out of sight, he sat down on the front bumper and leaned back against the hood. His driver had also gotten out of the jeep and was standing beside him. Greg fished into his pocket and pulled out a crumpled, half-empty cigarette pack and extended his hand up to the other soldier. "Cigarette?" he asked.

"Don't mind if I do," the soldier replied, reaching down to pull one of the cigarettes out of the pack.

Greg pulled one out for himself and then put it to his lips and lit it. He took a drag and looked around as he exhaled the smoke from his lungs. They were standing at the intersection of two dirt roads, in the middle of nowhere, waiting for no one to show up and try to get past them.

"This is ridiculous," he said to the other soldier.

"I don't think we have much choice. I sure don't want to get on the major's shit list. At least we don't have to stay out with the rest of the guys on recon training all weekend."

"That's true," Greg replied reluctantly.

He wondered how hard it would be for the Colonel to find the crash site. The woods were thick in this part of the country and the terrain was steep and hilly.

Blazing a trail through the woods in the darkness would be difficult, at best, and he didn't envy the men who had gone up the mountain to look for the plane.

He wondered why they were even there in the first place. "Do you think we shot it down by accident...or...do you think it might be one of those UFO's?" the driver asked Greg.

"Who knows," he replied.

They stood there talking to each other for almost an hour when they saw headlights and heard vehicles off in the distance coming toward them. They had heard nothing from the colonel since they had split up, but they knew this wasn't him because it was coming from the wrong direction. Whoever this was, they were headed toward the mountain. Most likely for the same reason he was there.

After a minute or so, the first vehicle came into view. As it approached the intersection where Greg was standing, he stepped out into the road with his flashlight to flag them down. He counted the headlights of five vehicles coming up the road toward them.

As the first vehicle pulled up to Greg and stopped, he could see the National Transportation Safety Board emblem on the passenger-side door. He motioned for the passenger of the vehicle to roll down the window.

When the window was down, Greg leaned over and looked in at the two men sitting in the front seat. "I'm sorry gentlemen, this is a restricted area."

"What?" they both replied, looking at each other and then back at Greg. "What do you mean a restricted area?" the passenger asked. "We've got a plane crashed on that mountain, and we gotta get up there."

"I'm sorry, sir. I've got my orders," Greg said. "I'm aware of the crash, but this matter is being handled by the United States Air Force. If you will wait here, sir, you can speak to my commanding officer when he returns from the crash site."

The driver of the car leaned over across the passenger and looked up at Greg. "Son, as far as I know, this is a civilian crash site, and we aren't on a military base. We've got jurisdiction on this, and we're going up that mountain."

"I'm sorry, sir. I was given strict orders not to let anyone up that mountain."

"Son, you don't have a choice," the driver said. "Now you can either let me and my people through, or I'll radio the local sheriff, and we'll let him resolve this."

"I'm sorry, sir. I can't let you past. You'll have to radio the sheriff, but I won't be able to let him past either. The colonel should be radioing down any minute now. If you can wait, I'm sure he'll be able to clear this up."

"Why don't you call him now?"

"I can't do that, sir. I have orders to maintain radio silence. I can't speak to the colonel until he calls me."

"This is bullshit!" the man exclaimed, obviously agitated with the situation. "What's your name, soldier?"

"Greg Jackson, sir...Lieutenant Greg Jackson," he replied calmly.

The man reached down toward the dashboard of his car and jerked the radio microphone out of its bracket. As he put the microphone up to his mouth, he pulled off to the side of the road by abruptly stepping on the accelerator and turning his wheels toward Greg, who had to take a couple of quick steps back to avoid having his feet run over. He looked back over his shoulder at the other soldier, who was still standing next to the jeep but now had an M-16 rifle in his hands. He signaled for him to call for some backup, and as he walked up to the vehicle, the doors swung open and the two occupants got out. The driver walked over to Greg, and the passenger headed back to the vehicle that had been traveling behind them.

"I don't know what the hell you guys are thinking, but the sheriff is on his way over here. What is goin' on up there? Why can't we go up? You didn't shoot the damn thing down, did you?"

"I certainly hope not, sir," Greg said, still wondering himself if that might not be the case. He didn't really know why he was out in the middle of the woods at night looking for this plane. The man in front of him was probably right, and they probably did have jurisdiction over a civilian crash site, but he had his orders, and they were not the ones who would have to deal with the consequences if he failed to follow those orders.

"I hope you know what you're doing, soldier. It looks like the Air Force has really crossed the line on this one."

"Sir, I apologize, but I have my orders. No one, and that means you or the sheriff, is going up that mountain until I hear otherwise from the colonel."

"We'll see about that when the damn sheriff gets here," the man said gruffly as he turned and walked back to the group of people that had been following them in the cars, most of whom had by now gotten out of their vehicles. Greg looked back over his shoulder and noticed that his driver, who had just run down the road, was now running back toward their jeep. Greg suddenly remembered they were under radio silence and realized that his driver had to run to alert the next soldier in the perimeter line. He walked back over to their jeep and waited for him to return.

"I ran down the road and told Private Wilson to get some of the men back here, sir," he said in between heavy breaths as he approached the jeep.

"That was good thinking, private," Greg said.

"Thanks," he replied, leaning over to catch his breath.

Just then, Greg thought he heard a sound coming from the woods alongside the road. He grabbed his flashlight and looked over at the group that he had just stopped. Most of them were out of their vehicles, standing around and talking to each other, but the sound hadn't come from their direction. Some of them had obviously heard it too, because they were also looking off into the woods. He turned back around, told the other soldier to follow, and headed up the road toward the apparent source of the sound.

They walked about a hundred yards up the road and stopped suddenly when they heard it again. This time it was clearly a person's voice. It sounded like it was coming from the nearby woods, just off the road.

They continued walking until they came to an old wooden bridge that stretched across a small, dry creek bed that wound itself down the side of the mountain. The sound seemed to have come from that area, and they stopped at the bridge to listen. They could hear leaves rustling off in the distance, and Greg thought that it was most likely some kind of animal. Then, from the darkness of the woods, they clearly heard someone saying, "Help." Whoever it was, it sounded like they were not far away. Greg and his driver both walked into the woods, using their flashlights to follow the creek bed.

After walking along the edge of the creek for a short distance, they found the source of the sound. It was a man in bloodstained clothes, lying motionless and face down on the ground. They rushed the last few feet to the injured man, nearly tripping over the roots and rocks that littered the ground alongside the creek. Greg dropped to his knees beside the man and gently rolled him over, carefully placing his hand under the man's head for support.

Greg turned to his driver, who was standing over him, and told him to go back to the jeep and get the first aid kit and the stretcher so they could carry him out of the woods and get him to a hospital. The driver immediately jumped up and ran back to the jeep. It wasn't long before he came running back along the creek bed with the first aid kit in hand. There were two other soldiers carrying the stretcher right behind him. Some of the civilians who had pulled up to the intersection earlier had also followed Greg's driver back into the woods, but he had his hands full and didn't pay any attention to them.

Greg had rolled the man over on his back and could see that he had a serious gash across his forehead that had been bleeding heavily. His clothes were ripped and covered in blood from his head wound, but he had apparently been able to cut or tear one of the sleeves off his shirt and use it as a bandage to slow the bleeding. Greg was no medic, but it was obvious that he needed immediate medical attention. They lifted him gently onto the stretcher and headed slowly back down the creek bed toward the bridge.

After they had carried the injured man back to the jeep, Greg looked him over more carefully. He was still breathing, but his breath was shallow, and he seemed to be slipping in and out of consciousness. His arm looked broken at the wrist, and it was obvious from his clothes that he had lost a lot of blood. It seemed to have stopped for the most part thanks to his makeshift bandage, but this man needed to get to a hospital immediately.

By the time they were ready to go, the local sheriff and several other soldiers had arrived at the intersection and were trying to figure out what was going on. As they were leaving, Greg told the sheriff what had happened and asked one of the soldiers to get the colonel on the radio and tell him that the NTSB and the FAA were there and that they had located what appeared to be a survivor and were driving him to the hospital.

"What about the colonel's order to maintain radio silence?" the soldier asked.

"I would call this an emergency," Greg replied. "Just get him on the radio."

They turned the jeep around and pulled out behind the sheriff, who was escorting them to the closest hospital. Greg sat in the back of the jeep where the stretcher was strapped down and talked to the man as he drifted in and out of consciousness, trying to reassure him. He opened his eyes several times. At one point, he looked at Greg as if he wanted to say something but couldn't get the words to come out of his mouth. Greg held the man's hand and leaned over him, telling him to hang on, that help was near, but before Greg could finish his sentence, the man had passed out again. The same thing happened several times during the ride to the hospital. A few times, Greg was able to make out what the man was saying, but it didn't make any sense.

*   *   *   *

They pulled up to the hospital in Shelbyville, Tennessee, about thirty minutes after leaving the mountain. The sheriff had called ahead, and the hospital staff was waiting outside the emergency entrance when they arrived. As they came to a stop, Greg quickly removed the straps that held the stretcher on the back of the jeep, and two large orderlies picked it up and carried the man inside with Greg following closely behind. As he was being carried in, Greg saw the injured man's eyes open. He looked straight at Greg, but then his eyes closed again and he went limp as he slipped back into unconsciousness. Greg tried to follow the man in but was stopped in the lobby by one of the nurses and told to wait.

Greg and his driver sat quietly in the lobby waiting on any news. Nearly half an hour had passed when the colonel walked through the sliding glass doors into the lobby where Greg and his driver were sitting. They immediately jumped to their feet when they saw him come in.

"Where is he, lieutenant?" the colonel asked sharply, dispensing completely with the pleasantries that usually preceded a conversation.

"He's being treated, sir," Greg replied, pointing back to the doors that the man had been taken through earlier. "We were told to stay out here in the waiting room."

"How did he look?"

"He was pretty banged up and had bled a lot, sir. I'm not sure if he's going to make it."

"Was he able to speak? Did he say anything?" The colonel was obviously very worried about this man, whoever he was.

"Nothing that made any sense, sir. He was unconscious most of the time but was babbling something about a key and something about a briefcase or something. It sounded like gibberish to me, sir."

The colonel, who had apparently heard enough from Greg, turned and walked over to the nurses' desk. He leaned over to talk to the nurse, but Greg couldn't hear what he was saying. He appeared to be telling the nurse that he wanted to go back and see the man, and the nurse was apparently refusing his request. After arguing with the nurse for a few minutes, the colonel walked back over to Greg, sat down in the empty seat next to him, and said, "We wait here."

What is so important about this man, and why is the colonel so interested in him? Greg wondered. He couldn't stop thinking about why the Air Force might have been called in anyway. Clearly, this did not seem like a military matter, and the civilian authorities obviously agreed, but he wasn't the one making decisions.

Before long, two soldiers that Greg didn't recognize came into the waiting room and walked toward them. The colonel noticed them coming in the door, got up from his seat, and walked over to meet them halfway. Greg was close enough to hear some of what they were saying, but they were being very careful to speak quietly. They had been looking for something at the crash site but couldn't find it. He heard them saying something about finding some kind of case that was full of phone books. Whatever they had been looking for, the colonel was obviously unhappy about what they'd found.

CHAPTER 5

▼

Jeff Patten opened his eyes slowly. He was in terrible pain and could hear voices all around him, but he couldn't make out what they were saying. He vaguely remembered being on an airplane and that something had gone terribly wrong, but he didn't know where he was or how he had gotten there. He struggled to break through the fog that seemed to fill his head, and a warm feeling began to spread through his body, starting from his fingers and toes. As the feeling spread up his arms and legs, the pain seemed to vanish and his panic and confusion receded into a strange sort of peacefulness. Slowly, the warmth spread over his whole body until all of his pain was gone.

He tried to speak but could not seem to open his mouth. He tried to open his eyes and focus on the people standing around him but could not make out anything more than shadows in the bright light that started to fill his vision. As the light spread, he felt a strange numbness working its way across his body replacing the warmth. When the light completely filled his vision, he had the strange sensation that he was floating and a nagging thought in the back of his mind that he had something to do.

*　　*　　*　　*

Lieutenant Jackson looked down at his watch. He'd been sitting in the waiting room for nearly two hours, and the colonel still seemed agitated. The two soldiers who had come in to talk to him had left nearly an hour ago, and he had been pacing the floors ever since.

The waiting room was nearly empty, and he was starting to fall asleep in his chair when he heard a commotion outside and saw a car pull up and screech to a halt in front of the glass doors that led into the waiting room. A young man jumped quickly out of the car and ran around to the passenger's side. He said something to the woman who was sitting in the passenger's seat and then ran into the waiting room and went straight to the nurses' station. As he approached the nurse sitting behind the desk, he said in a voice loud enough for everyone in the waiting room to hear, "My wife is having her baby right now."

The nurse quickly picked up the phone and motioned to the orderly, who was already on his way over to the door pushing a wheelchair. As he pushed the wheelchair outside, three more hospital employees burst through the emergency room doors into the waiting room. By the time they got outside, the orderly already had the wheelchair sitting next to the car and was talking to the woman in the passenger's seat.

Greg could see from the expression on her face that she was in pain. Two of the men helped get her out of the car and into the wheelchair while her husband stood by, watching helplessly. They rolled her across the waiting room and through the doors into the emergency room with the husband following closely behind.

After a few minutes had passed, the husband came back into the room where Greg was sitting. The nurse, whom he'd talked to when he first came in, was following closely behind with her hand on his shoulder. She escorted him over to a seat against the wall close to Greg, asked him to wait there, and then walked back to the nurses' station.

Greg looked at the man, who was sitting slumped over with his head in his hands. He looked over at the colonel, who was now standing in the corner and talking on one of the courtesy phones, completely oblivious to what was going on around him. Greg stood up slowly and walked over to where the man was sitting. He was obviously distraught and Greg didn't know exactly what he would say to him, but he thought the guy looked like he could use some company.

"I sure hope your wife is okay," Greg said as he approached.

The man looked up at Greg with a bewildered look on his face. "Thanks."

Greg sat down next to him, and they began to talk. He told Greg that they had been driving from Chattanooga to Nashville when his wife started to feel labor pains. The baby was not due for another three weeks, and the doctors could not find its heartbeat. Greg didn't know what to say to the man, so he mostly just listened to his story. He tried to reassure the man that the doctors would do everything they could and that he and his wife would be all right. They sat together for almost an hour, mostly in silence but occasionally talking to one another. The colonel, on the other hand, seemed to be oblivious to all the commotion and continued talking on the phone.

Finally, a nurse walked out into the waiting room and over to where Greg and the man were sitting. Almost immediately, another nurse walked out following the first. The first nurse walked up to the man sitting next to Greg and reached out to take his hand. He looked up at her with the same fearful and bewildered look on his face that he'd had when Greg first spoke to him. The nurse, on the other hand, had a great big smile on her face.

"Congratulations, Mr. Hixson," she said. "Your wife is fine. Would you like to come meet your son?"

The man smiled and reached out to take her hand. Greg could see tears welling up in his eyes. He turned to look at Greg, who stood up and patted him on the shoulder.

"See, I told you everything would be all right," he said, breathing a sigh of relief.

"Thanks again," the man said as he stood up. He shook Greg's hand vigorously and then looked back to the nurse.

"A son?" he said both excitedly and inquisitively. "We thought it was going to be a girl."

Greg watched him as he followed the nurse back through the doors where they had taken his wife. As they walked through the doors, the other nurse spoke up.

"I'm sorry to tell you this," she said in a gentle voice, "but we lost the man that you brought in."

The colonel obviously overheard her because he quickly put the phone down and walked over to them.

"We did everything we could, but he never regained consciousness," she said. "Did you know him?"

"No," Greg replied as the colonel approached.

The three of them stood silently for a few seconds.

"I'll need a minute alone with this nurse, lieutenant," the colonel said.

"Yes sir," Greg quickly replied. He stepped to the side and started walking to the doors that led outside, thinking about how ironic it seemed that he'd watched the end of one life and the beginning of another.

He'd been at the hospital all night, and the sun was just starting to come up. He breathed deeply, taking in the sweet smell of the honeysuckle vines that were growing just outside the door. It had been one of the strangest nights of his life and, despite the tragic ending, he was glad that it was finally over.

PART II

CHAPTER 1

▼

Spring had finally arrived in Chattanooga after an unusually nasty winter. Everywhere he looked, the trees were sprouting new leaves, the flowers were blooming and there was a fresh smell in the humid southern air. The sidewalk below was bustling with people as Jack Hixson looked out of his sixth-floor office window. He had skipped breakfast that morning, and his stomach was starting to grumble.

Jack was an attorney with the firm Cates & Stanley, one of the city's largest and most prestigious law firms. He had graduated from the University of Memphis law school a little over a year ago and was finally starting to settle into the practice of law. He was still not altogether comfortable with his decision to become a lawyer, but it paid well, and he had student loans to pay off, so he was resolved to stick it out. At least until something better came along.

It was almost noon when his phone rang. "Jack Hixson," he said as he put the receiver up to his ear. He heard a familiar female voice on the other end.

"Hello, Jack. This is Patricia Patten…Clark's mother."

"Hello!" he said enthusiastically. "How are you, Patricia?"

"Fine, thanks."

"Clark's not in trouble, is he?" Jack asked, only half kidding. Clark was an old friend of his. They had met in high school and ran around together until Jack moved to Memphis to go to law school. After he left town, he and Clark had completely lost touch with each other, but he still spoke with Patricia occasionally.

"No…this time it's not Clark," she said. "I wanted to see if you could help me with something."

"Sure. What's up?"

"Can you meet me somewhere for lunch one day this week?"

"I was actually just getting ready to get some lunch now," Jack said, remembering how hungry he was. "How about today?"

"That would be great!" she exclaimed. Do you want to meet at that little restaurant in the lobby of the Read House about noon?

"Sure. That'll be fine." Jack replied "I'll get us a table."

"Okay, Jack. That sounds great."

He hung up the phone and went back to large the stack documents sitting in front of him. He was reviewing the mortgage documents for a shopping mall in Panama City, Florida that one of the firm's clients was buying, and had a lot of dull and tedious contract provisions to decipher before he was finished.

When lunchtime came, he happily got up, grabbed his coat from its hanger on the back of his door, and started down the stairs to the street below. On the way down, he bumped into Elizabeth Pierce. She also worked for Cates & Stanley as a paralegal, and Jack knew her fairly well, but not as well as he would like. They had kissed each other after the firm's Christmas party last year, but decided that it would be unprofessional of them to pursue a romantic relationship between coworkers. Actually, the decision had been more hers than his, and Jack always thought it was a pity that they hadn't tried to make it work.

She was such an attractive girl, with long blond hair that hung down over her shoulders, an athletic body, and a beautiful face, and she always smelled so nice. Jack let out a sigh as he thought about the time they'd kissed. Most everyone had left the party, and they had each had a little too much to drink. He had called them both taxis and was waiting for hers to arrive when they started talking. One thing led to another, and the next thing he knew, they were making out in a doorway outside a fancy downtown restaurant.

Jack's daydream ended suddenly when he found that he had misjudged the length of the next step. He had to scramble to catch himself from falling the rest of the way down the stairs. When he regained his balance, he looked down to see her staring right at him with a silly grin on her face. He always seemed to be doing something stupid whenever he got around her, or else she always seemed to come around right when he was about to do something stupid. He wasn't sure which it was yet, but he pushed his embarrassment aside, said, "Hello," and kept walking past her. Once they had passed each other, he couldn't help himself from looking back over his shoulder to catch a quick glimpse of her backside as she made her way up the stairs. *What I wouldn't give for one more chance…*, he thought.

*   *   *   *

The Read House was an old hotel in downtown Chattanooga that had been built in the late 1800s. The Green Room was a restaurant in the hotel lobby. It was kind of pricey, and Jack had never eaten there, but he'd heard they had the best steak in town.

He arrived at the hotel and walked into the Green Room just as Patricia was arriving. They exchanged hellos and she gave Jack a big hug. In a lot of ways, Jack considered her to be like another mother to him. He had spent a lot of time around Clark's house during his high school years, and had gotten to know the family very well.

In the summer after high school, he and Clark had experimented with drugs and ended up in trouble. They had been pulled over with marijuana in the car and she had bailed both he and Clark out of jail. But she never said a word to Jack's parents. She had even helped him pay for his attorney. That was the turning point in Jack's life. He decided that he was going to try to be on the other side of the law next time he was in a courtroom.

After greeting each other, they followed an attractive, young hostess to a small table in the back corner of the restaurant and sat down across from one another. She set their menus down on the table in front of them and walked away. They talked for a few minutes and looked over their menus, and, at least twice, Patricia told Jack how proud she was of him and how happy she was that he was doing well. They talked about Clark too. He had moved out to California to work at a ski resort for the winter and was staying in a house that he and some friends had rented.

"That brings me to why I called you, Jack," she said, looking around as if to make sure that no one was eavesdropping on their conversation. "Actually…I want to talk about my father."

"Okay," he replied curiously. "I don't think I ever met Clark's grandfather."

"You didn't. He was killed in a plane crash in 1972, before Clark was born."

"And what is it that I can do for you?" he asked, wondering why she had called him in the first place.

"Jack, when my father died, he kind of left a mess behind him. You see…," she said, apparently pondering what to say next, or how to say it, "my father was an attorney too."

"Here in Chattanooga?" Jack said in a surprised voice. "I didn't know that."

"Yes. Right here in Chattanooga," she answered. "He actually worked for Cates & Stanley, the firm that you work for now, but he had gone out on his own about a year before he died. Anyway...he had a client that he was helping with some real estate business...or at least that's what they were supposed to be doing."

"What do you mean 'that's what they were supposed to be doing'?" Jack asked.

"They were looking at some property that they were going to develop, and my father was going to invest some money in the deal. Apparently, after my father died, the client just disappeared. My father was left holding money that he had taken from some of his friends and family, but he'd never invested it or turned it over to his client. When he died, there were some people who thought that he had ulterior motives for taking their money and that he was trying to run some kind of scam."

"Was he formally implicated in anything? I mean...were there ever any criminal charges filed against anyone?"

"Well, no. It wasn't like...Nobody actually lost any money or anything. All of the money that my father had collected was right there in the trust account where he normally kept money for his clients. But when the people he had taken the money from still wanted to invest, there wasn't any company to invest in, and they couldn't track down the client he had been dealing with. It looked like he had made the whole thing up."

"I hate to ask," Jack said hesitantly, "but that was a long time ago. Are you sure he wasn't planning to do something with the money?"

"Yes, I'm sure!" she exclaimed without hesitation. "I know my father, and he would never have taken anyone's money. He was not a thief!"

"I'm sorry...," Jack said apologetically. He could see that he had touched on a sore spot. "I didn't mean to imply that he was intentionally trying to deceive anyone. I just wanted to see if it was a possibility."

"It's okay, Jack. I didn't mean to sound irritated. I've just spent the last twenty-eight years defending my father over this, and I guess it's kinda second nature. I know you didn't mean any harm."

"What is it that I can do for you now?" he asked, still not sure where this conversation was leading.

"Remember, I told you that he died in a plane crash?"

"Yes, Ma'am," he replied.

"Well…there's more to it than that. Stella Allman—that was my father's secretary—told both me and my mother that there was supposed to be a million dollars in cash on the plane when it crashed."

"What?" he asked in obvious disbelief. "Are you serious?"

"I'm deadly serious. According to Stella, he got a call from his client the day before he died asking him to fly to Denver to meet with an investor. He was supposed to pick up the cash and bring it back here. Unfortunately, he never made it back."

"Was the money found with the plane?"

"I don't really know for sure, but I don't think so. I got a telephone call from a man the other day who claimed to have been a lieutenant in the Air Force at the same time that my father's plane went down."

"What does the Air Force have to do with your father's crash?" Jack was becoming more confused by the moment.

"His plane crashed into a mountain just north of Tullahoma. This man says that he was stationed at Arnold Air Force Base, which is very near where the plane went down, and that he was there at the crash site. He said that he drove my father to the hospital the night he died."

"Are you serious?" Jack asked incredulously. "And you believe him?"

"Yes, I do believe him. And this is what prompted me to call you." She slowly looked around the restaurant again, scanning each face as though she was afraid someone was watching them. She leaned over and picked up her purse that was sitting in the seat next to her. She set it on the table, reached in, and pulled out what appeared to be a black leather wallet, similar to the one Jack had in his own pocket. "He sent me this," she said, handing the wallet across the table to him.

He reached out and took the wallet from her and opened it up. It had some pictures and an old Tennessee driver's license with the name Jeffery R. Patten on it.

"That picture on top is me and the rest of my family. It was taken a month before my father died."

Jack was silent and looked it over for a moment. "So this is your father's wallet?" he finally asked. "How did he say he got it?"

"His name is Greg Jackson, and, like I said, he told me that he was one of the soldiers that responded to the crash. He says he found my father in the woods near the crash site. A few days later he found this wallet in the jeep they had used to drive him to the hospital. He says he meant to return it but just never got around to it. Anyway…he finally tracked me down after all these years, called me, and told me that he wanted to get the wallet back to its rightful owner. You'll notice that it still has money in it."

"I did notice that," he said, thumbing through a large stack of money that was still in the wallet. "It's strange," he said. "Why would the Air Force respond to a private plane crash?"

"Who knows?" she said inquisitively.

"Well, who was this client? And who was the investor? I would think that they would both be pretty unhappy about losing that kind of money."

"No one really knows who the client was. His last name was Gray, but, like I said, he just vanished after my father's death, and there weren't any documents or records, other than my father's files, that proved his existence. That's why everyone thought that my father was trying to rip them off. And this is where it gets really weird. When my mother and I got home from my father's funeral, our house had been torn apart. Someone was looking very hard for something. The police told us it was probably just a burglary. They said that someone probably read his obituary and then robbed the house while everyone was away at the funeral, but I don't believe that. Nothing was missing. The place was just torn apart. Whoever it was had paid special attention to his home office and to my parents' bedroom. They were obviously looking for something specific, and the man that sent me this wallet told me that they had been looking for something at the crash site too. Obviously, they didn't find it there or they would never have come to our house to search."

"So you think they were looking for the money at your house?"

"I don't know, but it's a theory."

"And you don't think that the money was recovered from the crash site?"

"I don't know the answer to that, Jack. Like I said, the man who returned my father's wallet told me that they had been looking for something that had been on the plane, but they apparently couldn't find it."

"Why would the Air Force be looking for the money?"

"I can't answer that either, Jack. I just don't know."

Jack could hardly believe what he was hearing. "I still don't understand what you want me to do."

"I know that you handle probates and estates," Patricia said quietly.

"Right. I do."

"They keep records of each probate at the courthouse, don't they?"

"Yes, they do."

"I want you to see if you could pull the records from my father's estate and see if there was any mention of fraud or anything relating to the work he was doing just before his death. To be honest, I'm not really concerned about finding the million dollars. In fact, I can't imagine that it would have been sitting around all these years without someone finding it. I just want to see if I can find anything that will prove that my father wasn't a crook."

"Of course. You know I'll be glad to help you any way that I can."

"I knew you would, Jack."

"So you just want me to pull the files from the probate court records?"

"That's it."

"I'll do it."

"Great. But let me tell you one more thing. You need to be very careful when you look into this."

"Why's that?"

"About a week after the funeral, some FBI agents came to our house asking us if my father had ever discussed his work with us, and if we knew what he had been doing in Colorado the day before he died. I remember my mother telling them that she had no idea what he had been doing. She told them that my father made it a point not to discuss his work. That he felt strongly about his clients' right to their privacy."

"But you said she did know about it."

"She knew about the trip to Denver and about the money, but I think she knew there was something strange going on and didn't want to tell them anything. I guess my point is that, between the Air Force responding to the crash and the FBI coming to ask us questions about whether we knew what he was doing in Denver, it appears that the government may have been involved in my father's death. It looks like they were trying to find the money for some reason, and that's why I'm telling you to be careful. I just want to clear his name. I know he didn't intentionally steal anyone's money, and I want to find a way to prove it, but I don't want anyone getting hurt. I think it's important that you know everything that happened so you can decide whether you really want to get involved. And don't worry, I'll pay you for your time."

"I'm not worried about getting paid," he said. "You'll get the family discount. I just hope I can find something that helps."

"I really appreciate it. You probably won't find anything, but it's worth trying. If you don't find anything, no harm done."

It wasn't likely that he would be able to find anything helpful in the probate files, and Patricia knew that, but she wanted to try anyway. Jack was happy to help and wondered if the money wasn't still out there somewhere. It was a strange story that was difficult to believe, but he agreed that it was at least worth a look.

When they were finished eating, Jack paid the check over Patricia's objections, and they headed out of the restaurant and back into the sunshine. When they got outside, they said their good-byes and Jack told her again that he would see what he could do and that he would call her in a couple of days.

"Oh…," he said before turning to walk away. "One more question. You said your father died in 1972. What was the date of the crash?"

"It was August 28th."

"August 28th, 1972," he repeated incredulously. "You know that's my birthday, and I was actually born in the Shelbyville hospital. My parents were traveling to Nashville when my mother went into labor. They pulled into the closest hospital, and I was born there in the Shelbyville emergency room. I could've been there in the hospital with your father."

"Maybe…that would be strange, wouldn't it?"

"Too strange," he said, shaking his head in agreement. As he walked down the sidewalk toward his office, he began to wonder whether his friend's mother had gone a little crazy. *Could her father really have gone out to Denver to pick up a million dollars?* he wondered. Stranger things have certainly happened, but moving that kind of cash around made Jack suspicious and certainly should've made Patricia's father suspicious too. But he had promised Patricia that he would help, and if what she had just told him was true, and the government was involved, then he had better take her advice and be careful.

He would go up to the courthouse the next day to pull the probate files, and see what he could find. He also had an uncle that happened to be an Air Force colonel. He would try to give him a call when he got back to his office and see what he could find out about Lieutenant Greg Jackson and why the Air Force might respond to a civilian plane crash.

CHAPTER 2

▼

Jack arrived at his office early the next morning. He had called his uncle the day before to inquire about the man who had sent the wallet to Patricia. Like Jack, his uncle was also curious about why the Air Force would've responded to a civilian plane crash. "Did it crash on the base?" he had asked. "Or did we shoot it down? I've been in the Air Force for twenty-seven years and I've never heard of the military responding to such a thing. They have civilian agencies that handle those matters." When they got off the phone, his uncle had agreed to make some calls and see what he could find out about the incident and the man who had sent Patricia the wallet.

He sat behind his desk sipping his coffee and looking back and forth between the window and the pile of work sitting in front of him when Elizabeth, the paralegal he'd seen yesterday in the stairwell, popped her head into his office.

"You're here early today," she said.

"Yeah. The early bird gets the worm." As soon as he said it, he felt silly. Could he not think of anything more clever to say? Elizabeth just smiled at him. She had the most beautiful smile.

"So what's going on in here?" she asked.

"Nothing really," he replied. "I'm just looking at some e-mails." He caught a whiff of her perfume and wondered how many times he was going to manage to put his foot in his mouth during this conversation. He seemed to have an uncanny ability to embarrass himself whenever she was around. He was also confused about her intentions. Had she changed her mind about him, or was this just a friendly visit? Either way, she seemed to be smiling at him a lot. Jack had always been a relatively bright kid. He had made straight A's in high school and college and was even in the top ten percent of his class at law school, but he was relatively sure that no matter how smart he was or how hard he worked at it, he would never...ever...understand women.

"So, where were you headed yesterday when I saw you in the stairwell?" she asked. "You looked kind of preoccupied."

"Oh," he said, remembering how he had almost fallen down a flight of stairs. "I had to meet an old friend's mother for lunch."

"That sounds like fun," she said sarcastically.

"Well...it wasn't that bad. She's kinda like my godmother or something. Her son Clark and I were best friends in high school. He and I went our separate ways, but I still talk to her every now and then...you know...just to keep up."

"How is your friend?"

"We didn't actually talk about him very much."

"What did you talk about?"

He began to tell Elizabeth about the conversation he and Patricia had the day before. She listened to his story intently, interjecting with questions every now and then. He told her the whole story about the call Jeff Patten had received from the mysterious client, the sudden trip to Denver, the plane crash, the wallet, and the million dollars.

When he finished the story, she looked at him curiously and said, "I think that would make a good movie, but do you really believe it? The million dollars...I mean, do you think that money is really just sitting somewhere?"

"Who knows where the money is, or if it ever really existed, but that's what she was told, and that's the story she told me. It isn't the money she's after. Her husband is a cardiologist and they live in a great big house on the mountain. I think they've got plenty of money. Before her father died in the crash, he had taken some money from some of his friends and family that he said he planned to invest in his client's real estate project. After he died, it turned out that the company he was supposedly going to invest their money in didn't even exist. Some of them thought that he might have been trying to swindle them out of their money and just died before he had the chance to spend it. She just wants to clear her father's name, and I told her I would look into it for her. I've got an uncle who is in the Air Force. I called him yesterday and asked him to make some phone calls to see if he could find out anything about the soldier who sent her father's wallet to her. Obviously, he was with her father at some point before he died. How else would he have gotten the wallet?"

"What about your uncle? Has he called you back?"

"No, not yet. I suspect that it will take him a couple of days to find anything."

"It seems strange that the Air Force would be involved in a civilian plane crash."

"That's one of the things I can't figure out. Patricia thinks the government is somehow involved, and if it weren't for the Air Force responding to the crash and the FBI coming to visit them after the funeral, I would think she's completely crazy. There had to be something out of the ordinary for them to get involved."

"Did you say that her father was an attorney here in Chattanooga?"

"Yeah. In fact, he worked here at Cates & Stanley during the '60s."

"It's a small world, isn't it? Why don't we check with the courthouse and see what we can find there?"

"So you're going to help me?" Jack asked in a surprised tone.

"Sure. This sounds interesting, and you could obviously use my help," she said sarcastically.

"Well, I seriously doubt that we will find anything, but if you want to help, that'll be just fine with me." He thought about the stack of files on his desk and how little extra work he needed to take on right then, but he wasn't about to pass on the opportunity to spend some time with Elizabeth.

"I've got to go up and file something with the probate court this afternoon," she said. "I'll see if I can get the clerk to pull up any records while I'm there. Was his estate was probated here in Hamilton County?"

"Yes, and it would have been done in 1972, but I don't know if they keep the files from that far back. It was more than thirty years ago."

"I'll check and see what I can find. It was a long time ago, but they probably still have archived copies somewhere."

They continued talking for a few minutes, and then she headed back down the hall to her office. Once again, he caught himself sneaking a quick glance at her backside as she turned and walked away. He hated to see their conversation coming to an end, but he really needed to get some work done. He had to meet with clients later that day and needed to spend the rest of the morning reviewing the loan documents he'd been working on. He worked diligently—right up to the meeting, which went well—and was about to call it a day when he heard a knock on his door and Elizabeth came walking in with a stack of papers.

"I found it," she said abruptly.

"You found what?"

"I found Jeff Patten's probate file. You were right. They don't keep the records that far back in the courthouse, but they went across the street for me and pulled the file from their archives."

"That was nice of them."

"I told you you'd need my help. They made copies of everything in the file and called me about a half-hour ago to tell me they were ready to be picked up. And you're not gonna believe this." She sat the stack of paper on the desk in front of him.

"Believe what?"

"Take a look at the name of the firm that filed all of these documents with the court."

Jack looked down at the first page and immediately saw the familiar signature block at the bottom. It read:

> **Respectfully Submitted and**
> **Approved for Entry :**
> **this 8th day of November, 1972**
> **Cates & Stanley, P.C.:**
> **By: _James P. Williams, Esq._**
> **For the Firm**

"That's us!" he said in an excited tone.

"Exactly. We probated his estate. I even recognize the name of the attorney who signed all of these documents. He died several years ago, before either of us came to work here, but I've seen his name around."

"I've heard of him too," he said. "At least I recognize the name. He was the one who had the heart attack and died in the fifth-floor conference room." Jack felt a shiver run down his spine as he said it.

"That's him," she replied. "He died right here in this building."

"What a way to go," Jack said sorrowfully. "Dying at work. That's pretty creepy, huh?

"No doubt about that. I'll tell you one thing. I sure don't plan to die in the office."

"Me neither," he said, laying his hand on the stack of papers she had just brought in. "Have you looked at any of this yet?"

"No," she replied. "I just picked it up and brought it straight back here."

"Okay, I'll take it home with me tonight and look at some of it, but it looks like there's a lot of documents here. Do you want to try to get together sometime to help me?"

"Sure. I'll call down to your office in the morning."

*   *   *   *

Downtown Chattanooga was bordered on the west by the Tennessee River, and Jack lived on the other side of the river. It only took him five minutes to get from the parking garage next to his office to his house. When he arrived, he walked inside and set the stack of papers from Jeff Patten's probate file on the coffee table in the front room.

He lived in a modest, two-bedroom bungalow-style house that he had recently bought. It was mostly furnished with hand-me-downs that he had accumulated from friends and family over the years, but now that he was making a little money, he was starting to think about buying some matching pieces.

The house sat on a hill on a small lot overlooking the river, and he could see the top of his office building from the back porch. Like most nights, he didn't feel like making himself anything for dinner, so he ordered a pizza, picked up the stack of papers, and headed out to the porch. He was hoping to find something in the court records relating to to the alleged fraud in which he'd been implicated—something that would show that the probate court had been aware of it.

He flipped through the pages, scanning each one carefully. He made it through about fifty pages, most of which were standard court filings—the petition for probate of the will, creditors' claims and payment receipts, a detailed accounting of the assets of the estate, and a motion to close the administration of the estate, but couldn't find anything relating directly to the mystery client or any fraud allegations, and he certainly didn't see anything about a million dollars in cash being found. There were some claims filed against the estate by several people who said that he was holding their money, in trust, for investment purposes, and there were receipts showing where money was returned to each of them, but there were no specific allegations of fraud in any of the claims. It looked like a dead end, which is exactly what he expected to find. He would check to see if Cates & Stanley still had their records when he got to work the next day.

*   *   *   *

He arrived at work at his usual time the next morning, got a cup of coffee, and sat down at his desk to read through the morning paper. Around 9:30, Elizabeth walked into his office wearing her beautiful smile.

"Did you look at the files last night?"

"Yes, I did," he responded, flashing his best smile, "but there wasn't anything there. Just the standard stuff you'd expect to find in a probate file. Nothing out of the ordinary, and nothing that would help Patricia."

"What about the money? Did it mention—"

"No," he said, cutting her off before she could get the rest of her sentence out.

"Have you checked to see if we still have a file on it?"

"No, but I thought about that too and was going to try to get it at some point today or tomorrow. I'm sure it'll have some stuff that isn't in the court's file. I don't know if we'll find anything helpful, though. I was gonna send out an e-mail today to see if one of the runners might be going over to our storage. If they are, we'll ask them to look around for us too."

"You're in luck," she said. "I'm sending a runner over there this afternoon to pull some files for another client. I'll have them look for Mr. Patten's file while they're there."

"Good. But I don't think we're going to find anything," he said matter-of-factly. "I looked through all of the documents you got yesterday and didn't see anything helpful."

"Well…I think it's worth a shot. If we don't find anything, then we've wasted a couple of hours. No big deal. At least you've helped your friend's mother out. I'll have the runner look for it. If it's there, I'll bring the file to you this afternoon."

"Thanks Elizabeth," he said as she turned and walked out of his office.

The phone rang shortly before lunch and he was pleasantly surprised when he picked up the receiver and heard his uncle's voice on the other end.

"Hey Jack. This is your uncle Bill."

"Hello, Uncle Bill," he replied cheerfully. "Did you find anything?"

"Well, I called around to some friends up at Tullahoma. They couldn't find any accident reports or anything else about any plane crash on or around the date you gave me. There is a record of a Lieutenant Greg Jackson that was stationed there, though. In fact, he was there at the base until he was discharged or retired in the early eighties. If there was a crash—and I'm not saying that there was or wasn't—but if there was one, and he was there, he didn't file a report."

"So there were no records on the crash?"

"None. There were no records or reports of any civilian crashes, and I didn't think there would be. Like I told you the other day, the military doesn't typically respond to those sorts of things, unless they need some kind of special help. If it's underwater, for instance, the Navy might be asked to help recover the wreckage, but generally that type of stuff is for the FAA and other civilian agencies to deal with."

"Well, I appreciate you checking on it for me. Looks like I'm hitting dead ends all the way around."

"That's okay. It was no problem. Just a couple of phone calls. I do hope you're able to find something, though."

"Thanks Bill. I'm really starting to think this may be a lost cause, but I'm not billing anyone for my time anyway, so it's probably just as well."

He hung up the phone and called Patricia to tell her the bad news. "Looks like we're gonna have trouble finding anything that will help you. I've looked at the probate court file and called my uncle to see if he could discover any records on Lieutenant Jackson or the crash, but neither turned up anything out of the ordinary. I did find some claims filed against the estate where people were asking to get money that they said your father was holding for investment purposes. No fraud is alleged in any of the claims and they don't really tell us any more than you already know. I could call the FAA and the NTSB to see if they have any records on the crash, but I don't think it will help us. They wouldn't have anything about your father specifically."

"Don't bother," she replied. "I guess I forgot to tell you the other day that I had tried that already. I called both of them several years ago when I first started looking into this. They both told me I had to send a written request for information relating to the crash, so I did. The FAA said that they had a file, but it was classified and couldn't be released. The NTSB said they didn't have any records at all relating to the crash."

"The FAA said it was classified?"

"Yes…their response said that all information relating to the crash was classified and required security clearance."

"That's strange," Jack said hesitantly, "that civilian records would be classified."

"That's what I thought too, so I called up there again after I got their letter. The man I spoke to said that they could not release any information to me, and I don't think there's anything we can do about it."

"We could file suit against them under the Freedom of Information Act. You know…to try and compel them to declassify and release the records, but it won't be cheap."

"No, Jack. I really don't want to make a big deal out of it, and I definitely don't want to attract the kind of attention that a lawsuit would bring."

"Well, you're the boss. I've got one more avenue to pursue, but I'm not hopeful. It turns out that my firm represented your father's estate during the probate, and I've got someone digging through our file storage today. I hate to say it, but if our firm's file doesn't have anything more than the probate court's file, then I think we're just out of luck."

"Regardless of what we find, I appreciate everything you've done, Jack."

"I'm glad to help you, Patricia. I just wish we could find something useful."

"Me too. I have been looking into this off and on for fifteen years now and all I ever find is more questions. I'm about ready to just give it up myself."

"Don't give up yet, Patricia. Maybe we'll find something in our files."

"I won't hold my breath and I don't want to take up any more of your time. Just call me if you find anything. If I don't hear from you, I'll assume you didn't."

"I'll call you either way. Maybe we can have lunch again sometime. I really enjoyed seeing you the other day. We need to do a better job of keeping in touch."

"That sounds good, Jack. I'd like that."

"Please tell Clark that I said hi, and tell him to call me sometime. I haven't heard from him in years, and I'd really like to catch up with him."

"I'll tell him," she said. "And thanks again for all your help."

They hung up and Jack headed out for a quick lunch. He was by himself, so he just picked up a sandwich and headed back to his office, where he spent the rest of the afternoon working and waiting for Elizabeth to come by.

*   *   *   *

Elizabeth walked into his office around 5:30 carrying a worn-out-looking accordion file that was crammed full of papers. She walked over to his desk with a smile on her face and dropped it right in front of him.

"I told you I'd find it," she said triumphantly.

"And you did," Jack replied, looking reluctantly at the huge and ancient file that now littered his desk. "Where was it?"

"It was in storage with the closed files," she answered playfully. "Just like I said it would be."

He reached out and put his hand on top of the file and then looked up at Elizabeth. She had an impish grin on her face that he found extremely attractive. Suddenly, a great idea popped into his head. "Do you want to go through this with me?" he asked.

"Sure, if you want. Do you need me to help you?"

"Well, it'd be nice, and it would save some time if we worked together. Besides, I've got a lot of other work to do right now and I'm not billing Patricia for this. You know how the partners love for us to spend time without billing," he said sarcastically.

"Yeah, they love that, don't they," she replied, chuckling.

"Like they love kidney stones. Why don't we get together this weekend and go through the file. We could meet here at the office on Saturday."

"Thanks," she said, "but I try to stay out of the office on the weekends. Why don't we meet at your house?"

This was working out better than he'd imagined. "We can do that," he said, hoping that the smile on his face didn't give away too much. "If you want to come over around lunchtime, we can order a pizza or get some carryout from somewhere."

"Sounds good. Why don't I just pick something up on the way over."

"That'll be great. There're plenty of restaurants nearby." As he spoke, he remembered that his little bachelor pad needed some serious cleaning before he could let Elizabeth see it.

"How do I get there?"

"It's easy. I live right across the river." He gave her directions and they talked for a few more minutes, and then, to his disappointment, she left his office and headed home for the evening.

Jack spent that and the next two nights cleaning up his house. By 10:30 Friday night, he had the house spic-and-span. He finished vacuuming the furniture and carpet, which he had saved for last, and sat down on the couch to relax in front of the TV. He didn't remember falling asleep but woke up on the couch to the sounds of Saturday-morning cartoons. He was still wearing his wrinkled clothes from the night before, his feet were still propped up on the coffee table, and the remote control was still in his hand. He slowly made his way to the kitchen to brew a pot of coffee, looked around at his newly clean house, and thought about how nice it would be if it could stay that way. He was usually too tired to clean it himself when he came home from work, and he certainly couldn't afford a maid, so it usually stayed messy.

He poured a cup of coffee and went back to the couch. After his second cup, he got up to take a shower and get ready.

Just before noon, he heard a car pull into his driveway. He looked out the window and saw Elizabeth getting out of her car.

"Right on time," he said as he walked outside to meet her, smiling like a child on Christmas morning.

"Hey Jack," she said. "I bought us some sandwiches from that little place down the road. I hope you like chicken salad."

"Anything's fine with me really, but I do love chicken salad. Come on in."

She handed the sandwiches to him and followed him inside. "I love your house," she said, looking around as he walked into the kitchen.

"You should've seen it earlier this week. I cleaned it up a little when I found out you were coming over."

"Well, I love it. It's so cute."

"It's small, but it's all I need," he said. "Come on; I'll give you the tour." He walked her through the house, pointing out the improvements he had made since he had bought the place. "I put the tile down in the bathrooms, and a buddy of mine does granite countertops, so I got these and the ones in the kitchen installed for free."

"You did a great job. You'd never know that a lawyer did it. It really looks great."

"Like I said, it's all I need right now," he said as they finished the tour. "Let me go get the file and we can sit in here and eat some lunch while we go through it."

"Okay," she said, standing next to the sliding glass door that led out from the kitchen onto the back porch. "I'm going to walk outside if you don't mind. It looks like you've got a pretty good view of the city from here."

"Yeah, I've got a great view. That's where I usually sit when I get home from work."

"I can see why," she said as she walked outside. She stood in the breeze next to a wrought-iron table and chairs, leaning against the railing and looking out across the river at the city.

"Do you want to eat out here?" he asked, sticking his head through the open doorway. "It's not too hot, and I can bring some plates out."

"Sure. That's fine. It's really nice out here with the breeze and all."

Jack walked out onto the deck, set the file on the table, and then headed back to the kitchen to get the sandwiches ready. "Can I get you something to drink?" he asked. "Coke, Sprite, iced tea, water…?"

"I'll have a beer actually," she replied. "If you have one."

"I'm sure I do," he said as he made his way into the kitchen. He pulled out plates, napkins, and silverware and took them out to the table, then went back inside and grabbed the bag with the sandwiches and two beers. When he was sure that he had everything they needed, he walked back out onto the deck and closed the sliding glass door behind him.

They sat down and began to eat and look through the files. Jack's file was labeled "Expenses" and contained receipts from a funeral home and some from the probate court, along with copies of invoices from his firm. There were various other receipts, most of which he had already seen, showing where the estate had paid claims that had been filed during the probate process. Elizabeth had the "Court Pleadings" file, which was full of motions and other documents that had been filed with the court.

They went through each file carefully, looking at every page, but they found nothing of interest. As it was with the "Expenses" file, Jack had already seen copies of most of the documents while he was going through the probate court's file earlier that week.

"I don't see anything," Elizabeth said sadly as she looked through the last file folder.

"I'm not finding anything either. It looks like we've been on a wild goose chase."

"I think you're right, but there was no harm in trying," she said. "Who knows, this may be the closest we ever get to a million dollars."

When they finished their lunch, Jack got up to take the empty plates back into the kitchen. "You want another beer?" he asked, standing up and reaching across the table to grab her plate.

"Sure, I'd love one. I'll have a couple more if you've got time."

Jack could feel his cheeks becoming flushed. In his excitement, he lost his grip and dropped the plate he was holding, knocking over the empty bottles that sat on the table. He quickly reached down to pick them up and, somewhere in the process, knocked the nearly empty accordion file off the table as well. When it hit the ground, a small blue envelope fell out. He set the bottles back on the table and leaned over to pick up the envelope. "What is this?" he asked curiously. "It must have gotten lost between the files." When he grabbed it, he could feel that there was something in it. He pulled open the flap, which was still glued shut and had obviously never been opened, and, looking inside, he saw a small brass key. "What do we have here?"

"I don't know," Elizabeth said. "What is it? What does it say?"

"It's a key," he said as he turned the envelope over and read the front. "It says 'Colorado Bank & Trust' across the top and just below that it says 'Box No. 240' and the date, 'August 28, 1972.' It looks like a key to a safe-deposit box."

"Are you kidding me?" Elizabeth asked with obvious excitement in her voice. "You mean he rented a safe-deposit box, in Colorado, on the day he was flying home? The day his plane crashed?"

"I don't know if it was him, but somebody rented a box that day. The envelope must have gotten lost in the file years ago. It doesn't look like it's ever been opened."

"But how would the key get into the file at all?" Elizabeth asked. "If he had it on him when the plane went down, I wouldn't think that it would have made it to the probate file."

"Good point," Jack said, rubbing his chin. "I don't know how it ended up here, but it did."

"Are you thinking what I'm thinking?" Elizabeth asked.

"If you're thinking that we need to go see if we can get in this box, then yes...I am definitely thinking what you are thinking."

"The money could be right there, Jack...just waiting for us to go and get it."

"Maybe so, but if he stashed the money there, it's probably gone by now. No one's paid rent on the box in over thirty years."

"I know," Elizabeth said reluctantly. "You sure know how to put a damper on things."

"I didn't say we shouldn't go look. Besides, if the money really has been sitting there for this long, I'm sure it's been forgotten about. If we were to find it, we could just split it up between you, me, and Patricia and keep our mouths shut."

"Now that's what I like to hear," she said as her lips curled back into that incredible smile she had been wearing just a few moments before.

"I'll call Patricia first thing Monday morning and let her know what we've found. I'll see if she wants me to go out there and see what's in the box. At least we could call out to the bank and see if it's still there."

They sat on the deck enjoying the sunshine and talking about what they would do with the money if they found it. Jack was really enjoying her company and didn't want the day to end. He had been focused so much on work lately and hadn't spent enough time pursuing any friendly relationships. He certainly hadn't met anyone recently that he liked as much as Elizabeth. She was beautiful and funny and so easy to get along with. He wondered why she didn't have a boyfriend already.

CHAPTER 3

▼

When Jack arrived at his office Monday morning, he immediately called Patricia to tell her what he had found over the weekend. He wasn't expecting her to be in her office yet and was surprised when she answered her phone.

"Did you find something?" she asked when he told her who it was.

"Yes. Well…maybe. We found something. I'm not sure if it is anything really, but it could lead somewhere."

"Well, what is it?"

"It's a key. Actually, a safe-deposit box key from a bank in Denver. It was rented the day your father flew home and must have gotten lost in the bottom of the file during the probate of his estate. The envelope it was in had never been opened, and I don't think anyone ever checked to see what was in there. I mean, there was no inventory of a safety-deposit box in the probate files or any correspondence from Colorado Bank & Trust. I just don't think anybody realized that this was out there."

Patricia was silent. "What do we do?" she finally asked.

"I suggest we call out there first to see if the bank is still around. Even if it's still in business, you need to keep in mind that this key has been sitting for a long time and that no one has been paying any rent on the box. It's not likely that we will find anything, but if the bank is still open, and they still have the box or its contents, then we should go out there and check it out."

"Jack, I didn't tell you the other day because I didn't think it was important, but when I talked to Lieutenant Jackson, the man who sent my father's wallet to me, he told me that my father kept saying something about a key while they were driving to the hospital. He said my father was delirious and slipping in and out of consciousness at the time, but he also told me that a small group of soldiers went up the mountain to the crash site to look for something, something that they couldn't find."

Jack could barely contain his excitement. "This may be it, Patricia! This may be the key he was talking about."

"I'll pay for it if you want to fly out there, Jack," Patricia said. She too was obviously excited about this turn of events.

"If I fly out there early Monday morning, I can go to the bank to check it out that afternoon and be back home on Tuesday. I'll call the bank today to see what happened to the box and what they're going to need in the way of paperwork so that I can get access to it."

"I'll sign or give you whatever you need, Jack. Just let me know."

"Good! I'll call out there this morning and make sure that Colorado Bank & Trust stil exists. If so, I'll talk to the bank manager and call you back when I know something."

It was only 8:30 in the morning in Chattanooga when they hung up the phone, and Colorado was two hours behind them; Jack had to wait a few hours before making the call. He called information to get the number and to verify that the bank was still operating and that the specific branch office he was looking for was still around. Fortunately it was, and he was able to get a phone number.

He waited until noon, then called and asked to speak to the branch manager. He explained who he was and that his firm had handled the probate of an estate some years back and that the contents of a safe-deposit box rented by the decedent had never been claimed or inventoried. "I'd like to come out and claim the contents of the box," he said, "and I need to know what paperwork I should bring to collect anything that was in there and bring it back here for the beneficiaries of the estate."

"Nineteen seventy-two," the voice on the other end of the call said in a surprised tone. "I'll have to check. We normally turn anything of value over to the state authorities after the lease on a box expires. We do keep some unclaimed items, those that aren't valuable, in our storage for a while, but I've got to tell you that I'm not very optimistic." The manager told him that he would look into the matter and that in order for him to get any of the items that were still around, he would need a picture ID of himself, a death certificate, a notarized affidavit from the beneficiaries of the estate giving him the authority to get into the box, and some kind of court document showing that his firm represented the estate. Luckily, the probate files he had already pulled out of storage and gone through still contained a certified death certificate and the original court documents naming his firm as attorneys for the estate. All he needed now was an affidavit signed by Patricia.

He got on his computer and quickly prepared an affidavit stating that Patricia was the sole surviving beneficiary of Jeff Patten's estate and that he, as the attorney for the estate, was authorized to examine and claim the contents of the box. When he was finished, he called Patricia to tell her the good news.

"I've already prepared the affidavit they requested. Do you want to come by my office to sign it?"

"No, I'd rather meet you somewhere away from your office if you don't mind. I really just want to keep this as quiet as possible."

"That's fine," he replied, thinking she was being a little too paranoid. "I can meet you somewhere, or I come by your house this evening after I get finished up at the office."

"Would you do that, Jack? Would you stop by my house this evening?"

"Yeah sure, I don't mind," he said. "I can be there around 6:30."

"Do you want me to make you some dinner?"

"No…that's okay. I appreciate the offer, though. I'll be there around 6:30."

"I'll be waiting on you."

"Oh yeah, one more thing," he said. "I'd like to set up a meeting with your father's old secretary if she's still around. You said her name was Stella, right?"

"That's right. It's Stella Allman, and as far as I know, she's living in a nursing home downtown."

"We need to see if she knows anything about this key. Who knows what she'll be able to tell us. She might just save us a trip to Colorado."

"That's a good idea."

"You said she lives downtown?"

"Yes. I think it's called Saint Barnabas Apartments."

As soon as they hung up, Jack called Elizabeth into his office to see if she would call over to the nursing home to set up a visit with Stella, which she happily agreed to do.

"You're gonna go with me, right?" she asked.

"Of course," he quickly replied.

"I don't mind," Elizabeth said, "but I can't do it today. I've got a ton of work to do. We'll have to try to go tomorrow."

Jack also had a lot of work piled up on his desk and didn't really have time to go, especially if he was going to fly out to Colorado next week, but he wasn't going to pass up the opportunity to spend more time with Elizabeth away from the office. "Are you sure you don't mind?" he asked.

"No, I don't mind. It'll be like our second date."

Jack could feel his cheeks growing red. "Oh, it's a date?" he said, smiling.

"It sure is, so you need to get dressed up," she replied with a big grin on her face. He was glad to see that her cheeks were turning a little red as well.

"Okay then, it's a date. We'll go see her tomorrow. Call her this afternoon and let her know that we are coming and that we want to ask her just a few questions about her old boss, Jeff Patten? You'll have to look her up in the phone book and find out what apartment she's in. We don't want to just show up unexpected and scare her half to death with a bunch of questions."

"I'll take care of all that," Elizabeth said, still smiling. "Don't worry."

Jack couldn't get enough of her smile. He was definitely starting to develop feelings for Elizabeth that went beyond friendship. Every time she spoke to him (or even looked in his direction) he felt nervous and excited at the same time. His stomach would tighten up into a ball and he would lose the ability to get the words from his brain to his mouth. It was exactly the feeling his mother had described to him in his childhood when he asked her how he would know if he was in love. He knew that he didn't know her well enough to be in love with her, but he sure wanted to have the chance. He even looked forward to spending time in a nursing home as long as she was going to be there with him.

CHAPTER 4

▼

When Jack arrived at his office the next morning, there was a note from Elizabeth stuck to his computer screen:

Talked to Stella. She is expecting us around noon. I'll be at your office at 15 till. Be ready—And remember this is a date. XXOO, Elizabeth

He was grinning from ear to ear as he read the note. Like everything else he knew about her, her handwriting was flawless. She had even written little X's and O's. He picked the note up and lifted it to his nose. It smelled like her perfume. He took in a deep whiff, closed his eyes, and smiled.

He sat in his office working and looking every few minutes at the clock that hung on his wall. He thought 11:45 would never come.

"Are you ready for our date?" she asked when she finally walked into his office.

Jack had always been shy around women and could never have been so forward, but he was glad that she didn't seem to share that trait with him. Even if she was just kidding about it being a date, he liked the sound of it. He couldn't think of anything witty to say in response, so he just smiled his best smile and said, "Yes, I am."

"What...no flowers?" she asked.

"Well," he said. "I would have bought you some, but they didn't have any that were as pretty as you."

"You're sweet, Jack."

He was proud of himself for having finally said something right. "I'm trying," he said softly, as his cheeks turned red again. He wondered if she felt as awkward or got tongue-twisted like he did when they were together. Probably not, but her confidence was one of the things that he liked best about her.

He stood up, walked around from behind the desk, and pulled his coat from the hanger on the back of his door. "Let's go see Stella," he said. "Your note said that she was expecting us."

"She should be. I talked to her yesterday afternoon and told her we were coming over to talk to her at lunchtime, but she seemed a little...you know...a little out of it. I hope she remembers."

Having spent some time in the estate planning business, Jack had dealt with his share of elderly people. The namesake of his own law firm, Mr. Charles Cates, was ninety-three years old, and he still came to work every day. He didn't do a whole lot of actual legal work, but he did come in and sit behind the desk for several hours each day, just as he had for the past 70 years.

Jack enjoyed spending time with older clients, listening to their stories. Most of the elderly he had dealt with were still very much sane and, in some instances, sharp. They usually had great stories from their lifetime of experience. But you never really knew what you were going to get. One day they could be as lucid as he was, and the next day they would be living in a fantasy world full of jumbled and mixed-up memories, dreams, and reality. He was hoping to find Stella, who was now eighty-seven years old, able to remember the events that had happened thirty years ago.

They left the office, and after a short walk, arrived at the Saint Barnabas Apartments. It was a large brick building that had ten floors of apartments. The furnishings in the lobby looked as though they had last been updated when Jeff Patten was still alive. They walked to the desk in the center of the lobby and informed the attendant that they were there to see Stella Allman.

The attendant was a somewhat large black woman in a starched white nurse's uniform. She was an older lady, probably in her mid-fifties, and had a grandmotherly look about her that made you want to crawl up in her lap and hug her around the neck.

"Okay," she said. "Just let me check with Mrs. Allman and see if she's takin' any vis'tors right now. What are your names, please?"

Elizabeth put her hand on the desk next to the base of the telephone that the attendant had picked up. "I spoke with her yesterday on the phone," she said, leaning forward. "Will you tell her it is Elizabeth Pierce and Jack Hixson, and we're here to see her about Jeff Patten?"

"Oh, yes ma'am. I'll tell 'er, but Mrs. Allman has Alzheimer's, you know. She may not remember talkin' to you yesterday, and she may not be able to talk to you today. We'll just have to call up there and see how she's doin'."

Jack and Elizabeth glanced at each other with disappointed looks on their faces. "No, we didn't know that," Jack said.

"Oh my…How long has she had it?" Elizabeth asked.

She's had it since she's been here, and that's goin' on 'bout two years. She's okay most days, but she has her moments. She likes to walk around, ya know, and we can't let her go outside unattended 'cause she might not find her way back. It's a shame really…a real terrible disease. I don't mean to sound so negative, though. She still has her good days too, and she loves to have visitors. She'll be so excited that you stopped by. If she's feelin' all right, that is. Now, are you folks relatives of hers?"

"Oh, no ma'am," Jack said. "We're not family. We're…uh…friends, I guess you could say. I guess friends of friends would be more precise."

"No matter. She'll be happy to see you just the same. You'll need to sign in here while I call her." As she spoke, she handed Jack a clipboard and a pen.

Jack signed his name and looked down at his watch to see what time it was while the attendant called upstairs to Stella.

"It's 11:55," Elizabeth said in a sweet voice. It made him feel good to know that she was paying attention to him. They looked into each other's eyes and smiled.

The nurse was on the phone for less than a minute before turning back to Jack and Elizabeth. "Well, I spoke to Mrs. Allman," she said, leaning her head forward and looking at them over the rims of the eyeglasses that were perched on the end of her nose, "and she say she don't really remember you folks. That being the case, we can't just let you go up to her room, you understand…but I'll have someone go upstairs and fetch her for you. She said she'd come down and talk to you."

"Great. That'll be fine," Jack said, relieved.

"Yes," Elizabeth said in agreement. "That would be just great."

"Well fine. She'll be right down. You folks can have a seat anywhere in the lobby here, and I'll bring her right over to you when she comes down. My name is Mrs. Pearlman, and you folks just let me know if you need anything. There's coffee in the corner over there," she said pointing to a table across the room, "and I'll be right here behind this desk."

"Thanks," Jack and Elizabeth both said at the same time.

They walked over and sat on a couch that was facing a TV. The couch, like the rest of the lobby, looked as though it had been there for quite some time. The exterior walls of the lobby had several large windows stretching from floor to ceiling, providing an abundance of sunlight. The interior walls were concrete blocks painted white, and the air smelled sterile, like a doctor's office. The place was in desperate need of some updating. They sat together and waited on the couch for Stella. Before too long, Mrs. Pearlman came walking across the lobby leading an elderly lady by the arm.

As she approached, Jack and Elizabeth stood up from their seats on the couch and Mrs. Pearlman said, "These are your visitors, Stella. These nice folks have come to see you today."

"Hello Mrs. Allman," Elizabeth said with a big smile on her face. "My name is Elizabeth Pierce. We spoke yesterday on the phone."

"Yes," Stella replied, looking confused.

Mrs. Pearlman obviously felt comfortable with Jack and Elizabeth at that point because she looked at Stella, pointed to the couch, and said, "Stella honey...why don't you have a seat here on the couch and talk to these nice folks. I'll be right over here at my desk if you need anything."

"Thank you, Rose," Stella said as Mrs. Pearlman helped her sit down on the couch and then turned and walked back across the lobby to her desk. Jack pulled up a chair that was sitting close to the couch, and Elizabeth took her seat on the couch next to Stella. They both smiled at Stella.

"Do you remember talking with me yesterday?" Elizabeth asked. "I asked you about your old boss, Jeff Patten."

The mention of Jeff Patten must have set off a lightbulb in her head, because she gave everyone a big smile and looked over at Mrs. Pearlman as if to say that everything was going to be all right. "I remember him," Stella said proudly, as she reached out to take Elizabeth's hand. "He was my boss." She paused for a moment, obviously thinking about something, and then she spoke again. "That poor man died. It made me so sad. He's been gone a long time now." Her smile was suddenly replaced with a frown. She had obviously cared for Mr. Patten a great deal. "What can I do for you young people?"

"Hello, Mrs. Allman," Jack said in a gentle voice. "My name is Jack Hixson. I'm a lawyer like Mr. Patten and I work for his daughter, Patricia. We wanted to ask you some questions about Mr. Patten's death if that's okay with you. Now, I don't want to upset you, so you just let me know if you don't want to talk about it. All right?"

"Oh...you mean little Patsy," she said, smiling at him. "I remember her. She was such a sweet child. She's not in any trouble, is she?"

"No ma'am," Elizabeth said, reaching out and touching Stella's hand. "She's not in any trouble."

"Mrs. Allman, like I told you, I am a lawyer, and I work for Patricia Patten, Jeff Patten's daughter, and this is my paralegal, Elizabeth. We wanted to come see you today to ask you if you can remember anything unusual about the days before Mr. Patten died in the plane crash." He sat silently for a moment, giving what he had just said to Stella a chance to sink in and jog her memory. "Patsy has asked us to look into it and see if her father was doing anything wrong as some people have suggested."

"He would never," Stella said sharply. "I told them all back then that Jeff Patten was a good man. And he was an honest man too. He would never steal a penny from anyone."

"No ma'am," Jack said. "We don't believe he did, and Patricia, or Patsy as you called her, has hired us to prove it. That's why we wanted to talk to you."

"Well, my memory isn't what it used to be, but I'll try to tell you what I can,"

"That's great, Mrs. Allman," Elizabeth chimed in. "We just appreciate your taking the time to see us today."

"We sure do," Jack said in agreement. "Why don't you tell us what you can remember about the situation. Do you know why he had to fly out to Colorado, or who he was working for?"

"I can't remember the gentleman's name," she replied. "But I believe that Jeff was working for a man that lived in Florida. He had never met the man...you know, face-to-face. They had just talked on the phone a couple of times and Jeff had helped him with some property he wanted to buy or was going to help him. He called one morning, out of the blue, and asked Mr. Patten to go to Denver, Colorado and meet with somebody to get some money. The poor thing went out there and never made it back. Bless his heart...his airplane crashed into a mountain on his way home." She stopped for a moment and stared into space, obviously sad at the memory of her former boss's death. "It was such a tragedy."

"You have a great memory, Stella," Jack said, patting her leg to comfort her. "Did he call you from Denver? Did he ever say anything about a safe-deposit box or going to a bank before he came home?"

Stella made a face as if she was straining hard to remember. "He didn't say anything about any of that, I don't think, but he did call me that morning...the morning he got on that airplane, I mean, and told me that something was wrong. He said he didn't know what it was but that he had been lied to. I remember that he sounded just as nervous and scared as I had ever heard him, and believe me, I knew Jeff Patten very well. Did Patsy tell you I had worked for her daddy for many, many years?"

"She sure did," Jack said. "She told us that you were his secretary for a long time and that he could never have gotten along without you."

Stella smiled as Jack told her that Patsy had said those nice things about her. It obviously meant a lot to her to be remembered. "I'm sorry I can't remember everything or be more help to you. It was such a long time ago."

"Oh…no, that's okay. It was a long time ago, and you're being very helpful by telling us what you can remember. Do you happen to remember him sending anything to the office from Colorado? Do you remember him sending you a key or a small blue envelope with the words 'Colorado Bank & Trust' written across the front?"

"I don't remember him sending any kind of key to me. He did send a letter or something to the office from Colorado. It was addressed to his wife, so I didn't open it, but it might have had a key in it. I just gave it to the attorneys at Cates & Stanley."

"Was there anything else that you can remember that you might have thought was strange?"

"Well, I do remember that some people came to my house during the funeral to ask me a bunch of questions."

"What do you mean? Do you mean that people came and asked you questions about Mr. Patten's death?"

"Yes. That's right. There were two of them. One of them was in an army uniform and the other said he was from one of those three-letter things. You know…the FBI or the CIA or one of those. I was sick and wasn't able to go to the funeral. It was so sad. I had worked for him all those years and couldn't even be there to see him buried."

Jack's eyes lit up. "And these people came to your house during the funeral?"

"That's right."

"Did they call first to tell you they were coming?"

"Not that I remember. I thought it was strange that they showed up then, because I should have been at the funeral, not at home."

"What did they want?"

"They asked me several questions about Jeff. Just like you, they wanted to know if he had contacted me before he got on that plane to come home. They were very rude, as I recall. Not at all like you nice folks. I told them just what I told you, but they just kept on and on. They asked me the same questions over and over again, and I just kept telling them that I didn't know anything else. I told them that he had gone to Colorado for one of his clients and that he had told me something was wrong, but he didn't tell me what it was. He didn't even know what it was."

"Is that all they asked?"

"Yes. I believe so. They just kept asking me what he had told me when he called that morning. When they were finally satisfied that I didn't know any more than I was telling them, they told me to forget that they had ever been there to see me, and they were gone just as quick as they came. I never saw those gentlemen again."

"Very interesting," Jack said. "You've been most helpful, Mrs. Allman. Is there anything else that you can remember about the time surrounding Mr. Patten's death that was strange or unusual in any way?"

"Well...someone broke into the office on the day of the funeral."

"What do you mean?"

"Somebody came in through the front door and went through everything. The day after the funeral, I went into the office to meet with the attorneys from Cates & Stanley and help them figure out what was what. When I got there, the place was just a mess. All of the files and desk drawers had been pulled out and everything from the coat closet was lying on the floor. It looked like someone had just torn the place apart."

"Was anything missing?"

"Not that I could tell. It was just a mess."

"Did they ever find out who did it?"

"I don't suppose they did because I never heard anything else about it."

"Is there anything else you can remember?"

"No. I can't think of anything else right now, but if I do I'll call you."

"Thanks. We really appreciate all your help, Stella," Jack said as he reached around to his back pocket and pulled out his wallet. He opened it up and grabbed one of his business cards. "If you do remember anything, anything at all, please give me a call. If I'm not there, you can ask for Elizabeth. You can reach her at this same phone number."

"I will call you if I can think of anything, but they say I'm going senile, so don't hold your breath." She laughed at herself, then sat silently for a moment with a funny look on her face. "Are you two married?" she asked.

Jack and Elizabeth both looked at each other and blushed. "No ma'am," Jack replied. "We're not married. We just work together."

"It's a pity. You two make such a handsome couple."

"Thank you," Elizabeth said, her cheeks still red with embarrassment.

"We sure do appreciate your time, Stella," Jack said, quickly trying to change the subject. "You've really been a lot of help. You just keep us in mind, and let us know if there is anything else you can remember or want to tell us."

"I will," she said. "Now you two don't forget to invite me to the wedding."

Jack reached out and took Stella's hand as he stood up. Elizabeth, taking her cue from Jack, stood up right behind him. They said their good-byes and headed out the door and back to their office.

"That was interesting," Jack said to Elizabeth as soon as they got out on the street.

"Yeah, who would've thought that we made such a handsome couple?"

He could feel himself blushing again. "That's not exactly what I was talking about."

"I know. I just couldn't resist."

"I'm talking about the people coming and questioning her, and the break-in. The same thing happened to Patricia and her mother. We've got the Air Force responding to a civilian plane crash, which they have no business doing. Now we have his home and office being burglarized within a week of his death and his secretary being questioned by the military about their conversation on the day of his death. I sure would like to know why the government was so worried about Jeff Patten's death."

"You don't really think the government had anything to do with his plane crashing, do you?"

"I don't know, but I'm not ruling anything out at this point. For all we know, they could have accidentally shot the thing out of the sky and then tried to cover it up. I do know that we should proceed with caution though. If the government was involved, and it looks as if they were, we better hope they've forgotten about it. We don't want to do anything that'll draw their attention to us."

"Like going to Denver and checking to see what was in that box?" she said sarcastically. "What if they're watching it to see if anyone ever comes to get it?"

"Yeah, I realize there's some risk here, but we've got to find out what was in there. What if the money's there?"

"And what if someone is watching it, Jack?"

"For thirty years? I don't think so. Besides, we're not doing anything wrong. We're just looking into something for a client."

"Well, maybe we're not doing anything wrong, Jack, but I'll bet Jeff Patten thought the same thing when he went to Denver. You better be careful while you're out there. I don't want your plane crashing into a mountain on your way home."

"I know," he said, wondering what had gone through Jeff's mind as his plane went down. "I'll be careful."

When he returned to his office, there was a voice mail from the bank manager he'd talked to the day before saying that the box had, in fact, been closed for non-payment of rent. He also said that he had located the contents of the box and would have them ready for Jack to pick up. After listening to the message, he called Patricia to tell her the good news and then booked himself a Monday morning flight to Denver.

CHAPTER 5

▼

Jack arrived in Denver Monday afternoon around 1:30 local time and got a taxi to his motel. He was tired from traveling but wanted to get to the bank as quickly as possible, so he asked the taxi driver to wait while he checked into his room. Ten minutes after arriving at the motel, he was back in the cab and on his way to the bank.

As he rode across town, he could think of little else besides the money. Occasionally, he would look at the mountains off in the distance, but his thoughts would almost immediately drift back to the money. He knew that, in reality, there was very little chance of the money being there. The bank manager said nothing about it in the voice mail he'd left, and there was no proof that it was ever put in that box to begin with. All he really knew was that Jeff Patten had rented the box and presumably put something in it on the morning of the day he died. But that was thirty years ago, and, if the money had ever been there, it had undoubtedly been emptied by now. Even so, there had to be some reason Mr. Patten had rented that box, and it was worth a look to find out why.

Eventually, the taxi pulled up in front of a tall downtown building.

"Here we are," the taxi driver said, looking back over his shoulder at Jack as they came to a stop. "Colorado Bank & Trust."

"Thanks," Jack replied. "What do I owe ya?"

"That'll be forty-five dollars," he quickly replied.

Jack pulled out his wallet and handed the driver a fifty and a ten. "Here's sixty. Will you come back in about thirty minutes to pick me up?"

The driver took the money out of Jack's hand and said, "No problem. I'll just wait here. You take as long as you need. I'll be right here when you get done."

"Thanks. I shouldn't be too long. Thirty minutes or so," Jack said as he got out of the cab and shut the door behind him.

"No problem," the cabby said as the door slammed shut.

Jack stood nervously in front of the bank holding the file he had brought with him. The file contained the affidavit that Patricia had signed and the original court order appointing Patricia's mother, Sarah Patten, as the administrator of the estate and naming his law firm as attorneys of record. Also in his pocket was the small blue envelope that he had found in the old probate files with the key to the safe-deposit box.

He took a deep breath to compose himself, walked in through the revolving door, and asked one of the tellers if he could speak to the branch manager. The teller got up and walked into one of the offices while Jack waited out in the lobby. Moments later, she walked back out of the office followed by a short, thin man with a receding hair line. She pointed across the lobby to Jack, who smiled back at her, and the man who had followed her out of the office walked over to him.

"Hello sir," the man said, approaching Jack with his hand out. "I'm Walter Kirby. I'm the branch manager. What can I do for you today?"

Jack stuck his hand out to meet Mr. Kirby's. As they shook hands, Jack noticed that he had a remarkably firm grasp for such a small person. "Yes sir, Mr. Kirby. I'm Jack Hixson. I am an attorney from Chattanooga, Tennessee. We spoke on the phone last week about a safe-deposit box."

Mr. Kirby's eyes lit up as he remembered their earlier telephone conversation. "Yes Mr. Hixson. It's good to see you. I guess you got my message. I did some checking after we talked last time, and we did still have the contents of that box in our basement storage."

"That's great!" Jack exclaimed. "I was wondering what you would find. It has been quite a while."

"You're right about that. It's been quite a long time indeed. Why don't we step into my office so we can talk."

"That's fine."

"Follow me," he said as he turned and started walking back toward his office. Jack followed him in and shut the door behind them. Mr. Kirby had a beautiful office. The marble floor was polished to a mirror like finish and covered by an intricately woven rug. In the middle of the office was a huge wooden desk that looked as though it had been there as long as the building. Jack sat in one of the high-backed leather chairs across the desk from Mr. Kirby and set the file folder he was carrying in front of him.

"Did you have a good flight?" Mr. Kirby asked after getting himself comfortable behind the desk.

"Yes. It was fine. Nice and smooth."

"That's good."

"Well, it certainly beats the alternative," Jack said, thinking of Jeff Patten's last flight.

"Were you able to bring the paperwork we discussed?" Mr. Kirby asked, looking down at Jack's file.

"Yes sir, Mr. Kirby. I sure did. I've actually got the original court order appointing my firm as counsel of record for the estate."

"That's great, Jack, and please…call me Walter."

"Okay, Walter," he replied as he pulled the papers out of the file. "This is the affidavit you requested from the beneficiaries of the estate. Actually, there's only one beneficiary, Patricia Patten, who is Mr. Patten's daughter. Her mother, Sarah Patten, passed away several years ago and she is the only surviving heir." He leaned forward and handed the paper across the desk to Mr. Kirby, who studied it intently before looking back up at Jack.

"That's fine," he said, smiling. "As long as I have what I need in my file."

"And here is the original court order from 1972 naming my firm, Cates & Stanley, as the attorneys of record in the probate. It's an old document, but it's authentic and has the court's seal, and I think that's everything you requested." Jack handed the documents across the desk, and Mr. Kirby took a moment to study them.

"I think that's all we need," he said after a few moments of silence. "You do have the key, don't you?"

"Yes, sir. I sure do," he responded, reaching into his pocket. He pulled out the tiny blue envelope and set it in the middle of the desk. Mr. Kirby reached out and picked it up. He read the outside and then flipped it over to see if there was anything on the back.

"August 28, 1972," he said as he looked at the envelope. "You know, I was working at this bank back then. Not this branch, but I was a teller at another location. It's been a long time since I've seen one of the little blue envelopes like this."

"Really?" Jack asked, trying his hardest to sound interested. He was so eager to see the box that it was all he could think about.

"Yes. It's been a while. Anyway…," he said after a brief pause, "you didn't come here to hear about my work history. I did some investigating after your call to see what I could find out about this box. It seems that it was rented on the date on this envelope by a Jeffery R. Patten. He paid six months' rent on the box in advance and then never made another payment. Now we know why. The box was closed for nonpayment, and its contents were put in our abandoned and unclaimed storage that we keep in the basement of this building." As he was finishing his sentence, he reached down and opened the bottom right-hand drawer of his desk and pulled out a large brown mailing envelope, which he set on the desk in front of Jack. "Here it is," he said.

Jack looked down at the envelope. He hoped his disappointment was not showing as he reached out in front of him to pick it up off the desk. From its weight (or lack of weight), he could tell that there was no money there, and he felt as though someone had punched him in the gut as he picked it up and peeked inside. All he could see were several sheets of paper. Not at all what he had hoped for.

"It seems," Mr. Kirby said, breaking Jack's concentration, "that someone got into the box shortly after Mr. Patten's death, but it doesn't say who."

Jack perked up suddenly. "Was anything removed from the box?"

"No, the records indicate that someone got into the box but they didn't take anything."

"How did someone get into the box without a key, and what does that mean?"

"Well, generally…if you don't have a key, you can't get in, and this person didn't even sign the normal paperwork we require. However, there is a note from the manager at that time, indicating that whoever it was had a federal search warrant. The manager's notes say that they looked through it but didn't take anything. I'm not sure exactly what that means."

"Are you sure that nothing was removed?"

"I don't think so, but again, I can't really be sure of that. There's not much of an explanation, but you can see where the entry date is noted and the words *federal warrant* are written in the space where a signature would normally go, but there is nothing showing what, if anything, was removed. That's really all I can tell you."

"That's fine then, I guess. There's not much we can do about it now," Jack said, "but I do appreciate your help."

"Is there anything else that I can do for you?"

"No. I think that will do it."

"Good, then if I could just get you to fill out this form here," he said, sliding a piece of paper across the desk to Jack, "showing where you claimed the contents of the box, then you can go ahead and take this stuff with you."

"Sure," Jack said, looking down at the form Mr. Kirby had just handed him. He filled it out, signed it, and handed it back across the desk. It made him nervous to sign his name, but he didn't really have a choice if he wanted to take the stuff with him. They stood up and shook hands, and Jack picked up the envelope and walked out of the bank.

He was more than a little disappointed as he walked out onto the street. He had just wasted two days, as well as several hundred dollars of Patricia's money. He got in the cab, which was still waiting for him outside by the curb, and asked the driver to take him back to the motel. Had he known that the box had nothing valuable in it, he never would've made the trip. *Oh well*, he thought to himself, *at least it's over, and I didn't find any trouble.* He would have to be happy with that.

CHAPTER 6

▼

He sat on the bed in his motel room watching TV and wondering how close he had been to the money. He wondered if there was ever any money at all. All he had to go on was the word of Patricia who, in turn, had heard it from her mother, who heard it from Stella. But there was no real proof that it ever really existed.

He kept going over the facts in his head. He was sure that Jeff Patten had made an unexpected trip to Denver the day before he died, and that he had told his secretary and his wife that he was going out there to pick up the money. But there was no way to confirm that he had ever received it. Stella had told them that Jeff had called her before getting on the plan and told her that something was amiss, but they didn't know what it was. Was there ever any money? And why did he go to all the trouble of renting the safe-deposit box? It just didn't add up. The circumstances surrounding the crash were strange too. Why would the military be interested in a civilian plane crash? And why would his house and office have been ransacked?

He knew that a soldier who claimed to have been at the crash site said that they'd been looking for something specific amongst the wreckage but couldn't find it, but there was no way to confirm that. He did have Jeff's wallet though, and that made his story somewhat believable. He wondered why his uncle, with all his connections in the Air Force, wasn't able to find any record of the incident. Stella and Patricia had also each told him that someone from the military had come to see them after the funeral asking all kinds of questions about Jeff and whether they were aware of what he had been doing. Looking at it objectively, there was undoubtedly something strange going on, but it was looking as if what happened to Jeff Paten and the million dollars would remain a mystery.

He hated that he had spent so much of his time chasing this down, but it had been exciting playing detective. It had certainly been more exciting than reviewing loan documents or drafting wills and trust agreements.

He opened the envelope that Mr. Kirby had given him, pulled out the contents, and spread them out on the bed. They were nothing more than standard corporate organizational documents. The kind Jack frequently prepared himself. There was a charter and a set of by-laws, and that was it.

Why go to all the trouble of renting a safe-deposit box? he wondered. *Why go to all that trouble just to store what looked like ordinary, run-of-the-mill corporate legal documents? Especially in a city that was halfway across the country from your office.* These weren't even finalized documents. They were just drafts with handwritten notes and changes made to them. *Why go to all the trouble?*

The company name on the charter was "Modular Home Construction Company, Inc.," But that had been changed. Someone, most likely Jeff himself, had scratched the original name out and handwritten "PAP Future Homes, Inc." in bold lettering just above it. The address of the company had also been changed from Tampa, Florida, to someplace called Black Hawk, Colorado.

Jack knew from his review of the probate files that the Modular Home Construction Company was the corporation that Jeff was working to get set up for his mystery client just prior to his death. He had supposedly come to Denver to collect a cash investment for that very company, and it was that very company that turned out to be a sham after his death, and that was why Patricia had come to him—to help her find evidence that he had not willingly or knowingly been involved in any kind of scam.

Why had he changed the name of the company on those documents? Jack racked his brain for almost an hour, but could not figure it out. Maybe he was planning on setting up another company for the same purpose and was using the documents as forms. Maybe he planned on having Stella retype the documents, but if that was the case, then why did he leave them in Colorado?

He read the documents over and over again, looking for a clue—something, anything, that might tell him whether there had been any money and, if so, where it was. After a while, he had read them so many times that he almost had them memorized, but there just wasn't anything that looked out of the ordinary. He finally decided that it was time to give up and call Elizabeth and Patricia and let them know that he hadn't found anything. Elizabeth's number was the first one he dialed. She answered the phone on the second ring.

"It was a dead end," he said sadly. "There was nothing in the box but some old paperwork."

"What do you mean? What happened?" she asked.

"Well, as I told you the other day, they had closed the box after Mr. Patten's death because no one was paying for it."

"But they still had everything that was in the box?"

"Yeah, they still had it. At least I think they had everything. But it was just one of those big brown mailing envelopes with drafts of some corporate documents."

"What kind of corporate documents?"

"There was a charter and a set of by-laws, but they were just drafts. They had handwritten revisions on them."

"That's all that was there?"

"That's it. The bank manager said that someone had gotten into the box at some point shortly after the crash but that he didn't think anything had been taken."

"Who got into it?"

"He didn't know, but whoever it was had a federal search warrant."

"That's strange."

"You're tellin' me. What I can't figure out is why anyone would go through all that trouble? He was in Denver for less than twenty-four hours. It just doesn't make any sense. Why in the world would he rent a safety-deposit box that far from home and put this kind of stuff in it? Documents that he seemed to be working on. I just don't understand."

"You're right, Jack. It doesn't seem to make any sense. There had to be something else in there that was taken out when whoever had that warrant went through it."

"I guess you're right, but there was no mention of anything being taken out, and what are these documents still doing there? Why weren't they taken as well? It doesn't make any sense that he would put these drafts in an envelope and put them in the box."

They talked for a few more minutes trying to figure it out. It didn't make sense no matter how they thought about it. He read the documents to Elizabeth, carefully pointing out each of the changes that had been written in, but they didn't seem to mean anything to either of them. Neither of them could figure out why anyone would go to all of that trouble. There must have been something else in the box—something that was removed long before Jack got there. Maybe the money had been there in the box after all and had been taken out back in 1972.

"How big is a million dollars?" Elizabeth asked. "I mean…I've never seen that much money in one place. Would it actually fit in a safe-deposit box?"

"Well…," Jack said, pondering her question. "I would imagine that a million dollars would take up quite a bit of space. It would be one thousand one-hundred-dollar bills. I guess it would probably fit, assuming it was hundred-dollar bills. Now if it was smaller bills…I don't know," he said, frustrated. "All I know is that it wasn't in the box when I got there."

"I'm sorry, Jack," she said, recognizing his frustration.

He could tell from her voice that she was truly concerned—not so much about the money, but about his feelings—and that made him feel much better. The more he thought about it, the happier he was that he had gone on this wild-goose chase because it had brought him close to Elizabeth. "It's all right," he said. "I'll be home tomorrow, and I'll just pick up where I left off. It sure would've been nice to find a pile of money, but what were the odds anyway? Right? I mean…what are the odds that a million dollars in cash is just going to sit around waiting to be found for thirty years? Somebody is going to notice that it's missing and they are going to go looking for it. If it was my million dollars, I would be looking for it, and I wouldn't stop looking until I found it."

"You're right, Jack…you're right. I would do the same thing."

"Anyway," he said in a melancholy voice, "I guess I need to call Patricia and tell her the bad news too."

"Yes. You should've called her first. I'm sure she's worried about you."

Jack didn't want to hang up the phone, and they talked for a few more minutes. The sound of her voice was comforting, and he could've talked to her all night, but he really did need to call Patricia and let her know that they'd found what was likely the final dead end. He wasn't looking forward to making that call.

Patricia wanted so badly to find something that showed her father's innocence, but he had to tell her that she wouldn't find it there. She had been so excited when he told her about the key. It had given her a glimmer of hope that she might find the "smoking gun" that would prove that her father wasn't knowingly involved in any deception. She didn't care so much about the money. She had plenty of that. It was exoneration she was after. She wanted something that would prove to herself, and anyone else who cared to know, that her father had not tried to defraud anyone, something that showed that he believed he was doing legitimate work for a legitimate client. She didn't know exactly what she was looking for, but there was nothing new in the box. They had seen the charter and the other documents before, and he was sure that Patricia was going to be disappointed.

He dialed her number and tried to prepare himself mentally for her disappointment. He didn't know how many times it rang before she answered.

"Hello."

"Hello, Patricia. This is Jack."

"Hello, Jack," she said. "What's the news?"

"Unfortunately, there isn't much," he responded reluctantly. He tried not to sound too disappointed but didn't think he was being very successful at it. "I hate to tell you this, but I didn't find anything we haven't already seen."

"Oh well…," she said with a sigh. "I can't say that I expected any more than that anyway. I had hoped you might find something, but, in all honesty, I didn't really expect you to."

Jack was pleasantly surprised by her response, not having expected her to take the news so well. "I'd hoped to find something too," he said, trying to make her feel a little better.

"It's been thirty years, Jack. I'm sure that whatever was there was gone a long time ago."

"Well…the box wasn't empty, but it didn't have anything in it that we hadn't already seen."

"What was in it?"

"There was a large mailing envelope that had drafts of some documents that your father had been working on for the client that sent him out here to get the money. There was a copy of the charter and some other documents relating to the corporation that he had been working on, but the name and address of that company had been scratched out, and he had handwritten some notes on it. It looked like he was either changing the name of that company or setting up a new one that was going to be based out here in Colorado. I'm not sure why, though. Maybe the man he was meeting with out here wanted to set up his own company and your dad was going to help him draw up the necessary papers. But that wouldn't make any sense," he said, thinking out loud, "because the guy he was meeting out here was supposedly investing his cash in the other company. Why would he be setting up his own company and invest in a competitor? And why would he leave the papers he was working on in a safe-deposit box a thousand miles from home?"

"You're right, Jack. It doesn't make any sense, but nothing about my father's death makes any sense. What was the name he had written on the papers you found?"

"PAP Future Homes, Inc., or something like that," he said.

Patricia sat silently on the other end of the line for a few moments and then said, "Will you repeat that?"

"Sure. It's PAP Future Homes, Inc." This time he read directly from the page in front of him.

"I don't know if this means anything, Jack, but my initials are PAP. Patricia Anne Patten…PAP. Those are my initials," she said, becoming more excited with each word. "Did you say that company, the PAP one, was going to be headquartered in Colorado?"

"Yes. At least that's what these papers say."

"What's the address? Is it in a place called Black Hawk, Colorado?"

Jack was a little stunned. "Yeah, it's 2112 Chase Gulch Road, in Black Hawk. How did you know that?"

"Jack, I think you may have just found a clue." She was obviously getting excited again.

"What do you mean?"

"My father's family owns a cabin in Black Hawk. It's about an hour from Denver, up in the mountains. My father used to go there with his father when he was a kid. Maybe he went to the cabin and hid the money before he got on the plane to fly home. That would make perfect sense."

"What's the address of the cabin?" Jack asked her, getting a little excited himself.

"I'm not sure, but I'll bet that it's the same one you just read to me. I can find out for sure. Like I said, my family still owns it as far as I know. No one goes out there anymore, but they still own it. It sits on a big piece of land, several hundred acres I think, and they lease it out to hunters. It used to be part of a mining operation. I went out there once when I was a kid. There's an abandoned mine shaft that my father showed me behind the house about a mile up an old dirt road where they mined for silver."

"Do you think…," Jack started to say.

But before he could finish his sentence, Patricia blurted out, "I'll bet that's where the money is! Jack, you've got to go up there to the cabin and check it out. You can rent a car there in Denver and drive up to Black Hawk. I'll get the directions and call you back. You've got to go up there, Jack," Patricia pleaded, but she didn't need to plead with him. He had already made up his mind.

"I'll head up there first thing in the morning," he said. "I'll go to the airport and rent a car tonight so that I can leave early. I'll call you back to get directions as soon as I get back here with the car."

"When are you supposed to fly home?"

Jack wasn't even thinking about that. He had all but forgotten that his return flight was scheduled for 8:00 the next morning. He would just have to miss it. Maybe he could call and reschedule for the next day. He would figure that out while he was getting his rental car. "I'm supposed to fly home tomorrow morning," he said, "but don't worry about that. I'll reschedule the flight and get home as soon as I can."

"Okay. Call me back in a couple of hours. I'll have the directions for you by then."

As they hung up the phone, a big smile appeared on Jack's face. He quickly went through the phone book and found the listing for the cab company that he had used earlier that day. They said they would have someone there to pick him up shortly. As soon as the cab arrived, he jumped into the backseat. "Can you take me to the airport to get a rental car please?" he said.

"No problem," the driver said. "I'll take you right there."

After a long ride that seemed to Jack as if it would take forever, they pulled up to the curb outside the baggage claim terminal at Denver International and Jack hopped out of the cab. As he was walking in, he noticed, out of the corner of his eye, a black sedan with dark tinted windows pull in behind his taxi. Such a thing wouldn't normally draw his attention, but he remembered seeing the same car (or an identical one) sitting in the parking lot of his motel when he had left to go to the bank that morning and again when he had gotten in the taxi. He tried to push his suspicions into the back of his head as he walked up to the counter.

After twenty minutes of filling out paperwork, speaking to the clerk behind the counter, and waiting patiently, Jack was handed a set of keys and directed outside to a shuttle that would take him to the lot where the rental cars were parked. The black sedan that he had noticed earlier was still sitting outside when he came back through the doors onto the sidewalk. He tried to avoid looking over at the car while waiting on the shuttle, but it was difficult to keep his eyes off of it. Even more so when he watched it pull away from the curb and follow closely behind the shuttle.

The shuttle arrived at the lot, and, after looking around for a few minutes, Jack got in his car and started to pull out. He looked out the window as he pulled away and noticed that the car he'd been watching was gone. It had followed him all the way to the rental lot, and he hadn't seen it leave, but it wasn't there anymore. Maybe it was all in his head. There had to be plenty of black sedans with tinted windows in Denver. He tried to convince himself that he was letting his imagination get the better of him as he headed back to the motel.

He called Patricia as soon as he got back in his room.

"Hey Jack," she said, recognizing his voice. "I got those directions to the—"

Jack cut her off before she could finish. "Don't say anything over the phone."

"Why? What's going on?" she asked worriedly.

"I'm not sure...," he responded. "Probably nothing, but I've seen this same suspicious-looking car a couple of times, and I think it may be following me."

"You think you're being followed?" she asked nervously.

"I'm not sure. I'll bet it's just my imagination, but we're better off safe than sorry. We probably shouldn't talk on the phone anymore tonight. I've got the street address from the paperwork I picked up this morning. I'm sure I can find the place on my own. Just hang tight, and I'll call you when I get the chance."

"All right, Jack," she said, her voice filled with concern. "Please be careful."

"I will, and don't worry. I'll be home before you know it." He hung up the phone and sat on the bed staring at the window in front of him. The drapes were pulled shut, which prevented him from seeing out into the parking lot, but his curiosity was becoming stronger by the minute. It was only a matter of time before it was too strong to fight. He made his way over to the window, pulled back the drapes just enough for him to see into the parking lot outside his door, and peeked through the glass. To his relief, he didn't see the black sedan outside. He pulled the drapes a little farther back from the window so that he could see the entire parking lot. It wasn't anywhere in sight, and he let out a big sigh of relief.

Jack got very little sleep that night; tossing and turning and wondering whether he was being watched and, if so, by whom. He dozed off at some point and was awakened abruptly the next morning by the alarm clock that was sitting next to the bed. When the alarm went off, he quickly got up and jumped in the shower. It was only 5:30 in the morning, which was 7:30 Chattanooga time, and Jack figured that he should be able to get to Black Hawk by 7:00 A.M. if he could get out of there before the rush-hour traffic started. He threw on his clothes and looked out the window to see if the black sedan was there. Once again, he didn't see it. He quickly gathered his luggage and headed toward the office to check out.

The girl sitting behind the desk must have been sleeping when he walked in. She was obviously startled and nearly fell out of her seat when he approached her. She was so embarrassed that she could hardly look up at him. Jack just smiled at her and set his room key on the counter.

"Checking out?" she asked, her face glowing bright red.

"Yes, ma'am," he replied. "You don't happen to have any maps around here, do you?"

"That depends. Where ya trying to go?"

"A place called Black Hawk. It's up in the mountains about an hour from here."

"Oh yeah…I know Black Hawk. You goin' up there to the casinos?"

"Yep," he replied. He had no idea that there were any casinos there, but it was much easier to say yes than trying to explain that he was trying to find an old cabin near an abandoned mining operation.

"I've got a map I'll give ya, but you really don't need one." She reached down behind the counter and pulled out a not so neatly folded map that showed the whole state. "Here you are," she said, pointing to a spot on the map in the western side of Denver. "Now, you need to go up the road here about a quarter mile or so," she said, tracing the route with her finger, "and then get on 470. That runs all the way around the city. Now, make sure the mountains are on your left. After a couple miles, you'll see Interstate 70. You're gonna head west on 70 towards the mountains until you get to the Idaho Springs exit. This map says that's Highway 6, but you just look for Idaho Springs, and then you're gonna head back east until you get to Highway 119, and that will you all the way into Black Hawk. You'll start seeing signs for it when you get toward the edge of town. Most of the land is Indian reservations up there," she said. "They used to mine that area for gold and silver, but the mines dried up years ago, and the only place you're gonna find any gold now is at the blackjack tables."

Jack stood at the counter listening intently and following her directions on the map. It looked like an easy drive, but Jack, like most men, had an uncanny ability to get himself lost. "That doesn't look too difficult," he said. "But can I take this map with me just in case?"

"Sure," she replied. "Be my guest."

He finished checking out, grabbed the map, and headed out the door, giving one last look around to make sure the black sedan wasn't in sight as he pulled away from the motel. He followed the instructions he had been given and pulled into Black Hawk about an hour and a half later. The drive was uneventful, for which he was grateful. He had checked his rearview mirror every few minutes to make sure he wasn't being followed and never saw any suspicious-looking vehicles, but he was still nervous and on edge waiting for the black sedan to show up again.

CHAPTER 7

▼

As he pulled into the small town of Black Hawk, he was intrigued by what looked like on Old West town that had recently gotten a face-lift. There must have been fifteen to twenty small hotels and casinos lining the road that ran through the center of town, which was appropriately named "Main Street." Jack who hadn't yet eaten that morning and was getting pretty hungry, and decided to stop and get some breakfast at one of the hotels while he looked at his map and tried to find the road that the cabin was on.

He pulled up in front of a three-story brick building with the words "The Gilpin Hotel" painted in large white letters across the top. He parked his car on the street and got out to see if they were serving breakfast. As he walked inside through the double doors, he noticed a sign offering valet parking. Getting his car off the road sounded like a great idea, and he needed a place to sit while he found and studied a better map than the one he had, so he walked over to the hotel's main desk.

"Do you guys serve breakfast?" he asked the man who was sitting behind the counter.

"We sure do," the man replied. "There's a restaurant upstairs."

"That sounds great," Jack said as his stomach let out a fierce rumble.

"You gonna' be checkin' into the hotel, sir?" the attendant asked politely.

"No. I'm just making my way through town and thought this looked like a good place to get some food."

"Yes, sir, it is. You picked the right place."

"My car is parked out on the street, and I noticed that you had valet parking. Could I get someone to park it off the street for me?" Jack reached out and offered his key to the attendant as he spoke.

"Oh…yes sir," the man said, reaching out to take the keys from him. "I'll have someone take care of that. Here is your number." He handed Jack a red poker chip with the number "08" printed on it. "Whenever you're ready, just bring your chip to the front desk here, and we'll have your car brought around for you."

"Thanks," Jack said. "You said the restaurant was upstairs?"

"That's right. Just head up those stairs," he said as he pointed toward the large staircase leading up to a mezzanine level.

"Thanks, and just one more thing. Do you have a local map that I could look at?"

"I sure do. Is there somethin' in particular you're lookin' for?"

"Well…," Jack said hesitantly. He wasn't sure that he wanted to tell anyone what he was looking for, but he wanted to get there as quickly as he could. After thinking about it for a few seconds, he decided to have a look at the map first. If he couldn't find what he was looking for, then he would ask for help. "I don't want to trouble you…not just yet, but thanks anyway," he said. "I'll see if I can't find it on the map. If I have any trouble, I'll come back and see you."

"That sounds fine, sir. I'll be right here all day, and I've lived here in Black Hawk all my life, so I know my way around. You take this map, and here's the phone book too. If you can't find what you're lookin' for…you just let me know." The man handed Jack a small map that showed the center of town and the surrounding area. The phone book, which was one of the thinnest Jack had ever seen, had a slightly more detailed map that showed all of Gilpin County. Surely he would be able to find the cabin on one of them.

"Thanks again," Jack said as he made his way over to the stairs and then up to the restaurant above him.

He was surprised to see how many people were in the restaurant when he walked in. He sat down at one of the empty tables, ordered some breakfast, and ate slowly while he studied the map and the phone book. He was looking for Chase Gulch Road, which was the name of the street that Mr. Patten had written on the documents he left at the bank, but he was having a hard time finding it on either of the maps. He still hadn't found it by the time he finished up his breakfast and decided to ask the man behind the counter for directions as he was leaving.

"Chase Gulch Road? I know exactly where that is. You go right up here on 119. That's the road you came into town on, and you're gonna turn left about a mile or so up the road, when you get to Chase Street. You're gonna stay on Chase Street for a couple miles, and then it'll turn into Chase Gulch Road. That's all there is to it. You can't see on the map here where the street name changes, but just trust me. It'll change as you head up through the gulch."

Jack thanked the man for the directions, handed back the poker chip he had been given earlier, and walked out on the porch to wait on his car. It wasn't long before he was headed up the road again, but this time he had a full belly and knew where he was going. He had not seen the black sedan since the day before and was starting to think that maybe it had just been his imagination after all, or maybe he had lost them. Either way, they were nowhere to be seen.

*   *   *   *

The road from Black Hawk to the cabin was a beautiful drive. He was high up in the mountains, and the road was tight and twisty. It was very different from what he was used to back home. Chattanooga was surrounded on all sides by mountains, but they looked more like hills compared to these.

He looked carefully for street numbers each time he passed a mailbox or building of any sort (which didn't happen very often), and eventually he came to a mailbox with the numbers 2112 on it. This was the address that Jeff Patten had written more than thirty years ago.

The mailbox was old and rusty and obviously hadn't been used for some time. It was set just off the street next to a disused dirt road that went back about fifty yards and then rounded a corner. Jack turned onto the driveway and slowly made his way toward the turn ahead. When he rounded the turn, he could see that the driveway continued to twist and turn up the side of a hill until it stopped in front of a dilapidated house.

His heart began to beat faster as he drove up the driveway, trying to avoid the ruts and potholes that littered his path. He stopped near the top when he came around one of the many turns and found that a large pine tree had fallen over and was blocking the road. It was half-rotted and looked as though it had been lying across the driveway for some time. He put the car in park and decided to walk the rest of the way. It was only another hundred yards or so to the end of the driveway, and Jack was standing in front of the cabin in no time.

He looked in the windows and saw that the place was dusty but still full of furniture. The gutters had come loose in several places and the eaves were starting to rot. The cabin had a weathered metal roof that was covered in rust and extended out over the front porch. After surveying the front of the cabin and wondering how he would get inside, he walked around to the backyard and found a door that led into the kitchen. The door had several small windowpanes, one of which he broke with a swift blow from his elbow. The sound of glass breaking made him nervous, even though he had looked around the place and was sure that there was no one there. In fact, he knew that there was probably no one within five miles of him, but he was still uncomfortable.

The broken window gave him just enough room to reach in and unlock the door from the inside. The hinges squeaked loudly as the door swung open for the first time in probably a decade. He went inside and looked through each room, trying to search thoroughly without disturbing things too much. It was a one-story building with four rooms. There were two bedrooms, a den and living room area, and an eat-in kitchen. It was musty and the air inside was stagnant.

He slowly and carefully searched each of the rooms, the closets, and the drawers and found nothing but dust. As he walked into one of the bedrooms, a small bird flew across the room to a hole in the wall. Apparently, nature had taken the place over. After a thorough search, there was no suitcase and no money that Jack could find anywhere in the cabin, and then he remembered that Patricia had said something about an abandoned mine shaft being somewhere on the property. She had said it was somewhere in the woods behind the cabin, but it could take the rest of his life to search all of those woods.

He walked back outside and looked around. The cabin was set in a shallow valley between two mountain ridges and was surrounded on all sides by large pine trees. The tree line where the forest began was about thirty yards from the back door, and he could see what looked like the head of an overgrown trail that disappeared off into the woods. The trail was old and had obviously not been traveled in a while, but it was the only path (other than the driveway) that led away from the house. The ridge behind the house looked to be about a mile or so away, and the trail seemed to lead in that general direction, so Jack started walking, hoping to find the mine shaft Patricia had talked about.

The forest was immediately thick, and it got thicker as he headed farther down the trail away from the house. He was surrounded by tall pines, and everything looked the same no matter which direction he chose.

This would be a terrible place to get lost, he thought, but he kept following the trail deeper into the wilderness that stretched in front of him as far as he could see. As he continued, he kept his eye on the ridgeline off in the distance in front of him. Standing at the back door of the cabin, he had noticed a small outcrop of rocks on top of the ridge that reminded him of a face, and he was using that feature to gauge his position relative to the cabin.

After following the trail for half a mile, he came to a clearing that sat on the side of a steep slope. The path continued uphill across the clearing and disappeared back into the forest. In the center of the clearing was a small stream that came out of the trees, wound down the hill past a large pile of boulders, and, like the trail, disappeared back into the forest to his right. There appeared to be an old road where the stream entered the forest.

He couldn't tell much from where he was standing, but the road looked similar to the driveway leading up to the cabin. It was a dirt road that had apparently been used at some time in the past but had fallen into disrepair. As he walked toward the boulders, he noticed that they had markings of some sort on them. As he got even closer, he could see that there were actually old wooden signs that had been affixed to the rocks long ago.

When he was finally close enough to read the signs, he realized that he had found what he was looking for. Most of the words had fallen away as the wooden sign had decomposed over the years, but what he could make out told him that this was the entrance to the "Bald Mountain" mine shaft. As he walked around the huge gray rocks in front of him, he realized that they had been placed there in an attempt to cover the entrance to the shaft that had been dug into the side of the hill. Fortunately, there was enough room for him to squeeze between two of the boulders, and after doing so, Jack found himself standing in a cave-like tunnel that continued forward into the darkness.

The walls and ceiling of the shaft were braced with large timbers, and there were still old lanterns hanging on spikes that had been driven into the walls every fifty feet or so. He wondered if they might still work. There was no telling how old they were and he doubted that they could still have any fuel in them after all those years. He didn't have a flashlight and was disappointed with himself for not having thought ahead enough to bring one along. He would need some form of illumination if he was going to search the cave, and all that he had with him was a disposable lighter that he had brought with him. He pulled one of the lanterns from the wall and slid back through the rocks blocking the entrance.

Once outside, he jiggled the lantern and heard the sound of liquid swishing around. He pulled the lighter out of his pocket and tried to ignite the wick, but he couldn't get it to stay lit. He tried several times, but it just wouldn't burn. He unscrewed the cap from the fuel tank and put the lantern up to his nose. It smelled like some sort of fuel, but it had turned to a dark colored sludge over the years and was undoubtedly too old to burn.

He wasn't sure what he should do. Should he go back to the cabin and look for a flashlight or a lantern? He knew he was not likely to find anything useful there either. Even if he were able to find a flashlight, he didn't have any batteries and wouldn't be able to use it.

He considered his alternatives for a minute and decided to go back into the cave and try to use his lighter. It wouldn't provide much in the way of light, but it was all he had without going back into town, and it would be better than nothing. So, he slid back into the shaft and slowly made his way into the darkness. Every few steps, he would light the lighter and hold it up for a few seconds so that he could see the next few steps.

After he had gone about a hundred yards into the shaft, he came to a fork in the path where it split into two separate shafts. The path on his left went downhill, deeper into the side of the mountain. The other seemed to stay level and turn to the right a little. He was not sure which path to take. Either of them might lead him to the money.

Jack was starting to question the intelligence of climbing down an abandoned mine shaft in the first place. After all, he was a lawyer, not a caver. He was used to sitting behind a desk and talking on the telephone, but now he was climbing down a hole in the ground a thousand miles from home, and he didn't even have a flashlight. After giving it some serious thought, he decided that he would go a short distance down each of the paths, and if he didn't find anything, he would turn around, go back to town, and get some lights.

The path on the left was first. It started steeply downhill for about twenty yards and then leveled off. Jack slowly made his way forward, holding up the lighter every few feet so that he could see his way. The metal wheel on top of the lighter was starting to get very hot—so hot that it was burning his thumb—and he was having trouble striking it. He proceeded slowly and was considering stopping for a moment to let the lighter cool off when suddenly and without warning, there was no ground beneath his front foot. He barely caught his balance and pulled back from the edge before toppling forward into the pit in front of him. He lit the lighter and saw that the shaft stopped abruptly in front of him and went straight down into the blackness.

"This is crazy!" he exclaimed out loud. His echo bounced off the walls of the shaft, repeating the phrase over and over again. His heart was beating so fast, he thought it might explode, and he was cursing his stupidity. He had nearly fallen to his death, and no one even knew where he was. It would have been days at best before anyone back home reported him missing, and only Patricia had any idea where he was. Had he gone over the edge, it would most certainly have been the end of him. He sat down and tried to catch his breath.

There was no light at all other than the lighter he held in his hands. He struck it again and saw another lantern hanging on the wall in front of him. He slowly inched his way to it on his hands and knees so that he could pull it off the wall and try to get it lit. He knew that it probably wouldn't work, but he had nearly killed himself in the darkness and was getting a little desperate for a better source of light.

As he crawled toward the lantern, his hand landed on something that was sitting on the ground at the base of the cave wall. He couldn't tell what it was exactly, but it felt like a wooden box.

He crawled all the way over to the object and struck the lighter again. In the limited light provided by his flame, he could barely make out a small wooden box with the words "DANGER—EXPLOSIVES" written in large red letters on the outside. On either side of the box were rope handles, and Jack grabbed one of them and pulled the box closer to him. It was fairly heavy, and as he tried to open it, he discovered that the top was nailed shut. He was a little reluctant to have an open flame near a box labeled "explosives," but he wanted to get another look at it, and he needed to try to orient himself so that he did not start walking again and end up at the bottom of the pit that he had almost fallen into moments before.

He struck the lighter again, confirmed his position relative to the pit, and gave the box another look. The top was nailed securely, and he couldn't see inside it at all, so he picked it up and slowly made his way back toward the entrance. Just as he had done on his way into the mine, he had to stop every ten yards or so, set the box down, and strike the lighter so that he could see his next few steps. The box was heavy, but his excitement grew with every step. Did he have it? Did the box he had in his hands contain the money he was searching for? Was this the end of his quest?

By the time he could see the entrance, he had all but forgotten about his brush with death. All he could think about was the box he carried and its potential contents.

As he reached the entrance, he had to hold the box up over his head and slide through the crack in the rocks to get outside. The sunlight nearly blinded him as he reached the outside and took in a deep breath of fresh air. The thick pine scent was a welcome relief from the stale air he had been breathing inside the shaft. He sat the box on the ground and then sat down next to it for a minute, waiting for his eyes to adjust to the light. When they did finally adjust, he got his first good look at the box he'd almost died to find.

It was an old dynamite box—not as old as the mine, but still pretty old. He had to treat this box as if it were actually full of dynamite, because it might, in fact, be, and he did not want to find that out the hard way. He was going to need some tools to pry the lid off, so he gingerly picked the box up and started back down the trail toward the cabin where he had seen a hammer and screwdriver in one of the kitchen drawers earlier.

It seemed as though the trip back to the cabin took forever. The box was getting heavier and heavier with every step. By the time he came back out of the woods and found himself in the backyard of the cabin, he was exhausted and wanted to sit and rest, but he was so excited that he couldn't. *I can rest later,* he thought to himself, and he immediately went back into the cabin and pulled the tools he needed out of the kitchen drawer.

He set the box on the kitchen table and got to work. Beads of sweat dripped from his forehead, and his hands were shaking as he pried the top off the box with the screwdriver. As he loosened the nails and raised a corner of the lid, he could see that whatever was in the box was wrapped in what looked like a black plastic garbage bag. *Definitely not left there by any miners,* he thought. He finally removed the lid completely and opened the bag, nearly passing out when he saw it's contents sitting there in front of him. Neatly wrapped in ten-thousand-dollar bundles was the largest pile of money he had ever seen.

He couldn't believe it. It was sitting right in front of him, staring him in the face, and he could not believe his eyes. Patricia had been right all along. Her father had hidden the money. Why he had hidden it didn't seem very important at the moment. All that mattered to Jack was that he had found it.

He sat there staring at the money for several minutes not knowing what to do next. This was a lot of money, more than just one million dollars and certainly more than he wanted to try to fly home with. He could imagine trying to explain that much cash to airport security. After staring at it for a few more minutes, he decided to count it. When he had finished counting it the second time, he was ten thousand dollars short of eight million, and he was wearing what could only be described as a "million-dollar smile."

Patricia had told him there was only supposed to be a million dollars. She would be pleasantly surprised when she found out what the actual total was. He placed the money back in the bag, put the bag back in the box, and nailed the lid shut. *It's time to go,* he thought to himself as he hammered the last nail back into place. He picked up the box and headed out of the cabin and back down the driveway to his car.

When he finally reached the car, he carefully placed the box in the trunk and covered it with an old blanket that he had found in the house. He turned the car around and headed back down the driveway and out onto the road. It was early afternoon and he had already missed his return flight from Denver, but now that he had found the money, he couldn't fly home anyway.

It had been quite a day for Jack Hixson—possibly the most exciting day of his life—and now it was over, and he was headed home. He had a long drive ahead of him, but he felt as though he had all the time in the world. He had done what, three days before, he had considered impossible. He had tracked down and recovered nearly eight million dollars in cash that had been hidden away in a cave for thirty years, and the best part was that he had to share it with only two other people. Patricia wasn't really expecting anything, but he would offer her half. After all, she was the one who got the search started. She had told him that the money was not important, that she was only in this to clear her father's name, but he felt obligated to split it with her. He wanted Elizabeth to have some as well, as she had certainly helped him find it. Even after giving both of them a share, he would be left with millions of dollars.

What would he buy? Where would he go? How would he explain all that money to the IRS? Those were the type of thoughts that were swimming around in his head as he drove the winding mountain roads between the cabin and the interstate—that is, until he drove around a sharp curve and noticed an all-too-familiar, black sedan with tinted windows heading toward him on the opposite side of the road. His heart leapt into his throat and his attention immediately focused on his rearview mirror as the two cars sped past one another. As soon as they passed, the black sedan slammed on its brakes and Jack stomped his foot on the accelerator, pushing it all the way to the floor.

Speeding through the twisty roads that sliced through the canyons, he nearly lost control several times. It would be a shame for the occupants of that car, whoever they were, to catch up with him now, and they weren't going to catch him without a chase. He stayed on the gas relentlessly, driving as fast as his rental car would take him, his tires screeching around every turn. He passed several roads that he could have turned onto to try to throw off any pursuit, but he kept moving past them, hoping he could outrun anyone that was trying to follow him. He knew, though, that the engine in the sedan was probably twice as powerful as his and that it would eventually catch up to him. After passing several side roads that, for one reason or another, didn't look promising, he came across a gravel driveway that led into a thick stand of pine trees near the main road on which he was traveling. Unlike the other roads he had passed, this one appealed to him because it would allow him to get his car quickly off the main road and out of sight. He was approaching the turn with a massive amount of speed and had to cut the wheel hard while pulling on the emergency brake to lock up the rear tires. The car slid sideways, and when he had turned a full ninety degrees, he released the brake and stomped the accelerator again, propelling him up the gravel drive toward the stand of trees he'd eyed before turning.

Once he was out of sight of the main road, he turned the car around, rolled the windows down, and waited. Within a minute, he heard the unmistakable sound of tires squealing as they rounded a nearby turn at high speed. He held his breath and listened as the sound of the car's engine whizzed past and faded into the distance. Jack sat silently, gripping the steering wheel tightly and waiting for his pursuer to realize his mistake and turn around to come after him.

He sat in his car on the gravel road and considered his predicament. He knew now that the black sedan was not part of his imagination. He'd seen it too many times to be coincidence, and it had actually chased after him this time. But who was driving it? He figured that, whoever it was, they wanted the money, but how did they know that he was looking for it as well. Did they know who he was or where he lived? This raised the stakes, and for the first time since he began this quest, he realized that he was in jeopardy—actual physical danger. But eight million dollars in cash was all the incentive he needed to keep pushing forward. Once he was safe at home, he would figure out his next move. But he was a long way from home.

He waited another few minutes, then headed back in the direction he'd come from. While waiting, he'd studied his map and found a few alternate routes that would take him back to the interstate without going through Black Hawk. They added some time to his trip, but that was the least of his concerns. He needed to get back to Denver and switch cars before trying to drive home.

The rest of the drive to Denver was uneventful, and for that, Jack was very thankful. He must have checked his rearview mirror thousands of times to make sure that the black sedan was not following him. As he pulled into town, he realized that he would need a place to put the money while he switched cars, so he decided to get a room there in Denver and stay an extra night.

He stopped at a hotel near the airport and got himself a room. "One with a minibar," he told the girl behind the counter as he checked in. He took the money and the rest of his luggage up to the room and got ready to head over and turn his car in. He hated to leave the money sitting in the room unprotected, but he couldn't carry it with him, and he figured it would be relatively safe there.

He took the car back and turned it in, and then went to another company to rent the car he would use to drive home. He paid in cash and headed back to the hotel to get a good night's rest.

He was asleep that night by eight o'clock and up the next morning at five. He showered and ate a small breakfast at the hotel and was on the road by six. The trip home was long and nerve-racking, but he never caught sight of the black sedan. He drove through the night, stopping at a rest area off the interstate some-where in Arkansas to get a little sleep and finally pulled into Chattanooga around seven o'clock in the evening of the second day.

CHAPTER 8

▼

Jack let out a sigh of relief as he felt the front tires hit the edge of his driveway. He pulled the car into the garage, closed the door behind him, and said a little prayer of thanks for the safe ride home. It was hard for him to believe that he'd actually made it and was sitting in his garage with eight million dollars in cash in the trunk.

As he walked inside, he wondered what he was going to do with the money. He certainly couldn't leave it in the car. He needed to hide it somewhere until he was sure that it was safe—somewhere no one would be able to find it. After much consideration, he decided to put the money in a hiding place he had discovered by accident while cleaning the house one day. He had been vacuuming the floor in his bedroom and hit the baseboard, knocking it away from the wall. When he reached down to pick it up, he noticed a small space where the drywall had been removed, leaving a hole in the wall. When the baseboard was put back into place, it looked like every other wall in the house. To find his hiding place, someone would have to either know it was there or go through the whole house kicking baseboards. *Not likely,* he thought.

Once again, he pulled the top off the box and emptied its contents onto his bed. He stared at the pile in front of him. This time, looking at it made him nervous, and he quickly stuffed all but one of the bundles of cash into the hiding place inside the wall.

After he had put the rest of his things away, he went into the kitchen to scrounge up some dinner. As usual, the cupboards were almost bare, reminding him of his need for the proverbial woman's touch. He thought of Elizabeth and realized how much he missed her while he'd been away. He hadn't told her about his feelings for her yet, but that would change tomorrow. He would take her out for lunch and tell her about his trip and his feelings.

Jack was exhausted after his long drive and was sound asleep by nine o'clock. As he dozed off, he imagined what his life would be like now that he was financially secure. He hoped more than anything that Elizabeth would be a part of it.

*   *   *   *

Jack awoke the next morning before his alarm clock went off. That was a rare event, as he usually found himself hitting the snooze button a couple of times before getting out of bed, but this day was different. He had a lot to look forward to and kept going over his plans for the day while he was in the shower. The first thing he needed to do was to call Patricia. It had been a couple of days since they'd talked, and she was probably very worried about him.

He was excited about the talk he planned to have with Elizabeth. He was clearly developing some strong feelings for her—feelings that he wanted to pursue and that he needed her to know about.

When he got to his office, he found a note from Elizabeth on his desk: "Call me as soon as you get in." Not wanting to disappoint her, he immediately picked up the phone and dialed her office extension.

"Hello," came her familiar, sweet voice across the line as she picked up her phone.

"I'm back," he said triumphantly.

"Jack. I'm so glad to hear your voice. I was starting to worry about you."

"No need to worry. I'm back and in my office."

"You didn't call for three days." Jack could hear a touch of anger in her voice.

"I'm sorry," he said apologetically. "Things got a little crazy out there, and I didn't have a chance to call. I'm sorry. I didn't mean to make you worry."

"As long as you're safe and back home in one piece."

"I am back," he said, "and I've got a lot to tell you."

"Did you find it?"

"Yeah, I found it, but—"

"I'll come to your office," she said, interrupting him.

"Wait," he replied quickly. He was so nervous. He wanted to talk to her, but he wanted to do it at the right moment. All he could think about at that moment was the rejection he faced should she not return the feelings he wanted to tell her about. "Give me some time to get caught up, and we'll talk later today. I've got to go meet Patricia at some point and tell her what I found. I was planning on doing that at lunch. Maybe we can get together this evening for a little while."

"Okay," she murmured, obviously unhappy about having to wait. Jack could clearly hear the resentment in her voice and hoped that she didn't feel like he was blowing her off. "I've waited this long to hear from you," she said. "I guess I can wait a little longer."

"I'm sorry, Elizabeth. I've just got to get caught up. I promise, we'll talk later today. I was also hoping that we could get together after work this evening."

"Sure. I'll have to check my schedule," she said sarcastically.

"I've got to return the rental car I drove home in. Do you think you could follow me out to the airport?"

"You drove home?"

"Yes, I couldn't fly home, but we'll talk about that later. I've got to call Patricia now and let her know that everything's all right. If you were worried, I can just imagine what she must be thinking."

"I missed you, Jack," Elizabeth said softly without a trace of bitterness.

His heartbeat accelerated and his palms began to sweat. It wasn't just what she said, but how she said it. "I missed you too," he replied. They ended their call, and he immediately dialed Patricia's number.

"I'm back," he said.

"Thank goodness," Patricia replied. "You had me worried sick."

"I'm sorry about that. I didn't mean to make you worry, but I didn't feel comfortable talking on the phone. The trip went well, though."

"Why don't we meet somewhere to talk about it?" Patricia asked excitedly.

"Sounds good. Do you have any plans for lunch today?"

"No. Where do you want to eat?"

"Same place we met last time. I've got some things I need to take care of here at my office, but I could be there at, say…twelve-thirty or one o'clock."

"Let's just say one o'clock."

"That sounds good. I'll see you there."

*   *   *   *

Jack worked in his office until twelve-forty-five. He had mountains of voice mails and e-mails to go through, each of which seemed to demand his immediate attention. He enjoyed practicing law, but he did not enjoy the schedule he was required to maintain in order to be financially successful doing it. Most of the attorneys that he knew who were making big money spent most of their waking hours in their office and very little time at home.

He struggled every day finding a balance between work and life outside the office. Now that he had the money, he would be able to be much more selective about the type and amount of work he would take on. He could also be more selective about who his clients were. No more nasty disputes among siblings over who got mamma's diamond rings or how they were going to divide daddy's farmland.

He had finished returning most of his phone messages by twelve-thirty, and needed to leave if he expected to meet Patricia on time. It was raining outside, and he decided to drive to lunch instead of walking. He didn't have far to go and was driving very carefully, so he was not concerned when he noticed a police car pull away from the curb outside the parking garage just as he pulled out onto the street. He looked in his rearview mirror and could see that the officer had pulled up right behind him. As he approached the next traffic light, he looked in the rearview mirror again and saw the flashing blue lights. He pulled to the side of the road to let the officer pass him, but he didn't pass. Instead, the cop pulled in right behind him.

Jack sat nervously waiting on the officer to get out of his car. He hadn't done anything wrong, but the sight of the police car behind him made him nervous—especially given the events of the last couple of weeks. An older-looking officer got out of the driver's side and walked slowly toward Jack's car. As he approached, Jack rolled down his window and said, "Is there a problem, officer?"

"Step out of the car, please," came the officer's quick response.

"Is there a problem, officer? I wasn't speeding."

"Just step out of the car, please, sir."

"Yes, sir," Jack said, opening his door and stepping out onto the road. He was annoyed by the way the cop had interrupted him, but he knew better than to say anything. He'd been pulled over before, but he'd never been asked to get out of the car; it made him a little nervous and he didn't want to push his luck.

"Please step over to the front of my vehicle," the officer said, pointing to the patrol car. "And put your hands out on the hood where I can see 'em."

Jack noticed that another officer had gotten out of the passenger's side of the patrol car and was walking toward his car. "What's the problem, officers? I wasn't speeding, was I?"

"Just stay right here, son," the first officer said gruffly.

"Look gentlemen. I don't know what's going on here, but I don't think I was doing anything wrong."

"We'll be the judge of that." The first officer turned to the other and told him to look in the car first and then to open the trunk. When Jack turned to look behind him, he noticed that the second officer had already opened the passenger-side door and was rifling through his glove compartment.

"What's going on?" Jack repeated earnestly. "You can't go through my car like that. Look…I happen to be an attorney, officers, and I know my rights. You can't search my car without a warrant or probable cause, and you have neither."

"Just keep your mouth shut," the first officer replied, "and this will go a lot easier for you."

"What?" Jack said, raising his voice. He couldn't believe what he was hearing. "I haven't done anything. You haven't even told me what you pulled me over for. Am I being arrested?"

"Not yet."

"What's that supposed to mean?"

"Son, I told you to keep your mouth shut. Now stay over there by my car and don't make this any more difficult for yourself."

Jack just stood there with his hands on the hood of the police car, staring at the officer in front of him in utter disbelief while the other officer rifled through his car. He couldn't believe this was happening, but he knew he was not going to make the situation any better by arguing with the cops, so he decided to just stay quiet and wait for them to finish looking through his car. He had a feeling that this had something to do with the money he'd found. If it was about the money, they weren't going to find it.

After searching through his car, the second officer popped open the trunk and began to look around. When he had finished searching the trunk, he turned around and held up a small plastic bag so that the other officer could see. "Look what I found," he said excitedly. "Looks like we got us some cocaine here."

"What the hell?" Jack exclaimed. "That wasn't in my trunk. You just planted that."

Within a second, the first officer was standing right next to Jack holding a pair of handcuffs. "Put your hands behind your back, boy."

"This is crazy!" Jack exclaimed in protest. "That's not mine. What the hell is going on here?"

"Just put your hands behind your back!"

Jack didn't know what to do. He was starting to panic. This was obviously no ordinary traffic stop. They were looking for something, most likely the money, but how did they know about that? It didn't take long before his impulse got the best of him, and he lifted his hands off the hood of the police car and turned to plead with the officers. He wasn't going to jail right now. Not over something he didn't do.

They must have thought he was going to run, and he didn't make it two steps away from the car before he was tackled from behind. As he fell, his head smacked the hard, wet pavement and he felt a stream of blood running from his forehead down the bridge of his nose. He could feel the officer's knee in the small of his back and a sharp pain in his wrist as the officer twisted it behind him and slapped handcuffs on him.

"I told you not to give us any trouble. Now look at what you've done. I oughta slap the shit out of you for getting blood on my uniform."

Jack was dumbfounded. He was lying facedown on the concrete in a slowly forming pool of his own blood. The cop had both wrists secured with handcuffs and was still digging his knee into Jack's back so that he couldn't move. He wanted to get away, but there was no chance of that now. The officer stood up and pulled Jack to his feet. As he stood, he heard the voice of the other officer talking to someone on the phone.

"No, it ain't here," he said. "No, we searched the whole car. He doesn't have it with him, but we're bringing him in. You can ask him when we get there. Do you want us to look through his house?"

Jack was sure now that they were looking for the money. How did the Chattanooga police get involved in this?

He sat quietly in the back of the police car, his head swimming in a mixture of pain and rage. The blood was starting to dry and cake up on his forehead, and the handcuffs cut deeper into his wrists with every move he made. It was everything he could do to keep his mouth shut. He wondered what he had gotten himself into and, more important, how he was ever going to get out of it.

"Where are you taking me?" he asked as soon as the officers got into the car with him.

"Where do you think we're taking you, dumb ass? You're going to jail."

"Oh, I wasn't sure," he said sarcastically. "The way you assholes operate, I was worried we were going out to a deserted field somewhere."

"That sounds like a pretty good idea, but there are some folks at the station that are real eager to talk to you first."

"And who would that be?" Jack demanded.

"Look boy…we'll ask the questions around here. Who they are don't really concern you anyway. All you need to know is that you better answer all their questions. If you don't, we may just get to take a trip to the field after all."

"Go to hell," Jack muttered under his breath.

The rest of the ride to the police station was made in silence. Jack's mind was racing. He was angry, but he had to calm down and figure a way out of this. A bag of cocaine like the one the officers had planted could land him under the jail, and he didn't have time for any of this right now.

CHAPTER 9

▼

They drove the short distance to the jail and pulled into an alley that led up to a large metal door. The officer driving the squad car said a few words into his radio and the door began to open. When it had rolled all the way up, they pulled in under it and Jack found himself in an enclosed garage area with another metal door at the other end.

They stopped the car, and the officer that was sitting in the passenger seat got out, opened Jack's door, and told him to get out of the car. As he got out of the car, a door opened and another officer walked out of the building.

"I'll take him from here," the officer said.

"No, we got him. He needs to go straight upstairs. There are a couple of feds waiting for him up there."

"He's got blood all over him."

"We'll get him a rag or something to clean up with once he gets upstairs. He just bumped his head. He's all right. Ain't ya, boy?"

The officer didn't give Jack time to answer and walked him straight through the door. They made a couple of turns and went up a flight of stairs. He led Jack to a small interrogation room that was empty except for a table and chairs that sat in front of a large mirror.

"Sit down at that table," the officer said smartly and gave Jack a little shove through the door. He was still wearing handcuffs and almost fell again, but somehow made it to one of the chairs before completely losing his balance. He sat down, looked across the table at the mirror, and wondered who was watching from behind the glass. The door was shut behind him, and he found himself alone, staring at a clock that hung on the wall above the mirror.

A few minutes later, the door swung open again, and the officer who had just pushed him into the room walked in carrying a couple of clean white towels. "Here," he said, standing in the doorway and tossing them across the room. "Clean yourself up."

Jack was unable to reach out and catch them because of the handcuffs, and after landing squarely on top of his head, they fell on the table in front of him.

"Sorry 'bout that," the officer quipped. "I forgot about your bracelets." He walked across the room to where Jack was sitting and unlocked the handcuffs, freeing Jack to wipe away the blood that was crusted across his face. The officer, who was still chuckling at himself, took the handcuffs and walked out of the room, shutting the door loudly behind him. It was nearly twenty minutes before he heard the sound of a key sliding into the lock on the outside of the door.

The door slowly opened and two men walked in and sat down across the table from him. They were both wearing nice suits—the kind of suits that police officers could not afford—and Jack was sure that these were the "feds" that he had heard mentioned earlier. One of them was carrying a laptop computer and the other had a briefcase. They put their things on the table in front of him and sat down.

"Hello Jack, I'm Special Agent Anderson," said the taller of the two men as he opened his briefcase and pulled out a file folder. "This is Special Agent Smith. We'd like to ask you a few questions if you don't mind."

"That's great. Can I see some badges?" Jack said, noticing the label on the folder Agent Anderson carried. It had the words "FOUR HORSEMEN" written across the file's tab and the words "CONFIDENTIAL—AUTHORIZED PERSONNEL ONLY" stamped in big red letters across the front cover. "And I have a few questions of my own. Like what in the hell am I doing here, and what do you guys want with me. I've done nothing wrong."

Jack had already made up his mind that he wasn't going to answer any questions. In fact, he would be downright belligerent. He was looking at spending the next twenty-five years sharing a cell with some Bubba anyway. How much worse could it get?

"We ask the questions here, Jack. You just got caught with a half-pound of cocaine, and I don't think you're in any position to be asking for anything."

"That's bullshit! That cocaine was planted by the cops that pulled me over, and besides, it doesn't have a damn thing to do with why I'm here. A half-pound of cocaine is a local police matter, and you are definitely not local cops. You're probably not cops at all. You want something from me, and you went through an awful lot of trouble to get me here, but I'll tell you this. You went about getting my help the wrong way. I'm not going to tell you a damn thing."

"Well, it looks like were going to skip the small talk," Agent Anderson said.

"Look Mr. Hixson, there are two ways we can do this," Agent Smith chimed in with a twisted smile on his face. "You can either cooperate with us now, or we can move you to a federal prison for a few months…maybe a year or so…and then we can check up on you to see if you have decided to be any more cooperative."

"Really…, That sounds threatening," Jack said with sarcasm dripping from his lips, "but I'll already be doing twenty years for the cocaine you planted. If a year in prison is all you got to threaten me with, you better come up with something else. If I'm already headed there, your threats don't mean too much. You both better put your heads together and find a way to get your information now."

"Listen, you little smart-ass!" Smith said excitedly. "We've got some pretty interesting ways to make you more talkative, but we'd rather avoid all that. Did you notice that you weren't booked when they brought you in? In fact, there is absolutely no record of you being here. People may miss you, but no one will find you. We can make you beg to tell us what we want to know. We can take you to places where every breath is pain and the sweet release of death is so close but yet so far from your grasp. Do you think you'll want to talk then? Do you think it matters when we get what we want? We've been waiting for quite a while to find what we are looking for, and we can wait a bit longer if we have to. Now you're going to tell us what you were doing in Denver and what you brought back from there."

Was he kidding? "The sweet release of death"…How many times had he used that line before? "Are you kidding me?"

"Does it look like we're kidding?"

"I guess not, but…'the sweet release of death'? Give me a fucking break. That's about the corniest thing I've ever heard." Jack could see the anger in their eyes, but they acted like they didn't even hear what he'd just said.

"What were you doing in Denver?"

"I was snow-skiing," he replied, looking across the table with a sarcastic grin. Jack wasn't sure how the belligerence was going to pay off for him, but if they wanted to know where the money was, they were going to have to work harder than throwing out a few cheesy lines.

"Skiing, huh…really? You know, Jack, that's not the kind of cooperation we were looking for."

"Well, it's the most cooperation you're going to get unless you let me out of here."

They again ignored his comments and moved right to the next question. "What do you know about Jeff Patten?"

"Jeff who?"

"Jeff Patten…Look, Jack, don't fuck with us. We know that you went to Denver, and we know that you checked a safe-deposit box he had rented there. How did you know about the box?" As he spoke, Agent Anderson pulled several pictures out of the file he had brought into the room with him and spread them out on the table. Jack was shocked when he realized that they were all pictures of him entering and leaving the bank in Denver. Whoever was driving that black sedan must have been working for these agents, but how did they know he was going to be there? They had obviously been tipped off that he was coming to the bank. It must have been the bank manager. There was no other logical explanation that Jack could think of. He must have notified the feds when Jack had called out there to check on the box. He knew from his discussions with the bank manager that someone with a warrant had gone through the box shortly after Jeff's death. They must have left instructions to notify the authorities if anyone ever tried to claim it.

"I don't know what you're talking about," he said, looking down at the pictures in front of him. "That's not me. Well, maybe it's me, but I don't know anything about any safe-deposit box. I was probably just looking for a bathroom."

"How did you get the key to that box?" Anderson asked in an increasingly irritated tone. He seemed to be losing his patience, and Jack was starting to wonder if he shouldn't tone it down a bit.

"Look, I told you that I don't know what you're talking about," he said softly, trying to sound more sincere. "I just got back from a snow-skiing vacation, and I don't know anything about any Jeff Patrick or whoever, and I don't know anything about any safe-deposit box. I went into that bank to use the bathroom, and come to think of it…you should be hassling them. That was one of the dirtiest bathrooms I've ever seen."

The two agents went back and forth, working Jack over for more than an hour. They kept asking questions about Jeff Patten and Jack's trip to Colorado, and Jack kept refusing to answer.

"This isn't going anywhere," Smith finally interjected with a disgusted look on his face.

"I told you it wouldn't," Jack said. "Not unless I can walk out of here."

"You're not going anywhere until we have what we are looking for." With that, both agents stood and walked to the door. As soon as they were gone, another officer came through the door.

"Let's go," he said, barely making eye contact. "We've got a cell ready for you."

Jack followed the officer out of the room, down some stairs, and past what Jack assumed was the booking area. "Am I going to be booked?" he asked, remembering what he'd been told in the interrogation room.

"I don't know," the officer replied. "Ain't you been booked already?"

"No. The feds that I was talking to upstairs said that they weren't going to book me."

"What?"

"They said that they were just going to keep me in here without booking me until I told them what they wanted to know. The problem is that I don't know what they want me to tell them."

"I'll look into it," the officer said suspiciously. He probably heard all kinds of accusations from all kinds of prisoners, and Jack knew that he probably didn't believe a word of it.

"Thanks. I sure do appreciate that, and I'd also be grateful if I could use a phone for just a few minutes to let someone know I'm here."

"I'll see what I can do for you."

Jack followed the officer past the booking area and into a hallway that was lined on either side with jail cells. There were between two and four people in each of the cells, and very few of the occupants looked friendly. The officer stopped at the end of the hallway and slid open the door to the last cell on the left. "In ya go," he said. There was one other person in the cell, and it reeked of vomit and Lysol.

Jack's cellmate was lying on the bottom bunk of the beds that were bolted to the back wall reading a magazine.

"What you in here for?" the man asked as soon as the guard had shut the door and walked away.

"Bullshit!" Jack responded.

"Hey, that's what I'm here for too. Hell, we're all in here for bullshit, man. What kinda bullshit do they say you did?"

"Drugs, if you really wanna know."

"Drugs ain't exactly bullshit, my friend."

Yeah, well…this was bullshit. They planted a half-pound of cocaine in my car."

"Planted it, huh?" the man asked, looking Jack over carefully.

"They sure did. Right in front of my eyes. But that doesn't help me very much. Who would believe me, right?"

"Well, I don't believe ya, if that's any help."

"I appreciate your concern, and I don't mean to be rude, but I'm not really worried right now about what you believe or don't believe." Jack climbed to the top bunk and stretched out, laying his head down on the mattress. "No pillows?" he asked, not really expecting a reply.

"No pillows, no sheets, and the roughest toilet paper you'll ever see."

Jack had noticed the toilet sitting next to the beds when he first entered the cell. He hoped he would not be here long enough to use it or to see it used. He lay quietly on his back, staring up at the concrete ceiling above him and reading the messages that had been written by various inmates over the years. A shiver ran down his spine as he read one message saying "Don't drop the soap." This was the stuff that his nightmares were made of.

As he lay there, he couldn't help but wonder about his cellmate. There was something not right about him. Like Jack, he just didn't seem to look like the other prisoners. He was muscular and clean cut. Jack eyed him suspiciously, but there was no way to know for sure whether he was just another prisoner like himself or a cop, planted to get information. Either way, Jack could see no harm in assuming that he was the later.

On the other hand, he didn't want to piss this guy off too much either. He needed to make some friends if he was going to stay there for any length of time, and smarting off to everyone who tried to talk to him probably wasn't the best way to do it. In fact, it could get him hurt. He decided that it would be better to be friendly but keep his mouth shut about anything that he might not want to get back to the feds, Anderson or Smith.

"My name is Jack, by the way," he finally said, breaking the silence that had fallen over the cell. "What are you in for?" He wanted to have a conversation and try to figure this guy out.

"Same as you, man," he responded. "They got me for a couple pounds of weed, but it wasn't mine, ya know. I was just holding it for a friend. Those sons of bitches busted down my door and trashed my place."

"How'd they know you were holding it?"

"Well...I apparently sold some of it to a cop."

"So you were selling it while you were holding it?"

"I just sold a little to help my friend out...you know...and pay some bills. He was just going to sell it anyway. I was trying to help him out a little."

"Yeah, well...selling it to a cop is a bad idea. I'd imagine that's going to make it pretty hard to get out of."

"Yeah...tell me about it. This is the first time I've ever been busted for anything, though. I figure I'll be out of here on probation. I just hope I still got a job when I get out."

"So, selling weed isn't your only job?"

"No man. I fix cars."

"That's good. Be sure to let the judge know that. He might go easier on you."

"What? Are you some kinda lawyer or something?"

"Yeah, actually I am...or at least I was. I'd say this is going to cost me my license."

"Just tell 'em the cops planted the shit on ya."

"I'm sure they will believe that. Just like you did."

"Prob'ly so, man," his cellmate said, shaking his head.

"So anyway, what did you say your name was?" Jack asked, trying to change the subject.

"I didn't...but the name's Sammy."

"Well, Sammy, it's a pleasure to meet you. I only wish it was under better circumstances."

"It's good to meet you too, Jack. It's always good to know a lawyer, and I guess it's especially good to share your cell with one," he said chuckling. "If you have to share it with someone, that is."

"Yeah...I guess you're right," Jack said, nodding his head and trying to laugh but not feeling very amused.

"What kinda law do you do?"

"I do mostly business and real estate stuff. Buying and selling businesses and commercial buildings like shopping malls and strip malls...that type of thing."

"You're not a criminal lawyer?"

"Well...I'm a lawyer, and these bastards are trying to make me look like a criminal, but I don't practice any criminal law."

"Shit. I'll bet you're wishin' you did criminal law now."

"I guess so. It would be nice to be able to help myself out of this mess."

The two men lay in their bunks talking to each other for another hour or so. Sammy, whom Jack quickly determined to be the typical loudmouth, said he was married and had a couple of girlfriends on the side. Sammy kept trying to get Jack to talk about what he was doing in jail and why he thought the cops would be planting drugs in his car. Jack avoided any discussions about his trip to Denver or the money or anything else that might give Sammy the idea that Jack knew what was going on. It was going to be strictly small talk until he was sure that his cellmate was not a threat.

After a couple of hours of their on-and-off conversation, the officer who had escorted Jack to the cell came back to the door. Jack had nearly dozed off and was startled awake by the sound of the key being slid into the lock. He looked over as the guard slid the door open.

"You got your phone call, Mr. Hixson," he said, staring into the cell at Jack.

"Me?" Jack asked.

"Yeah, you wanted to make a call, didn't ya?" the guard asked rhetorically.

"Yes sir."

"Well...come with me then." The guard stood outside the cell motioning for Jack to come out. He sprang out of his bunk and walked through the door. "That way," the officer said, pointing down the hallway that Jack had walked through earlier. "Take a right through the door at the end of this hallway. When you get to the end of that hallway, there's a door. That's where the phone is. I'll stand outside while you talk, but you only got five minutes. Make it quick."

Jack followed the guard's instructions and headed down the hallway. *Who should I call?* he wondered as he made his way toward the phone. Should he call his parents, his law firm, Elizabeth, Patricia?...He had only one call to make, so it had to count, and he had to decide quickly. After giving it all the consideration he had time for, he decided to call Elizabeth. He wanted her to hear about this from him directly, and he trusted that she would do what she could to help. At least she would be able to get one of the attorneys at his firm on the case. Perhaps they could do something to get him out.

When he got to the end of the hallway, there was a thick wooden door that was propped open. It had a small Plexiglas window so that he could be monitored while he made his call. Jack walked through the door into a closet-sized room that was completely barren except for the phone that hung on one of the walls. He closed the door behind him, picked up the phone, and dialed Elizabeth's direct line, praying that she would answer and that he wouldn't have to talk to the receptionist.

"Hello. This is Elizabeth Pierce." It was the sweetest sound Jack could ever remember hearing.

"Elizabeth...this is Jack. PLEASE DON'T HANG UP!"

"Jack. What's going on? You never made it back from lunch. I thought we were going to try to get together this evening."

"I know. I know. I'm sorry I missed it, but I'm in trouble here. I've been arrested and I'm in jail."

"What are you talking about?" Elizabeth was obviously very concerned and very confused.

"Elizabeth…listen to me…I've only got a few minutes to talk. I don't really know what's going on, but it has something to do with my trip to Denver. The cops pulled me over on my way to meet Patricia and planted drugs in my car."

"Are you all right?"

"I've got a little bump on my head, but I'm okay. I need someone to get me out of here."

"Jack, I'll come bail you out. How much is your bail?"

"They haven't booked me, so you can't bail me out. Something strange is going on and I've got to get out of here."

"What do you mean they haven't booked you?"

"Just what I said. They haven't booked me, and I'm pretty sure they don't intend to. I've been questioned by some federal agents about what I was doing in Denver. I told them that I was out there on a skiing trip. Apparently, they think otherwise and said that I was going to rot in my cell if I didn't tell them what they wanted to know. I need your help, Elizabeth."

"What can I do?"

"I'm not sure yet, but I need you to stay by the phone in case I call."

"Of course. I'll keep my cell phone with me. I'll be right there if you need me. I'll come post bail for you and get you out of there as soon as I can."

"You can try to call down here tomorrow, but I don't think they are going to set any kind of bail. I think I'm in big trouble here. I think I've stumbled into something that I shouldn't have and stepped on some mighty big toes in the process. Can you to do me a favor?"

"Sure Jack. Name it."

"First, I want you to get one of the attorneys there at the firm to try and get me out. I also need you to do some research and see what you can find out about a government operation called the Four Horsemen."

"What?"

"The Four Horsemen…and I don't mean the ones in the Bible. It's some kind of government operation or agency or something. That's all I know right now. Just see what you can find, if anything, and I'll be in touch as soon as possible."

"I'll check it out, but what does it have to do with you?"

"I don't know, but I'm sure it's got something to do with why I'm here. Just find out anything you can."

As Jack finished his sentence, the guard knocked on the door and motioned through the window for Jack to wrap it up. "Look…I've got to go, Elizabeth.

The guard is here. You've got to trust me. Please believe that I didn't do what they are accusing me of. The drugs were planted. They were not mine, and I'm going to need your help to prove it. But first, I've got to figure a way out of here. Talk to Scott Hall on the third floor. I think he does some criminal practice. Tell him what you know and see if he can get me out of here."

"I believe you, Jack. I'll talk to Scott and try to find out something about the Four Horsemen thing. I'll be waiting for you to call."

"Thanks, Elizabeth."

"You're welcome, Jack." She sounded as if she was holding back tears. "Please be careful. I'll see what I can do to get you out."

"I will…and thanks again," Jack said as he hung up the phone.

The guard followed him back to his cell, which he found empty. His cellmate was gone and Jack had the place all to himself. He walked over and sat glumly on the bottom bunk.

He sat on the edge of the bed, leaning forward with his head in his hands, wondering how he was going to get out of this. He tried to remember anything he could from his criminal law classes in law school that might help, but until they booked him and actually put him in "the system," there was very little that he, or anyone else for that matter, could do. The only condition Smith and Anderson had given him—to tell them where the money was—was not an option. He couldn't tell them where it was. That was his only leverage.

His captors obviously had some influence, and Jack had the feeling that there would be few, if any, questions asked of them if he were to disappear. He had to hold out. He needed to get them to tip their hand so that he could figure out what this was about. Why were they after the money? Who did it actually belong to, and how, or why, did Jeff Patten get involved? They were clearly up to no good, and Jack could use that against them if he could just figure out what was going on. From what he'd seen of the file that Anderson had pulled out earlier, whatever they were up to, it was top secret.

A voice from the next cell broke the silence and Jack's concentration. "I think your buddy is a cop."

Jack looked over to the cell next to him and saw the face of a young man pressed up to the bars that separated his cell from the next. "What?" Jack asked, sounding very annoyed.

"I said, I think your buddy is a cop."

"What are you talking about?" Jack asked, even more annoyed.

"Your buddy…your cellmate…you know, you were talking to him before they took you to use the phone."

"Why do you say that? Where is he?"

"Right after you left, a couple of guys in suits came down and got him out of the cell. They were trying to be quiet, but I could hear them on their way out asking him what you had told him."

"What did he say?"

"I couldn't hear them real good. They were walking down the hallway."

"Did you hear anything?"

"Yeah…he said you didn't say nothin' helpful."

"Were there two guys in suits? One of them kind of tall and the other about average height?"

"Sounds like them."

"Did you happen to hear their names?"

"No, I didn't catch the names."

Jack was suspicious about his cellmate from the moment they'd started talking. Now his suspicions were being confirmed. He had wondered why Sammy had been so interested in him, but thought maybe he was just trying to make conversation. Obviously, he'd been wrong about that. He was going to have to be very careful about what he said and who he spoke to. He was going to have to find somebody he could trust, but for the time being, he was stuck.

"Is that all he said?" Jack asked after a moment of silence.

"Like I said, they were on their way out, so I couldn't hear real good, but they were talking like they knew each other. I mean…they was a lot nicer to him than they are to me. My name is Dave, by the way."

"I'm Jack…Jack Hixson," he replied, smiling through the bars.

"Nice to meet ya, Jack."

"Same here."

"I wasn't trying to listen in on your conversation or anything, but I couldn't help but overhear you talking to your cellmate earlier. Are you really a lawyer?"

"Yes. That's right."

"And they got you in here on some cocaine?"

"Yes, unfortunately. A lot of it."

Dave looked back through the bars, shaking his head, with a scowl on his face. "That's some nasty shit…cocaine, I mean. That's what put me in here, too. I was just a drinker, but then I started smoking crack with some of the guys that I worked with. It just got a hold of me. Had me doin' some stupid shit that I never would of done if I'd been sober."

"What did you do?"

"I started stealin'…from my friends and family and lyin' to my old lady…just stupid shit like that. I was out of my mind and finally got caught trying to rob a liquor store." He chuckled as if remembering something funny and then said, "I had a cap gun and the guy behind the counter had a .357 Magnum. He pointed it right at my head and told me to get down on the ground, and that's exactly what I did."

"You said lying to your old lady. You're married?"

"No. I've got a girlfriend who, for some reason, is still waitin' for me. We had a little trailer that we bought together, and she's goin' to school to be a nurse."

"Sounds like a good girl."

"Yeah, she sure is. She's certainly better than I deserve. I know she hates it, but I think bein' in here is the best thing that's happened to me since I started smokin' that stuff."

"Why do you say that?"

"Well, it sobered me up for one reason. I used to have a job. I wasn't a lawyer or anything like that, but I had a job and it paid the bills. I was workin' as an electrician's apprentice since I got out of high school. I'd been doin' that for almost five years and was about to get certified as an electrician, but it didn't take me long after I started on that stuff to mess it all up, though."

"That's rough. When do you get out of here?"

"Well, my court date is next month, and I've been in here since I got arrested six months ago. They set bail for me, but I can't afford it."

"Was this the first time you've ever been in trouble with the law?"

"Yeah…the first and the last. Once I'm outta here, I ain't ever gonna start smokin' again. I'm gonna lay off the booze too." He let out a long sigh and then started in again. "It ain't no good…me being in here while my girlfriend's out there trying to go to school and get by. I know I messed up, but I'm gonna try to make it right once I get out."

"Do you have a lawyer?"

"The judge gave me one when I had my last court date, but I ain't seen or heard from her since then."

"So you've got a public defender?"

"I think that's what you call 'em. I didn't have no money for my own lawyer. Hell, I didn't even have the money to get bailed outta here."

"If I can get myself out, I may be able to get you some help. I do real estate law and wouldn't be any help to you myself, but I know some attorneys that do criminal defense work. I'll bet I could get one of them to help you."

"I appreciate that," Dave replied with a friendly grin, "but I can't really afford all that."

"I know. I'm talking about getting someone to do it for free."

"Would they do that?"

"They might. Contrary to what a lot of people say about lawyers, we're not such a bad crowd. In fact, we're just people trying to get by like everyone else. You sound serious about getting your life back on track, and I'll bet I can find someone who'll appreciate that and help you out."

"Man, that would be great. I just want another chance, ya know. I know I screwed up, but if I could have another chance..."

"Yeah, I know," Jack said, not needing for him to finish his sentence.

"I heard you telling your cellmate that the cops planted drugs on you. Is that for real?"

"They planted it in my car while they were 'searching' it."

"Ain't nobody goin' to believe that, ya know. I've been in here for a while, and you're not the only one saying that the cops set you up."

"Yeah, I know, and up until today, I wouldn't have believed them either. Now I'm wondering how many of them were actually set up."

"Why would they go and do a thing like that to you?"

"I don't know," Jack said cautiously, suddenly aware of the fact that he didn't really know the person he was talking to. He needed to be very careful about what he said.

"You don't know...or you can't say? I may not be the sharpest tool in the shed, but if they really planted drugs on you...I mean, if they wanted you in here so bad, you gotta know why. Or at least have some idea."

"Well, I'm pretty sure I know why they want me, but I'd really rather not discuss it. I'm not trying to be rude, but I don't know if I can trust you. No offense, Dave, but I'm not sure that you're not one of them."

"I guess you're right. You can't be sure that I'm not one of them, but it don't really matter to me. I'm just makin' conversation. We can talk about somethin' else."

"Yeah, I would rather find something else to talk about if you don't mind. What's the food like in here?"

"It sucks, but it comes three times a day."

"And what do you do all day? Just sit in your cell?"

"I been doing a little work here and there while I've been in here. You know, just helpin' out, sweepin' and moppin' and doin' some light electrical stuff when they need it. I made a few friends outta the cops at this place, and sometimes they'll bring me some donuts or the leftovers from their dinner the night before. Like I said, I've been in here for a while, and they've gotten to know me pretty well. And hell…I ain't such a bad guy."

"No. You seem nice enough."

They sat on their bunks and talked to each other through the bars until they heard footsteps coming down the hall. They looked up and saw one of the guards walking down the hallway between the cells. He walked all the way to the end of the hallway and turned around in front of Jack's cell. "Light's out," he said as he made his way back toward the doorway that he had just come through. When the footsteps reached the end of the hallway, the lights abruptly went dim, and those who weren't already in their bunks like Jack were crawling into them.

Jack lay back on his bunk thinking about everything that had happened to him that day. He wondered if he would be able to trust his new friend, Dave. Being an attorney had taught Jack to think on his toes and to uncover inconsistencies in people's stories, and he felt pretty confident that Dave had been honest with him—especially the part about his cellmate, Sammy, who'd been gone for some time and still hadn't come back to the cell. Why would he tell Jack that he thought Sammy was a cop if he was also a cop? It wouldn't make sense, but nothing made sense to Jack at that point.

He needed to focus on getting himself out of jail and back on the street, where he would have a chance to fight back. He was not going to just let this happen to him without a fight. He knew that getting out was not enough though. His captors undoubtedly had the connections and the resources to track him down anywhere he cared to go, and would surely follow him to the ends of the earth to get what they wanted. He was going to have to figure out why they wanted the money and use it against them if he ever wanted to be a free man again.

He sat quietly on his bunk thinking of all the prison escape stories he'd heard and watched on the television over the years. All he could think about was getting out of there quickly, and he lay in bed thinking about it until he fell asleep.

CHAPTER 10

▼

Jack woke up early the next morning. He opened his eyes slowly and looked around at the concrete walls and steel bars surrounding him. He let out a long, anguished sigh when he realized that he hadn't been dreaming. His head still hurt from its encounter with the pavement, and he was still wearing his bloodied clothes from the day before. It was like being in a nightmare from which he couldn't wake up.

He lay in bed staring up at the ceiling and thinking. He had been in custody for almost twenty-four hours and still hadn't been booked. Maybe Anderson's words were more than empty threats. Maybe they were just going to wait him out. The money had been hidden away for all those years. Nobody knew where it was or what had happened to it. If they had waited this long to find it, they could surely wait a while longer.

He was starting to get depressed. He was a lawyer, but he didn't know enough about criminal defense work to help himself. He didn't even really know why he was there. He knew it had something to do with the money, but he didn't know why the feds would be so desperate to get their hands on it. Whatever the reason, he was going to have to try to connect the dots to figure it out. Why did they want the money? He was sure the money itself was not what they were after. The feds had plenty of money at their disposal. It must be what the money represented that they were worried about. Whatever this money had been intended for, it was probably not legal, and he hoped that would be his saving grace. He had stumbled into something big that the federal government (or at least some part of the government) was involved in. Something that they undoubtedly didn't want the public to know about. He had to figure out what was going on and who was involved. If he wanted his freedom, he would have to get some proof and confront the people that were holding him. But first, he needed to get out of jail.

He was startled by a voice at the door of his cell. "Good morning, Mr. Hixson. Rise and shine," the voice said. He turned his head and saw the guard who had taken him to use the phone the day before. *He is far too cheerful for this sort of place,* Jack thought to himself.

He slid his key into the lock and pulled the door open. "You need to follow me please, Mr. Hixson."

"Where are we going?" Jack asked. "I'm starving. I haven't had anything to eat since yesterday."

The guard laughed. "You're not missing anything. Believe me. Now get up and come with me. You've got some folks that are eager to talk to you this morning. You can have your breakfast after that."

Jack sat up and rubbed the knot on his head. He took in a deep breath and realized that he'd almost gotten used to the smell of the place. "You know, I didn't get anything to eat yesterday either. Are you guys ever going to feed me?" he asked, looking up at the guard. There was no reply. He just stood by the door staring at Jack with an annoyed look on his face.

Jack rubbed his eyes, let out a big yawn, and stretched his arms up over and behind his head. His back was sore from sleeping on the worn-out excuse for a mattress, but that was the least of his worries. He stood up and walked out of his cell into the hallway, looking around at the other cells while the guard closed his cell door behind them.

His cellmate, Sammy, was still missing, and Dave was asleep in the cell next to his. There was no activity in any of the cells, and Jack wondered what time it was. It must have been early, he surmised, because everyone else in the place was still sleeping.

"Come on," the guard said, motioning for Jack to head down the hallway. "I'm following you. Do your remember how to get back upstairs?"

"No...not really," Jack replied. He didn't remember but would memorize everything he could about the place. He was going to have to get himself out of here, and he needed to be ready to take advantage of any opportunity that presented itself. That meant he needed to know the layout of the place—especially the locations of any exits.

"Just follow me," the guard said, pointing down the hallway and motioning for Jack to start walking.

Jack started down the hall with the guard right behind him. As he walked past the booking area, he turned back to the officer and asked again whether they were going to book him.

"You still haven't been booked?" the officer asked with a curious look on his face. "Has anyone taken your mug shots or fingerprints?"

"Not yet," Jack replied. "And I've been here for almost twenty-four hours." The officer told Jack that he would check into it. He was obviously puzzled by the fact that Jack had not been booked. Whatever was going on, the guard didn't seem to be a part of it, and Jack made a mental note of that.

They walked up the stairs and came to the steel door that Jack had walked through the day before. The officer walked past him and unlocked the door. "Now when we go through this door, you're going to take a left and then take your first left. You should recognize it once you see it." Jack did as he was told and found himself in the familiar hallway where the interrogation rooms were. It was about forty feet long and had four doors on each side.

Standing outside of the third door on his left was Agent Smith, one of the two men who had questioned him the day before.

"Good morning, Mr. Hixson," Smith said as he approached. "Did you sleep well?" Sarcasm seemed to fit him well.

"Best night's sleep I've had in a long while," Jack replied with equal sarcasm.

Smith looked over at the officer who had escorted Jack. "That'll be all, officer," he said in an unnecessarily sharp tone of voice.

The officer didn't take kindly to the tone. He glared back at the agent indignantly and then looked over at Jack. "Yeah, thanks...I'm going to book him when ya'll get done, so let me know as soon as you're finished. We need to get a set of prints and process him if he's going to stay here."

"We can handle him, thanks," the agent said in the same sharp tone he'd used earlier.

"I'm sure you could, but that's my job. If he's going to stay in my jail, on my shift, I'm going to book him myself." He looked over and made eye contact with Jack as he spoke to Agent Smith. "He also needs to get some breakfast, so either get this over with and get him back downstairs or give him a break, and we'll bring some food to him."

This was obviously starting to upset Agent Smith, who was apparently not used to being challenged. Jack, who was getting a lot of pleasure watching this exchange, was starting to like this particular officer. He seemed to be one of the good guys. There were those police officers who thought they were above the law because they wore a badge, and then there were the ones who wore the badge because they respected the law. In Jack's experience, the latter usually tried to apply the law fairly and justly to everyone including themselves, while the former used the law to their own ends or to satisfy their twisted desire to control other people.

"Look, Officer...Speakman," Smith said, looking down at the officer's name badge. "I said we'll handle him. You will feed him when I say feed him, and you will book him when I say book him. In fact, you will not take him to the bathroom without asking me. Is that clear?"

"Whatever you say...Agent...uh...what did you say your name was?" It was delightfully clear to Jack that these two were not going to be friends. Perhaps he would be able to use that to his advantage. Agent Smith was a jackass in every sense of the word.

"Smith...my name is Special Agent Smith," the agent said, maintaining his harsh tone while responding to the officer's question. He looked at Officer Speakman, feeling very superior, and said, "That will be all, officer. You're excused." Jack could see the red starting to overtake Speakman's complexion. Two veins popped out on his forehead, and the hair on the back of his neck was starting to stand on end. Without saying another word, he turned and walked back down the hallway in the direction from which they had come, leaving Jack alone with Smith outside the interrogation room.

"Come in and have a seat, Jack," Smith said, turning his attention back to Jack and pointing to the table in the middle of the room. Jack walked in and sat down at the table as he had the day before, only this time with his back to the mirror. "Will you please sit on the other side of the table?" the agent asked.

"Sorry," he replied sarcastically. "I guess your buddy can't see my face through the mirror if I sit here." He stood up as he spoke and made his way around to the other side of the table, raising his middle finger and flipping a bird at whoever was on the other side of the mirror.

"I see that we are still a smart-ass today, Mr. Hixson. I had hoped that spending the night in a jail cell would've helped you change your mind."

"I'm afraid you were wrong. Not only did it not help change my mind, but it pissed me off. So now I've decided that I wouldn't answer your questions if you put a gun to my head."

"That can be arranged, Mr. Hixson. That can be arranged."

Jack looked at Smith with a cold stare and replied, "I'm sure it can be arranged, Smitty, but if you wanted me dead, something tells me that I'd already be that way. And as far as giving you ideas...somebody's got to do it. You don't look like the type that has too many ideas of your own." Apparently that comment went a little too far. Before he realized what was happening, Smith came across the table and landed a hard right hook squarely on Jack's jaw. The next thing Jack knew, he was sitting on the floor leaning up against the wall. Smith was a prick, no doubt about that, who obviously considered himself to be above the law, which made Jack's situation more dire and his desire to get himself out of jail more intense.

Smith was standing over him, rubbing his fist. He picked the chair that Jack had been sitting in up off the floor and set it back by the table. He looked down at Jack and told him to get back up in the chair. The sucker punch had definitely taken the fight out of Jack for the moment. He was not going to be helpful, but he was giving up on the smart-ass routine for now.

"There are two ways we can go about this. You just got a taste of the hard way...and believe me, it can get a lot harder. But we can also do this the easy way, which means you tell me what I want to know." He paused for a minute and then finished his thought, saying, "Without being a smart-ass."

Neither of the options Jack had just been given were acceptable. He was not too keen on the idea of getting hit again, but he was certainly not about to tell this asshole whether he had the money or where it might be. He was going to have to shoot for a third option, which was silence. From that moment on, Jack would not speak to Smith or his partner. They could beat him all they wanted, but he wasn't going to tell them what they wanted to know.

Jack stayed on the floor rubbing his jaw for a second and then pulled himself up and back into the chair.

"Let's try this again now. I'm going to ask you some questions, and you're going to give me some answers. Right?"

Jack looked up at him and smiled.

"What were you doing in Denver?"

Jack continued to stare, not making a sound.

"Jack, I asked you what you were doing in Denver. Now you're supposed to answer me." They both sat in silence for what seemed like an eternity. Jack expected the next punch to come at any moment.

"Are you going to answer me?" Smith asked in a stern voice. Jack just continued staring up at him. "Boy...," Smith said menacingly, "I'm telling you. You are all alone here. It's just you and me. Nobody's going to help you. Not even your lawyer friends. We've made sure of that. It would be a shame for you to fall down some staircase somewhere or get hurt or shot or something while trying to escape." Jack could hear the frustration and rage building in his voice, which both scared and pleased him at the same time. He just sat there, silently staring at this man, who was looking less like a human and more like a monster.

"Let's try this another way, Jack. I know about your phone call yesterday. I know you talked to your little girlfriend at work. What's her name…Elizabeth. I'm sure she told you that she would help you get out of here, but don't think for a second that she can follow through on that. Don't think that she can do anything for you; she can't. She's been trying, but it's not going to do you any good. In fact, one of the attorneys from your office called here several times yesterday evening, but as far as anybody knows, you're not here."

The mention of Elizabeth made Jack very uncomfortable. He didn't expect her name to be brought up, and it must have shown, because Smith suddenly got a big smile on his face. "You don't want anything to happen to your girlfriend, do you?"

Threatening Elizabeth was more than Jack could take. "You leave her out of this, you son of a bitch," he blurted in a blind rage. "This is between you and me. If you so much as breathe in her direction, then you'll never get your damn money. In fact, if anything happens to either one of us, then there are going to be an awful lot of people asking an awful lot of questions about where that money came from."

"So you do have the money?" Agent Smith said excitedly.

Jack realized that, in his rage and excitement, he had just made a huge mistake. He had let Smith know that he had the money. "Yes, damn it, I've got your money, but you'll never find it without me, and if I don't come get it in the next few days, then the case will be opened and the instructions that I put with the money will be followed, and then somebody is going to have a lot of explaining to do."

Jack was never good at poker, in part because he couldn't bluff. If he was betting strong with a weak hand, he invariably gave himself away, but not this time. There was just too much at stake. He was bluffing and he had to make it work.

"Don't threaten me, Jack," Agent Smith said. "I'm in charge here." The moment of excitement had passed and he was once again an angry man.

"Fuck you!" Jack said, lifting his middle finger toward Agent Smith's face.

"Look, you little shit, you better tell me what I want to know. You tell me where the money is and help me go get it, and you walk out of here a free man. It's that simple. If you don't tell me, you stay here…for a while. Then you go to a federal prison where you can rot while we keep an eye on you."

"A free man, huh…," Jack said sarcastically. "What about the half-pound of cocaine they found in my car?"

"That can be dealt with. After all, it was planted in your car, and I just happen to have a videotape of the whole thing."

"What are you talking about?"

"I just happen to have a video showing the officer getting the drugs out of his car and planting them in yours."

"A video, huh?…"

"Yes, it was made by…let's say…an anonymous, concerned citizen, who just happened to be standing in a parking lot across the street with their new video camera when you got pulled over. I've seen the tape myself. It pretty clearly shows you being set up by a bad cop who was about to lose his job and needed a good 'bust' on his record so he wouldn't get fired."

Jack couldn't believe what he was hearing. This son of a bitch would go to any length to get what he wanted and didn't care who he hurt in the process. Jack had no love for the cop who had planted the drugs on him, but at least now it made some sense. He was about to lose his job and was asked to do this "favor" for the feds, but he didn't know that they were making a video of the whole thing. He was set up just like Jack, only he didn't know it yet. These federal agents were true monsters.

"We also know, Jack, that you were busted for marijuana when you were eighteen. That's certainly not going to help you. If that information gets out, it won't be hard for anybody to believe that you were still using drugs. You know, once a druggie, always a druggie. It's up to you, Jack. Somebody's going down here; it's either you or the cop that set you up. It's your choice. Don't make the wrong one."

"And what about the money?" Jack asked angrily. "If I go down, you'll never find it. What are you going to do then?"

"You're a fool, Jack. I don't give a damn about the money. I'm only concerned with loose ends, and right now you and that money are loose ends. If you go down for a half-pound of cocaine, and the money is discovered, then it was obviously your drug money and we have nothing to explain. If you tell me where the money is, then the nasty cop goes to jail, we get our money back, your name is cleared, and everyone is happy. Think about it, Jack…think about it."

"I'll think about it," Jack said, leaning back in his chair. *What should I do?* he wondered. *Give up the money and let this bastard win? No!* That was a last resort. For that to happen, the cop who set Jack up would have to go down. His life along with the lives of his family would be ruined, and regardless of what he had done, Jack didn't want to see that happen. Jack couldn't trust that Smith was even telling him the truth. How could he be sure there was a video? How could he be sure that Smith wouldn't just take the money and let Jack sit in jail on some trumped-up charges? Or worse, get his hands on the money and then take Jack out to a field and let him "try" to escape? No, giving Smith what he wanted was definitely a last resort. It appeared at that moment that Smith couldn't loose: no matter what he did. But Jack also knew that given some time to analyze the situation, he would find a way out. Smith also seemed too sure of his position, and that, Jack thought, could be his undoing.

"You think about it, Jack," he said, standing up from his chair and walking over to the door. He walked out of the room and slammed the door behind him, leaving Jack alone to consider his choices. Smith believed he had presented Jack with his only viable option: to tell him where the money was so that he could go home. He didn't realize, however, that Jack didn't always do things the easy way. Jack liked to do things Jack's way; right now, Jack's way wasn't going to involve helping Agent Smith.

He sat alone in the interrogation room, rubbing his jaw and staring into the mirror. He knew Smith and his partner were watching him from the other side, and it was no surprise when, fifteen minutes later, the door opened again and Agent Anderson slipped into the room.

"Good morning, Jack," Anderson said, smiling politely. "I'm Special Agent Anderson. We talked a little bit yesterday."

"I remember you," Jack replied smugly, still rubbing his jaw.

"I see you got a little red mark there on your chin." Anderson was pointing to his own jaw in the area where Jack had been struck. "Is everything okay?"

"If okay means that your partner is allowed to slap people around while he's interrogating them, then yes, everything is okay."

"Of course he's not allowed to slap people around. You're not suggesting that Agent Smith struck you, are you?"

"I'm not suggesting anything at all. I'm flat-out telling you that the son of a bitch punched me in the face. I gave the wrong answer, and the asshole cracked my jaw, but I'm sure you're not here to do anything about that, are you?"

"No Jack, I'm not. I'm actually here to see if you would like any breakfast. I've got a few questions I would like to ask you, but if you're hungry, I'll have one of the officers come and take you back to your cell, and we can finish this up after you eat."

Jack knew the old "good cop—bad cop" routine, and this was a classic case. In comes Smith to terrorize and beat on him. After a couple of good smacks, bad cop leaves and then the good cop Anderson comes in to protect Jack from his nasty, abusive partner. He knew that this was just a ploy to get him to talk. Smith never expected Jack to break, but he would continue to beat up on him until he told Anderson what they wanted to know.

They didn't know it yet, but they were toying with the wrong man. Jack knew that they were involved in something illegal, or, at least, unethical and that whatever they were doing, it involved a lot of money and had been going on since at least 1972. He also know that his captors were too sure of themselves. He just needed to find a way to turn what he know to his advantage. Whatever happened, he had no intention of telling either of them anything, but he would take advantage of Anderson for as long as he was willing to play the good cop. "I would love some breakfast," Jack replied.

"We'll take care of that then, and you and I can talk later." Anderson walked out of the room, and Jack was left alone to stare at the mirror again. He looked up at the clock for the first time and realized that it wasn't even 6:00 A.M. He knew they were just on the other side of the glass, watching him and talking about him, and he imagined that they were plotting the best way to break him down.

Jack was stubborn and could be ornery when cornered, but he knew that if he stayed in this place too long, they would eventually break him. Given time, he would eventually tell them what they wanted to know, and he knew that he couldn't let that happen. It was the only thing that was keeping him, and possibly even Elizabeth, alive. There was something big going on here. The government was involved, and he needed to know what it was and expose it. He needed to bring these roaches into the light of day so that they could pay for what they had done to him over the last twenty-four hours; he would do his best to make sure that they paid dearly.

After several minutes had passed, there was a knock at the door. "Please come in," Jack said sarcastically, expecting Smith to come back for round two. He was starting to get very annoyed with his captivity. The door opened and in walked the officer who had brought him upstairs earlier. Seeing his face made Jack feel a little more at ease. In a strange way, he felt that the officer was on his side. "It's Officer Speakman, right?" Jack said as he walked into the room.

"Yeah...that's right," he replied with an empathetic look on his face. "I've come to take you to breakfast if you're hungry."

"Thanks," Jack said. "I'm starving. I haven't eaten since dinner two nights ago." His jaw was still sore and must have still been red because Officer Speakman asked what had happened.

"Agent Smith happened," Jack replied gruffly. "I answered one of his questions wrong."

"You mean he hit you?" Speakman asked. He didn't sound surprised but was definitely irritated.

"He did, and something tells me he plans on doing it again."

"Maybe not…Why don't you follow me back downstairs."

Maybe not, Jack mused as he stood up. *What is that supposed to mean?* It wasn't exactly reassuring, but it sounded as if there was more to what he was saying then was readily apparent.

Officer Speakman waited until they were out of the room and headed down the hallway before looking at Jack and saying, "I looked for your file, Jack. You don't have one. I don't think they plan on booking you. In fact, there is no report on your arrest. There's no warrant for your arrest and nothing in the evidence room linking you to any crime. I don't know what you did, or who you did it to, but you've pissed somebody off."

Jack was a little shocked by this. He didn't expect a police officer to care enough to look into it or to be speaking so candidly with him about what he'd found. "All I can tell you is that I haven't done anything illegal," he said, hoping that Officer Speakman believed him

"Seems that way to me too, Jack. Now follow me," he said, leading Jack back down to his cell.

CHAPTER 11

▼

When Jack got back to his cell, his cellmate, Sammy, was nowhere to be found and his neighbor, Dave, was still asleep in his bunk. Being in no mood for conversation, he was glad to see it. He walked in and sat down on the bottom bunk, waiting on breakfast. This would be his first jailhouse breakfast and he wasn't really looking forward to it, but it was certainly better than sitting in the interrogation room being slapped around by the worst asshole that Jack had ever had the displeasure of meeting.

Before too long, he heard footsteps and a clanking metallic sound coming down the hallway. He looked down the hall to see one of the guards pushing a metal cart down the hallway between the cells. The cart was full of trays and resembled those used to serve food on an airplane, but Jack's confinement was much less exciting than a plane ride.

As the cart was pushed down the hall, the other inmates started to wake up. Its wheels had obviously not been oiled recently and one of them appeared to be broken, because they were squeaking and the whole cart was vibrating. One by one, the other inmates sat up in their bunks, yawning and stretching and trying to wake up for another day of confinement. Jack thought to himself that he'd go crazy if he had to spend a significant amount of time locked up like this. Finally, the cart arrived outside Jack's cell. "Eat this carefully and drink your coffee, but don't do anything until you hear from me," the officer said as he slid Jack's tray through the slit in the bars.

"What?" Jack asked, not sure whether he'd actually heard what the officer said.

"Just eat your breakfast and do as you're told until you hear differently," he replied in a hushed tone that was almost a whisper.

"Okay," Jack tried to say, but by the time he could say it, the officer was already heading back up the hallway with an empty cart. Jack took his tray of food and carried it back to his bunk where he sat down to eat.

The tray reminded him of his elementary school days. It was a large rectangular piece of plastic with little sections to separate the different foods. Sitting on the tray were scrambled eggs, what appeared to be grits, two pieces of extra crispy bacon, two pieces of soggy toast, a Styrofoam cup with lukewarm coffee, and a plastic spoon. None of it looked very appetizing.

He picked up a piece of bacon and ate it first. He liked his bacon a little less cooked than this, but it would do. The eggs were a little too salty but not that bad, and the grits were edible. He wolfed down everything on his plate without even taking a sip of his coffee, which, by the time he picked it up, was already cold.

He put the cup to his lips and turned it up to take a big swallow and wash his food down. As the cool liquid made its way into his mouth and down his throat, he felt something hard hit his tongue. He stopped swallowing and slowly let the coffee drain out of his mouth back into the cup. He could feel a metallic object in his mouth and looked around to make sure that no one was paying attention to him. When he was satisfied that everyone was more interested in their own breakfast than in him, he took the object out of his mouth and was absolutely shocked to find himself holding a key.

He had no idea what it went to, but it appeared to be a door key of some sort. It was not the key to his cell. He had seen one of those, and they were much larger than the one he held in his hand now. *What in the hell is going on?* he thought to himself. What did this key go to, and why was it in his coffee? Obviously, it was meant to help him. But what did it open, and when was he supposed to use it?

Suddenly, he remembered the officer's instructions. "Eat carefully and don't do anything until you hear differently," he had said. Why was this officer helping him? Was he actually going to help him escape, or was this an excuse for Anderson and Smith to get rid of him?

When he was finished, he placed his empty tray on the floor in front of his cell and walked back over to his bunk. He had a bewildered look on his face that must have given away his confusion.

"Was it that bad?" Dave asked, startling Jack. "You look sick."

Jack snapped out of his train of thought and looked over at Dave, who was still shoveling eggs into his mouth. "No. It's not the food."

"Must be the coffee," Dave said with a strange, almost knowing, smile on his face.

Jack wondered if he knew what had been put in his coffee. His smile indicated that he knew something was up, but he needed to be careful about what he said. He still didn't really know Dave, and if the officer was trying to help him, he didn't want to jeopardize the opportunity.

He sat silently for a moment thinking about how to respond. "Yeah, the coffee was a little bitter."

"Bitter, huh," Dave said as he moved to the end of his bunk and leaned right up to the bars between their cells. "Did it have a metallic taste."

Jack stared at Dave with a curious look on his face. Dave just smiled back. He obviously knew something, and that meant that he knew more than Jack, who, at this point, knew nothing more than the fact that someone had put a key in his coffee. "What else do you know about the coffee?"

Dave looked around at the other cells and then back to Jack, who was staring at him intently. "Let's keep it down a little bit," Dave said. "You never know who might be listening." He looked around again and then back at Jack. "Was there a key in your coffee?"

"Yeah," Jack said hesitantly, "but I don't know what it goes to."

"That's where I come in. That key will get you into the desk and file cabinet in the office where visiting law enforcement people, like federal agents, keep their files."

"What? You mean it'll get me into their file cabinet?"

"And their desk, where they would keep files on the people they are investigating."

"That's great," Jack said sincerely, "but how am I supposed to get into the office? I don't even know where it is."

"Like I said, that's where I come in. You offered to help me, so now I'll help you."

"But how?" Jack asked inquisitively.

"I told you that I helped out around here from time to time. I'll be polishing the floors up there this afternoon during lunchtime, and I know exactly where the office is. You'll come with me, and one of us is going to pull the files while we're up there."

"Not that I don't appreciate all this, Dave, but how is that supposed to help me? What can I do with the files while I'm stuck in here?"

"Who says you're gonna be stuck in here, Jack?. After we get the files, you're going to slip out the door."

"You mean escape?" he whispered. Jack looked around carefully to make sure that no one was paying any attention to them.

"That's right," Dave replied. "You're getting out of here today."

Jack couldn't believe what he was hearing. "What about you?"

"I'll be out soon enough. Don't worry about that. Officer Speakman told me they ain't even booked you yet, and they don't have a record of your arrest. They can't tell anyone that you're gone after you escape, or else they'll have to explain why there are no records of your arrest. That ain't likely, from what I understand. Speakman has a pretty strong suspicion that they don't want anyone poking around."

"Why are you doing this?"

"We're just trying to help. Something's happening here that ain't right. I don't think you done anything and Speakman don't think you did anything either. It ain't right that you're here, so we gonna get you out."

Jack didn't know what to say. After giving it some thought, the only word that came to mind was "thanks."

"Don't mention it, my friend, but be ready to go this afternoon. As soon as the feds go to lunch, Speakman will come get us. We're gonna have to move pretty fast. We won't have very long to get in and out of that office, so be ready, 'cause, if we get caught…"

Dave didn't have to finish his sentence. Jack knew that both of them were taking a huge chance by helping him, but he couldn't come up with the words to express his gratitude. All he could do was repeat the word "thanks," to which Dave replied, "Just be ready to go."

They didn't have time to discuss it anymore. There were footsteps in the hallway and Jack quickly slid the key under his mattress. He was relieved when he saw that it was Officer Speakman coming around the corner. He walked down the hall and then up to Jack's cell. "You finished with your breakfast?" he asked. From the look on his face, he did not want Jack to say a word about what he had just discussed with Dave.

"Yeah," Jack responded. "It sure was good." He noticed that Speakman was holding a pair of coveralls in his hands.

"That's a good attitude. Now here," he said, tossing the coveralls to Jack. "Put these on. We're gonna wash your clothes up for you."

"Thanks," Jack replied.

"And they're ready for you upstairs again."

Jack didn't look forward to another session with the feds. He hoped it would be the "good cop" this time. Either way, he was dreading it. He had let the cat out of the bag last time and was sure the questions would be more intense. They were going to want to know where the money was, and Jack now knew that they were going to use all means at their disposal, including physical violence, to get their questions answered.

He took some comfort in the hope that this would be their last session and that, by the end of the day, he would be out of there. He would be on the run, but he would be on the outside, where he stood at least some chance of finding out what was really going on and proving his innocence. Of equal importance now, however, was proving the guilt of Smith and Anderson. In order to clear himself, he was going to have to find out exactly what they were up to. If he played his cards right, he would come out of this thing free and wealthy, but he had to play his cards right, and at this point, he didn't even know the name of the game he was playing.

"You get those clothes on, and I'll be right back."

By the time he had changed, Speakman was standing back at the door to his cell. "Let's go," he said, sliding the door open.

They made their way down the hall and past the booking area. When they entered the stairwell that led upstairs to the main floor and the interrogation room, Speakman leaned forward so that he was right against Jack and said in a barely audible whisper, "Did you get the key?"

"Yes," Jack whispered back.

"Did you talk to Dave?"

Jack smiled and nodded silently.

"Good. Now, you better be ready when the time comes, and whatever happens, don't mention my name. Do we have a deal?"

Again, Jack looked at the officer and nodded in agreement.

"Good," he said as they reached the door at the top of the stairs. He unlocked the door and escorted Jack back to the interrogation room where once again Agent Smith was standing outside the door waiting.

"Here ya go," he said to Smith as they approached. He obviously wanted to avoid the hostility that occurred last time he brought Jack up to be questioned.

"Thanks, officer. I'll let you know when we're done with him." He made eye contact with Jack and pointed to the now familiar interrogation room as if to tell him to go in. Jack followed his apparent instructions without a word as Speakman turned and walked back down the hallway without speaking.

As Jack entered the room, he saw that Anderson was already at the table and sat down opposite from him. As he sat in the hard wooden chair, he looked up at Smith, who was still standing in the doorway. He wasn't looking forward to the conversation that was about to happen. They were apparently both going to work him over at the same time, but he took some relief in the thought that this would be their last opportunity to interrogate him. If all went well, they could damn well catch him if they wanted to talk to him again. This time, however, he would know they were coming and it wouldn't be so easy.

Jack sat in his chair, silently waiting for Smith to walk in and the beating to begin, but was very relieved when Smith turned toward the door, walked out into the hallway, and closed the door behind him.

"How was your breakfast, Jack?" Anderson asked.

"Just delicious," he muttered sarcastically. "Thanks so much for asking."

"Good. I see they gave you some fresh clothes."

"Yep," Jack replied shortly.

"Are you ready to talk a little bit?"

"I guess I'm as ready as I'll ever be."

"That's good, Jack. That's good. You know that this will go much easier for all of us if you'll cooperate and just tell us what you know."

"Unfortunately, Mr. Anderson, I'm afraid that will also get me killed, and I'm trying hard to stay alive."

"Why would you think that, Jack?" Anderson asked, looking uncomfortable for a brief moment. He was probably trying to think of what he could say that might ease Jack's fears.

"Well…I'll tell you. It seems to me that you don't have to follow the same laws I have to follow. First you plant drugs in my car, then bring me in here and hold me illegally. Your partner starts slapping me around because I won't answer his questions, and then, without any remorse at all, he tells me that he will be perfectly happy to turn this whole thing around and blame the cop that you asked to plant the drugs in the first place. It looks to me like you're a bunch of sociopaths. You don't care about anyone or anything but your mission, whatever that might be. Frankly, you guys scare the hell out of me."

"That's good Jack. You should be scared," he interrupted in a calm voice, "but you should also know that we don't kill our friends. We're just soldiers, Jack. Fighting a war that most people aren't aware of. People die in a war. Sometimes those people are civilians. It's regrettable, but true. We're fighting to keep your world safe. We don't kill our own people, though, and you have to trust me on that. It's up to you to decide which team you are playing for. If you tell us what we need to know, you have my word that you'll go free."

Jack wondered if this guy was crazy. *What war? What the hell is he talking about?* "Hey," he said hesitantly. "I don't know anything about any war. I don't know what your side is and I don't know what the other side is, but I do know that I've been caught in the middle, and I don't like it."

"I don't like it either, Jack, but you've got to choose."

"The only way I'm gonna feel safe is if I have either something that you want or something that you're scared of. Right now, I've got both. If I give you what you want, you'll have nothing to be scared of and I'll have nothing at all."

"You seem to be a pretty smart fellow, Jack. Hell, I might even offer you a job after this is said and done, but right now, I need a decision."

"What can you tell me about this war you're fighting?" Jack knew he was not going to get an answer that would satisfy him, but he wanted to stall. Each minute that passed brought him closer to his chance at freedom. "Maybe, if I knew what you were talking about, I would agree with you. Maybe I would cooperate, but right now I just want to save my own skin."

"I can't tell you anything about that, Jack. You're just going to have to trust me. You're going to have to trust your government."

That's the same government that put a half-pound of cocaine in my car. The same government that is holding me without booking me, and that would not regret for a moment seeing me killed as an unfortunate casualty of its secret war. No thanks, he thought to himself. *How can I trust this guy?* If he told him where the money was now, it would be the end for him.

"What's it gonna be, Jack?"

"I'm gonna have to think about it some more."

"You do that, Jack. We've got all the time in the world, and neither one of us is going anywhere until you tell me what I want to know. Do you understand me, Jack? You will not leave this jail until you tell me where the money is." He was growing more and more agitated with each word and slammed his fists on the table. "I also want to know how you found out about the money and who you've talked about it with. If your girlfriend, your mother, your friends know about it, we want to know that. We want to know exactly who you've told and what you've told them."

They had just changed the game. Until that moment, Jack had considered only his safety. Now he knew that they would not stop with him. They would go after anyone they thought might be a "loose end—as Smith had put it—and Jack had led them to believe in their session earlier that morning that he had told others about the money. That was keeping them from disposing of him at that moment, but now he was worried about the safety of Elizabeth, his mother, his coworkers, and his friends. He knew now, more than ever, that he had no choice but to reverse the situation on them: to take control and get the upper hand on them. They would not stop with him, and they would use anyone they could to get their hands on him. Once he escaped from the jail, he would have to make his move and make it quickly, because it was clear that they would stop at nothing. "I haven't told anybody anything," Jack finally said in a sheepish voice.

"That's not what you told Agent Smith this morning, is it?"

"I don't know anything to tell," he said with a trace of desperation in his voice. Anderson smiled. "I just told some folks that if anything happened to me…you know…that they were to let everyone know that I was missing and that I had found something before I went missing and that the government, or part of the government, was somehow involved."

"That's good, Jack, and who did you tell?"

Jack was starting to feel the pressure. If he talked anymore, he was sure he was going to cause someone else problems, but if he didn't say anything else, then the people that he cared most about were going to get a visit from Smith and Anderson, and Jack wouldn't wish that on his worst enemy. He had to say something.

Agent Anderson just stared across the table at him with cold blue eyes. It was obvious that he got some sort of sick, perverse pleasure out of watching Jack squirm. He knew that Jack had talked himself into a corner, and he was pleased with himself.

Finally, Jack looked boldly into Anderson's eyes and said, "I'm sorry, but I'm not telling you anything. Not until I have your full assurance that once you get what you want, you'll be gone. I want to know that you will never bother me or anyone I know ever again. If I tell you what you want to know, I have to know that it will be over."

"It will be, Jack. You have my assurance that it will be over."

Jack knew it was a lie, but Jack was himself lying. He wasn't going to turn eight million dollars over to these people. He knew that what little information he had about his captors was too much and that, at some point, they would have to do something about that. That could mean trouble, and not just for Jack. He had to get the upper hand. He had to win this battle. If he won, he would be rich and free; if he lost, he didn't want to think about the consequences. He imagined that, at best, they would beat the information out of him; at worst, after they beat it out of him, they would try to confirm his coerced confession through Elizabeth. He couldn't allow that to happen. "I need more than your assurances."

"What exactly are you looking for, Jack?"

He wasn't sure how to answer that question. How could they possibly satisfy him? There was no way that he would ever be comfortable. No matter what they said or did, he would likely spend the rest of his life looking over his shoulder. He also feared that the rest of his life could be a very short period of time. All he needed was a little time. Just a couple of hours, and he would have his chance to escape. All he needed to do was to stall them until after lunch. He looked nervously at Anderson, who was already gloating over the fact that he had won. At least, he believed that he had won.

"I don't know," Jack said. "You've got to give me some time to think about it." *Just a couple of hours should do,* he thought slyly. "Give me a couple of hours to think."

"As I said before, we've got all the time in the world; eventually I'm going to get sick of waiting, and when I do, you will tell us exactly what we want to know. And believe me, Jack, we have some very persuasive methods. I want you to make the right decision here. You're going to help your country, Jack, whether you like it or not, and you can do it with or without pain. Now I would prefer, as you would, that we avoid the pain. I will do what I can to reassure you that this will end once we have what we came for. But you need to figure out what you want and quickly. I get impatient when I don't get what I want."

"I'll think as quickly as I can, but don't push me. Remember, I've got what you are looking for. I have your money and it will be uncovered for all to see if anything happens to me; then someone, maybe not you or Agent Smith, but somebody, will have to start explaining. Eight million dollars is a lot of money, and I'm sure the media will have plenty of questions." Jack wasn't feeling half as bold as he was hoping to look. In fact, he felt like he was about to vomit. They had him by the short hairs, and he knew it.

"I think you better not threaten me, Jack. We hold the cards here, not you. It's not the money we're after, but you're right about one thing. We don't like to answer questions, and the thought of you making people curious has a lot of very powerful people feeling very nervous. So be very careful, Jack. You're a small fish in an ocean full of sharks, and you're starting to bleed. You don't want to start a feeding frenzy, because you and all of the other little fish will be eaten alive. Now make your goddamn decision and make it fast." With that, Anderson stood up and walked out of the room, slamming the door behind him.

Jack sat in his chair shaking. A bead of sweat ran down his forehead, and his hands were clammy and trembling. He wondered if Anderson had noticed. He also wondered if Smith had enjoyed the show. Jack was sure that he had watched the whole thing through the mirror and that he had a big smile on his face. These were a special breed of men—those who enjoyed the suffering of others. They were the most dangerous of people because they, in their own minds, had a reason and a justification for their actions. They were not unlike radical, religious terrorists because they believed that they were operating for a higher purpose, one that superseded the laws of man. Nothing would ever justify their behavior to Jack or any other sane person, but they saw their actions as being for the greater good, and it did not matter who or what got in their way. Whatever or whoever stood between them and their ultimate goal would be destroyed swiftly and without remorse.

After a couple of minutes the door opened again and Jack braced himself. He expected Smith to come through the door with a car battery and some jumper cables to attach to his testicles. He was relieved to see the unfamiliar face of a uniformed police officer come through the door. "Come with me," the officer said.

Jack's knees almost buckled when he stood up. He felt weak and his whole body was trembling as he walked back to his cell, followed closely by the officer. When he got to his cell, he noticed that Dave was not in his. He walked over to his bunk and looked around to make sure no one was watching him. When he was sure that no one was looking, he slid his hand under the mattress and felt the key that he had put there earlier. He smiled, let out a long sigh, and then lay quietly in his bunk waiting for Dave to return.

It wasn't long before he heard Dave's voice coming up the hallway. He was singing a not-so-accurate version of Elvis's "Jailhouse Rock." The singing stopped, and a minute later, Dave came through the door that led out from the cell area to the hallway where the booking station was. He was escorted by Officer Speakman and the officer who had delivered Jack's breakfast to him earlier that morning. The three of them walked up to Jack's cell and Speakman slid his key into the lock.

"We got some work for you, Jack," he said gruffly as he unlocked the door and slid it open. "You didn't think we were going to let you just sleep all afternoon, did you?"

"No, I guess not," Jack replied, trying not to sound excited. He was now moments away from his shot at freedom, and he was hyped with excitement. He had to tell himself to slow down and pay attention before he screwed up his chance.

"You're going to go with Mr. Holder here," Speakman said, pointing to Dave. "He'll take you upstairs and show you what you need to do. Officer Hodges here is going to follow you and make sure you don't get in any trouble. Is that clear?"

"Yes sir. Crystal clear," Jack replied, giving Officer Speakman a smile.

He flashed a smile back at Jack and said, "Good luck son." Then he turned and walked back up the hallway.

"Come on, Jack. We've got to go upstairs and do the floors and then we've got to go out in the yard and wash some patrol cars."

"Sounds good to me. At least it's better than sitting in this cell all day."

"Yeah, I thought you'd prefer a little work to just sitting around. Here, put this on so they'll know you're allowed out of your cell." He handed Jack an orange vest to put on over the coveralls he had been wearing since earlier that morning. He slipped it on and followed Dave and the officer up the stairwell that Jack had traveled several times over the past two days. They walked out of the stairwell into a hallway that looked very similar to the one beneath them.

"Follow me," Hodges said, motioning with his hand. They walked down the hallway past several doors until they came to an office that had the door shut and the lights off.

"We'll start with this one," Dave said, looking straight at Jack.

"Clean up in there and I'll wait out here," Hodges replied. He looked a little nervous as he spoke, and Jack vowed at that moment that he would never again say anything about cops not being around when you needed them.

Dave opened the door, reached in, and flipped the light switch, revealing a small room with little more than an old desk, a couple of chairs, and a large metal file cabinet in the back corner. The walls were bare and there were no pictures or other items that a typical office would have.

"You got the key?" Dave asked quietly as he made his way over to the file cabinet.

"Right here," Jack said, reaching down and pulling it out of his sock.

"Well, there it is," Dave said, pointing to the file cabinet in the corner of the room. "Let's hurry up and get what we came for so we can get the hell out of here."

Jack slid the key into the lock, and it turned easily. He slid the top drawer open, only to find it empty. He quickly opened the second drawer, careful to minimize the noise. "Jackpot," he said in a hushed voice. There was only one set of files in the drawer, and it appeared to be what Jack was looking for. It was the same set of files they had brought into the interrogation room.

Each of the file folders had the words "Four Horsemen—Top Secret" written on their label tabs, and just below that on each of the file folders were names. One of the files had his name, another had Jeff Patten's name, and he didn't flip through the others to see what they had. It didn't really matter anyway, because he was going to take the whole thing. He pulled the files out of the drawer and pushed it shut, making sure it had locked. "This is it!" he told Dave excitedly. "This is the one I need."

"Good," Dave replied. "Now, hand it to me and let's get out of here."

Jack handed the files to Dave, who put them in the garbage can that was sitting next to the desk.

"What are you doing?" Jack asked.

"You don't think we can just walk around with that file in our hands, do ya?" Dave asked as he closed the plastic bag that was in the garbage can around the file, pulled it out of the garbage can, and tucked it under his arm.

"I guess not," Jack replied, feeling kind of silly. "Just let me check the desk before we get out of here."

"All right, but be quick about it." Dave walked over to the door and put his ear up to the glass to listen and see if there was any activity in the hallway.

Jack looked down at the small metal desk that was sitting up against the wall opposite the file cabinet. It looked as though it had probably been around for a while. It had a large, shallow drawer in the center and three drawers down either side. He pulled on the center drawer. "Damn," he said quietly. "It's locked." He slid the key in and was relieved to discover, once more, that it easily turned. He pulled the drawer open, and there in front of him was a black laptop computer with a label that said:

PROPERTY OF THE UNITED STATES OF AMERICA
DRUG ENFORCEMENT AGENCY

"Jackpot!" he said again, only this time he was a little louder.

"Come on, man," Dave said impatiently. "We've gotta go."

Jack grabbed the laptop and tried to put it in the garbage can but it wouldn't fit. "Damn," he said. "It won't fit."

"Just leave it. You've got the files."

Jack didn't know what to do. He was sure that the laptop would have more information than the files, probably enough information to ensure his safety forever, and he wanted to take it as well. How was he going to get it out of the office?

"Just put it in this bag with the files," Dave said, holding the trash bag out to him.

Jack quickly opened it, slid the computer in, and wrapped it all back up. "All right," he said. "Let's go."

They opened the door and walked slowly back out into the hallway where Hodges was still standing. "That took long enough," he said to Jack and Dave with a disgusted look on his face. "Y'all are gonna get us all caught."

"Sorry," Jack said apologetically, "but we got what we needed."

"That's great," Officer Hodges replied sharply. "Now let's get the hell out of here."

They walked down the hall and back to the stairwell that led down to the lower floors. Jack followed Dave's brisk pace down the stairs, holding the garbage bag close to his chest with both arms around it. Officer Hodges was right behind them. When they got to the bottom floor, they stopped in front of the door that led out to the booking area and the cells.

"Now we're gonna go out to the parking garage," he said to Jack. Then he looked over at Dave and said, "You know what to do, right?"

"Yeah," Dave replied confidently. "Give me five minutes."

"Give us about ten minutes," Hodges said, "then pull it."

"Ten minutes," Dave repeated, looking down at his watch. "I got it."

Jack had no idea what they were talking about, but apparently they had a plan. Whatever it was, he would have to trust them. He looked over at Dave to say thanks. Dave looked back at him, and it was clear from the look on his face that he understood what Jack was about to say. "Thanks," he said anyway.

"No problem, just remember me when you get out. You said you'd help me get a lawyer, and I expect you to follow through." He reached out as he spoke and handed Jack a piece of paper. "This is my old lady's phone number. Her name's Tonya and she'll help you if she can. I've already talked to her and told her that you would probably be needin' some help. She's a good person and knows that you're in a jam. She'll let you hide out at our place till the heat blows over. Just give her a call, and she'll come and pick you up somewhere."

"Man, I don't know what to say…"

"You don't have to say anything. Just be sure to tell her that I love her."

"I'll do it," Jack replied. "Thanks again, man, and don't worry—I'll keep my promise."

They shook hands and Dave turned and walked through the door ahead of the other two, who followed close behind. Dave turned left and walked past the booking area, and Jack and Hodges turned right and headed toward the doors that Jack had come through when he was first brought to the jail. They walked through the doors, and Jack found himself back in the garage area where he'd been dropped off when he arrived. They walked out through a door on the other side of the garage and into the sunlight. It took a second for his eyes to adjust, but once they did, Jack found himself standing outside in a parking lot full of police cruisers. It was surrounded by a large fence that stood no less than twenty feet tall and was topped with razor wire. *There won't be any climbing over that fence,* he thought.

"Follow me," Officer Hodges said, quickly walking across the lot. They walked down the row of cars until they came to the end. On the other side of the last car was a door in the fence with a sign that said "Emergency Exit Only—Alarm Will Sound." *Well that's no good,* he thought to himself. If the door was opened, the alarm would go off and he probably wouldn't get too far before he had every car in that lot on top of him.

"The clothes you had when you came in are there in the back seat," Officer Hodges said, pointing to the car. "Get in there and change clothes, and when I give you the signal, I want you to walk slowly through that door, and then you're on your own." He pointed to the door in the fence and Jack thought about the alarm, but this wasn't the time to be asking questions. If the alarm went off, he would just run twice as fast.

Jack was starting to get very worried. How was he going to pull this off? They would be all over him as soon as that alarm went off. Nevertheless, it was his only chance, and he would have to give it his best try. He set down the garbage bag that he was still clutching tightly to his chest and got in the backseat of the police car to change clothes. He pulled off the orange vest and the coveralls and slid into his old clothes, which had been washed and neatly folded. Everything was there: pants, shirt, shoes, belt, and his wallet, which still had the money he had put in there before leaving his house to go to work. He was glad to have his street clothes back, knowing that he would be easily apprehended in the jumpsuit.

As he was tying his shoe, he heard a clicking sound and looked up through the car window at the jail. He noticed that all the lights had gone off inside, as had all the lights in the parking lot. He realized that Dave must have shut down the power.

"It's time…go now!" Hodges said before Jack had finished tying his shoe. He didn't look back as he jumped out of the patrol car, opened the door in the fence, and walked quickly down the sidewalk carrying the black plastic bag containing what he hoped would prove to be the key to his freedom. As soon as he got to the end of the block and rounded the corner, he broke into a dead sprint, running several blocks before ducking into an alley between two office buildings, where he sat, trying to catch his breath.

He knew that he should be trying to look inconspicuous, but sweat was running down his forehead and his heart was racing. He knew that he didn't have very long before someone figured out that he was missing. The alley he found himself in was one he had driven past so many times in his life. He never would have imagined that he would one day be crouched down behind a dumpster in that alley hiding from the police. He was sure they would be after him as soon as they figured out that he was gone, but he had no idea how long that would take. They would probably do a roll call once they got the power back on, but his name wouldn't be on it. He smiled when he realized that their plan to hold him without booking him was actually helping him out.

Unfortunately, he hadn't had time to plan his escape very well and wasn't exactly sure what his next move should be. He didn't want to call Patricia for fear that her phone would be tapped. Likewise, he didn't want to try to contact Elizabeth because he didn't want to jeopardize her safety. Anderson and Smith were obviously aware of her role in this thing, and even though he wanted desperately to talk to her, he didn't want her to be in any more danger.

Whatever he did, he couldn't just sit there in the alley waiting on the cops to catch up with him. Once the feds got back from lunch, he was sure they would figure out that he was gone. When they did, they would come after him, and they wouldn't stop until they had him. He had to get out of downtown. There were a lot of police in the area, more than any other part of the city, and the last thing he wanted to do was to run into any of them.

He couldn't just walk around the streets either. The cops would soon be combing the area and someone would eventually see him. The lunch hour was ending and the streets were not crowded enough for him to blend in. *At least I'm in my street clothes,* he thought to himself.

He was also worried about his new friends back at the jail—especially the two officers who had helped him. They had a lot to lose by helping a prisoner escape. If they were to get caught, they would end up in the same cells they had guarded, and Jack imagined that they hadn't made too many friends among the inmates. He was impressed with the fact that they had seen a crime being committed by the agents, and they had risked their jobs, their very lives, to right a wrong. They were the type of men who needed to be cops, and he would never forget what they had done for him.

After a few minutes, he stood up from behind the dumpster and made his way back to the sidewalk. He had to get somewhere safe, but where? He needed to find a phone, and he wanted desperately to go by his house to retrieve the money before someone found it. It was well hidden, but if they searched hard enough, he was afraid that they would eventually find it. He knew that he couldn't go home, though. That was the first place they would be looking for him.

He would try to call a friend, but it had to be someone who lived in Chattanooga whom Anderson and Smith wouldn't go see. It could not be someone he normally associated with. The feds obviously knew a lot about him, but he had their file, so it would likely take them a while to track him down.

He would have to call Dave's girlfriend. He didn't know her and felt uncomfortable asking a complete stranger for help. Dave had told her that he would be calling, and he hoped Dave didn't get caught switching off the power. If he had been caught, they might figure that he had given Jack more help. These were not stupid men he was dealing with; they would undoubtedly track down every lead they had.

He decided he would try to get in touch with her and then hide at her place for a couple of days while he figured out his next move. He just hoped that she would really be willing to help him.

CHAPTER 12

▼

He decided that he would head over to the river where there would most likely be a crowd of tourists that he could blend into. He could see the tops of the buildings on the riverfront from where he was standing and decided to make his way there. He would call Tonya from a pay phone and wait for her in a nearby parking lot. There was a large park on the river banks where the *Southern Belle* riverboat was docked, and that parking lot was usually crowded, and he felt that it would be as good a place as any to wait for her if could find a place where he would be able to see everyone that pulled in or out of the lot.

As he headed toward the river, he thought about the look on Anderson's and Smith's faces when they realized he was gone. He would love to have seen it. They thought they had been so close to breaking him. He wondered how long it would take for them to figure out that their files and one of their computers were also missing. He imagined the expressions on their faces when they did figure it out. Not only had he escaped, but he'd taken all the information they had on him. It was like salt in an open wound. Jack relished the thought, but he also knew that the missing files would make finding him more urgent. They would also have to realize that he had some inside help. There wasn't any other explanation. How could he have gotten into that office or the file cabinet and desk without a key, and how could he have gotten a key without someone's help?

Once at the riverfront, he pulled the piece of paper that Dave had handed him out of his pocket and looked at it for the first time. The handwriting was terrible, but Jack was able to make out the name Tonya Fields and a phone number. He located a pay phone and dialed the number.

"Hello Tonya," he said when she answered. "You don't know me, but I'm a friend of David's. I'm really sorry to bother you, but I need some help right now, and Dave said that I should give you a call."

"Oh yeah. You're the one he told me about on the phone. It's Jack, right?" She sounded surprised. Apparently she wasn't expecting to hear from him so soon, if at all.

"Yeah, that's me. I know that you don't know me, and I hate to ask, but I need a place to crash for a few days. I wouldn't normally do this, but my back's against the wall." Jack couldn't believe what he was doing: asking a complete stranger for a place to stay so that he could hide from federal agents.

"Sure," she said, cutting him off. Jack could hear the hesitation in her voice, but he didn't have anywhere else to turn.

"I've got people after me and I just need a place where I can figure out what I'm going to do. I won't stay long, and you won't even know I'm there."

"It's okay. Dave told me you really needed some help, and I told him that I would do what I could for you. He says you're a good guy."

"I don't want to be any trouble, but I don't have anywhere else I can go. I'm sure they're watching my house and my office, and I'll bet they'll be watching my friends and family too. I just don't know where else to turn."

"It's all right. Just tell me where you are, and I'll come get you."

"Thanks Tonya. You don't know what this means to me."

"Really, Jack…it's okay. I've been expecting your call. Where are you now?"

"I'm downtown by the river. I can meet you in the parking lot across from the aquarium. You know, where they dock the riverboat."

"I know right where that is," she responded quickly. "If you can stay put for forty-five minutes or so, I'll come get you."

"You're a lifesaver. I'll wait as long as it takes. Just pull in the parking lot and wait there. When I see that it's safe, I'll come get in the car. What are you driving?"

"I'll be in a little blue Ford Ranger pickup truck and I'll park near the back of the lot by the river."

"I'll be waiting. Just pull in and park, and again…I really appreciate this."

"It's not a problem. I don't mind helping someone who's in a jam, and from what I hear, you're really in a big one. Sit tight, and I'll be there as soon as I can."

Jack put the receiver back in its cradle and looked around to make sure no one had been paying attention to him. Drawing attention to himself was the last thing he wanted to do. When he was satisfied that no one was paying attention to him, he walked a little further down the road so that he could see the parking lot where he was supposed to meet Tonya. He sat on a bench across the street from the parking lot and waited for her to arrive.

After what seemed like much longer than forty-five minutes, he finally saw a blue pickup truck pull up and slowly circle the parking lot. Jack looked around carefully and then slowly made his way across the street. He had no idea what Tonya looked like but felt confident it was her. The girl driving the truck was alone. She was petite and her hair was blond and frizzy, as if she had gotten one-too-many perms. As he walked across the parking lot toward the car, he saw her head moving around as though she was looking for something. She apparently didn't see him walk up to the truck and was obviously startled when he tapped on the window.

"Are you Tonya?" he asked hesitantly as she rolled down her window.

"You must be Jack," she said, looking him up and down and then reaching across to unlock his door. "Get in."

Jack opened the passenger door and slid quickly into the cab of the truck. Closing the door gently, he looked over and smiled at her. "I really appreciate this."

"Like I said before…it's fine. I'm glad to help." She smiled back at him and then turned back to watch the road. They sat in silence for several minutes while they drove through downtown toward the interstate. They stayed on the freeway for a good thirty minutes and eventually got off in a rural area outside of town that Jack seldom visited. The ride was awkward and neither of them spoke much. It wasn't that he didn't want to talk; he just couldn't think of anything to say.

"Hey, will you pull over up here at this gas station?" Jack asked when they got off the interstate.

"You hungry? 'Cause I got some food at the house."

"No. I'm not getting food, but thanks. I'm going to see if they have those pre-paid cell phones in here. I need to make some calls and don't want to use a line that they can trace back to you."

"Makes sense to me," she said as he got out of the truck. "I'll be waiting right out here."

As he walked into the store, he saw the phones he was looking for behind the counter. He walked up to the counter and asked the cashier to hand him two of them. He knew better than to use his credit card, and luckily he had enough cash in his wallet.

He got back in the truck, and another ten minutes later, they turned off the county road and pulled down a long gravel driveway. *No wonder it had taken her so long to get downtown.*

The driveway was full of ruts and potholes, and the truck bounced its way down to a double-wide trailer surrounded by woods.

"It ain't much," Tonya said as they pulled up, "but it's home."

"It's fine by me," Jack said, trying to sound sincere. He didn't want her to think that he was a snob. At that point, he would have been happy to sleep in a barn as long as he thought it was safe, and he felt safe here. It was far out in the country, and no one could make it up that driveway without him knowing it. It was more than a quarter-mile long, and the trailer couldn't be seen from the main road. Thick woods stretched out for miles behind it. If Anderson or his people found out where he was and tried to capture him, he would escape into the woods and be long gone before they could get to the door.

They got out of the truck, and Jack followed Tonya inside. When they got through the door, he looked around and found himself standing in a fairly large room. Looking around, he felt bad about all the "trailer jokes" he'd made in the past. It was a lot bigger than it looked from the outside, and he really didn't get the feeling that he was in a mobile home. The room he was standing in contained both the kitchen and den. The kitchen area had a tile floor, and a bar separated it from the den, which was carpeted and took up most of the open space. On his left was a hallway that led back to the bedrooms.

"There's two full bathrooms and three bedrooms," Tonya said, pointing down the hallway. "You can have the first bedroom on your right there."

"That's great," Jack said as he made his way over to the bar area where he placed the files and computer he had been carrying.

"I'm gonna' make sumthin' to eat. You want anything?"

"Sure. As long as it's no trouble. I'll have whatever you're having." He didn't want to wear out his welcome too soon.

"I'm just gonna heat up some lasagna that I've got from last night. I think there's plenty for both of us," she said, leaning into the refrigerator.

"That sounds good. I love lasagna."

"Good. What about a drink? You want a beer or anything?"

"I'll just take a glass of water if you don't mind."

"No offense," she said looking up from the fridge, "but you look like you could use a shower too."

Jack was a little embarrassed, and he could feel his cheeks getting flushed, but he knew she was right. He hadn't had one in a couple of days and he was sure that he smelled ripe. "Yes. I would love a shower."

"Why don't you take a shower while I get the food ready. The bathroom is right down the hallway there. There's towels and washcloths in the closet and there should be plenty of soap and shampoo and all that. Nobody ever uses that bathroom, so check to make sure you got everything you need, and let me know if you don't. You can just wear some of Dave's old clothes. I'll grab something for you out of our bedroom."

"All right. That sounds great. And I hate to be a bother, but does, uh, David have any razor blades?" Jack also hadn't shaved since the morning he was arrested and he was looking pretty scruffy.

"Sure. They're back in our bathroom. I'll get you one."

He followed her back into her bedroom and waited by the door while she gathered up the razor and some shaving cream. He thanked her as she handed it to him and went into the other bathroom and closed the door behind him.

CHAPTER 13

▼

Jack stood in front of the mirror, dripping. It felt great to be clean again. His mother would have been disappointed about the fact that he was running around without clean underwear. He thought about how worried she'd be if she knew what was going on. He needed to give her a call to let her know that he was alive and well. Jack didn't talk to his parents every day, but it had been more than a week since the last time they talked, and for all he knew they were out looking for him by now. They might have even heard that he had been arrested.

He dried himself off with the towel and put on the clothes that Tonya had given him. Dave was the same height but a little bigger around than Jack, and the clothes were baggy on him. He walked out on the front porch with one of the phones he'd purchased and dialed his parents' number. After several rings, his mother finally answered.

"Hello, Mom."

"Jack Hixson," she said in the voice she used whenever he was in trouble. "Where are you? Where have you been?"

"I can't say, Mom."

"What do you mean you can't say?"

"I can't say where I am right now. There are people looking for me. Dangerous and powerful people, and they might be listening to us right now."

"What are you talking about, young man?" she asked forcefully. She still called him "young man" whenever she was upset with him. "The FBI has already been here looking for you, and your father went over to your house two days ago. It looks like a tornado went through the place. What in the world have you gotten yourself into?"

"I swear, Mom. I didn't do anything wrong."

"That's not what they are saying, Jack."

"What who's saying?"

"The police, Jack. We had a little visit from the FBI and the DEA. In fact, they just left here a little while ago."

"And what are they saying, Mom?"

"They said you have been selling drugs, and they said you escaped from jail. You know your father is just beside himself right now. I just can't believe that our son—"

"I wasn't selling drugs, Mom. I promise."

"Then what were you doing?"

"I was driving to lunch."

"They don't arrest people for driving to lunch, Jack. This is your mother that you're talking to. I wasn't born yesterday." She was obviously upset and on the verge of tears and he felt terrible about it, but he hadn't caused this. He had to focus on getting himself out of the mess that he was in.

"You're right, Mom. Not unless they want to. Look, I didn't call to argue about this with you. You've just got to trust me right now, and I'll be able to prove it to you. I just wanted to tell you and Dad that I'm okay."

"You can't tell your mother where you are?"

"No, Mom. I told you. The people that are after me are killers."

"It's the police, Jack. The police are not killers."

"Unfortunately, Mom, some of them are. There are some bad cops out there, and I've found something that they want to get back very badly. It's something that could get a lot of people in trouble. I wasn't trying to get myself in trouble, but I found something and that's what happened. There's nothing I can do now but try to get myself out of it, and I can't do that from jail."

"How did you get out of the jail?"

"I can't tell you that either. I don't know who's listening to this call. If they've already been there, then I'll bet they're listening right now. I've got to go, Mom. I've got to go before they trace this call. You've got to trust me. You and Dad both. I swear, Mom, I didn't do anything wrong."

"Okay, Jack...okay. What can your father and I do to help?"

"There's nothing you can do for me right now. Tell Dad that I'm alive, and I'll try to call you back as soon as I can. I wish I could stay on the phone longer, but I've got to go now."

"Don't hang up, Jack."

"I've got to go."

"Just promise you'll call back to let us know you're all right."

"I will. I will, just as soon as I can. Now, I've got to hang up. I love you both, and I'll call you as soon as I can." He could hear his mother sniffling and fighting back her tears on the other end of the line. He almost wished he hadn't called her, but he knew he had done the right thing by letting her know that he was all right. He had also found out the FBI and DEA had already contacted his parents. *They didn't waste any time, did they?* he thought to himself. At least he knew for sure that they were aware of his escape.

He was relieved to have that phone call out of the way. Talking to his mother usually made him feel better, but this time there was very little she could say that would help him. He needed to focus his attention on the items he had taken during his escape. The key to his freedom could be in the files, and he was eager to examine them.

"Your food is ready," Tonya said as he walked back inside.

He sat down at the kitchen table where she had put his plate and looked at the files that were sitting on the table in front of him. They were each labeled "Confidential—Top Secret" across their covers. The one he was holding had Jeff Patten's name on the label, and there was another with his name.

Attached to the cover on the inside of the folder were pictures of a man that had been taken from a distance, apparently without his knowledge. There were six or seven pictures there, and they were all old. Jack figured that they must have been pictures of Jeff Patten, but he had never seen him and had no idea what he looked like; it was impossible to be sure.

Along with the pictures were several office memos, which he started reading. The first one read like an employment evaluation. There was a brief physical description (which confirmed the identity of the man in the photographs to be Mr. Patten) along with a chronology of his adult life. It said where he had attended college and law school and listed every job he had since he was sixteen years old. It also described his family, including his wife and his daughter, Patricia. The final paragraph of the memo concluded that he "would be an ideal candidate for the courier role." The memo confirmed Jack's suspicion that Patricia's father hadn't been a part of it. He was thoroughly checked out by the "Four Horsemen," whoever they were, before he was chosen to carry the money, but it was obvious that he didn't know what was going on.

The next memo in the file talked about the plane crash that killed him. It was very quickly evident from that memo that the crash was not part of the plan. It referred several times to a lost package, which Jack assumed was the money, and said that it had not been found among the wreckage. The case had been found, but it was full of phone books rather than money. It also said that Jeff had been found near the crash site and taken by Air Force personnel to the nearest hospital, but that he had died shortly after he was admitted. Jack thought it was interesting that the FAA crash report was also attached to the memo. It said that the Air Force had initially responded to the crash and had prevented the FAA officials from getting to the site. That's probably why they had told Patricia that the accident report was classified when she had called to see about getting a copy.

There was also a memo detailing the investigation that had been conducted after Jeff died. It described the FBI's interviews of Jeff's family and their interview with Stella. It also discussed the safety-deposit box in Denver. It said that the box had been checked out but that no money was found. There were also photocopies of each document that Jack had found in the box when he went through it.

The next file had Jack's name on it. It was the file that Agent Anderson had brought into the interrogation room the first time they had questioned Jack. Like the other file he had gone through, it contained several photographs. He had seen most of them when Anderson had laid them on the table in the interrogation room. Some of the others he recognized as having been taken outside the motel where he had stayed in Denver. He did not recognize the location of some of the pictures, but he was sure now that he had been followed from the time he left the bank.

The files confirmed most of Patricia's story and what Jack already suspected: that the government was paying someone lots of money (or receiving lots of money from someone) and that unsuspecting, innocent people were being used as mules to carry it across the country. It was not clear what the money was for, or which direction it was flowing, but it was clear that Jeff Patten had been one of the unfortunate people who had been selected to carry it.

Apparently he figured out that something was wrong and had stashed the money before getting on the plane. Jack now knew the who, the what, and the when, but he still didn't know where the money had been headed or why. He hoped that, if he was able to get into the files on the laptop, he could figure that out.

He put the laptop in front of him and turned it on but very quickly discovered that it was protected by a password. He tried typing in a few obvious words, but none of them worked. He knew that he needed to get into the files on that computer. His life depended on it, and luckily he knew just the person for the job.

*   *   *   *

Sean Pickett was an old friend and a whiz with computers. He had his own store where he built and serviced computers and other gadgets and was the person Jack called when he had problems with anything electronic. If anybody could crack the password, he could, and Jack hoped that he would be willing to help.

"Hey buddy," he said as Sean answered the phone. "This is Jack."

"Hey dude. What's goin' on?"

"I need your help, Sean."

"Did you download another virus?" he asked, laughing quietly. "You need to stop looking at all that Internet pornography."

"No, this is serious. I'm in trouble and I need some help."

Sean suddenly quit laughing and became serious. "What's going on?"

"I've been set up. I don't know if you've heard, and I don't guess there's any reason why you would have, but I was in jail for the last couple of days. I'm out now, and let's just say I left without permission. I'm out and I need some help to prove that I didn't do anything wrong."

"What happened? Why were you put in jail?"

"I got set up. The cops planted the drugs on me."

"Uh huh," Sean said sarcastically. "They planted it on ya…right."

"Listen, man. I know it sounds crazy, but you gotta believe me," Jack said, sounding desperate.

"I believe you, but what can I do?"

Jack could tell from the tone of his voice that he didn't really believe him. Who would? This wasn't the first time somebody claimed to have been set up. "I have evidence…I mean, I can prove it," he stammered. "I think I can prove it, but I need your help."

"Look man, I'm your buddy, and you know that I'll do whatever I can to help, but you've got to understand that I don't want to get involved in any trouble. I got a wife and kids to think about. What exactly do you need me to do?"

"I need your computer skills. That's all I'm saying right now, but trust me, this is big. You know I wouldn't ask if it weren't important. I need you to crack a password. Can you do that?"

"Can I crack a password? Are you kidding me?"

"No, I'm not kidding. I'm as serious as a heart attack. I really need your help on this one."

"Of course I can crack a password. I've got software that'll bust through just about any known encryption. I'm assuming that you've got the computer with you."

"Yeah. It's a laptop, and I'm looking at it as we speak."

"Can you bring it to me here at the shop?"

"Sure. When can I stop by?"

"I'll be here for the rest of the day. Just swing by and drop it off. I'll see what I can do."

"I'll be there as soon as I can, and I don't want to be pushy, but I need you to get to this as soon as you can."

"I'll take a look at it tonight if you can get it over here."

"That's great. I really appreciate this, Sean."

"It's okay. I know you'd do the same for me."

"I owe you one."

Sean sounded nervous on the phone and Jack knew that he had every reason to be. Jack was asking a lot for him to get involved, but he didn't have anywhere else to turn. He needed to see what was on that computer, and Sean was the only person that he trusted enough to ask for help who also had the necessary skills.

He was eager to get the computer to Sean so that he could get started trying to crack the password, but before he did that, he needed to get in touch with Patricia and Elizabeth to let them know that he was all right. As soon as he got through making those calls, he would have to figure out how he was going to get over there to drop off the computer. He would probably have to get Tonya to drop him off closer to town and then get a taxi to take him the rest of the way. He was more than a little nervous about being out on the streets and didn't want Tonya implicated in his escape, so he didn't want to ask her to drive him all the way into town. Once they got close, she could drop him off at a gas station; then he'd call a taxi.

He picked the phone up and dialed Patricia's number. The last time they'd talked, he was supposed to meet her for lunch, but that was on the day he got arrested, and not only had he failed to show up, but he hadn't been able to call and tell her why. He could only imagine what she must be thinking, but he was sure that she was worried about him. Jack put the phone up to his ear and listened to it ring until she picked up. "Patricia. It's me," he said after hearing her say hello.

"JACK!" she said excitedly back into the phone. "Jack, where have you been? What is going on?"

"It's OK. I'm OK. I'm somewhere safe."

"Where have you been? You didn't show up for lunch. Did something happen?"

"I've been in jail."

"What? In jail...why?"

"I was on my way to meet you for lunch the other day and I got pulled over downtown. They planted drugs in my car and took me to jail."

"Drugs?"

"Yeah. They put half a pound of cocaine in my trunk. It was a setup. I'm not sure how they knew anything, but they were all over me as soon as I left my office."

"Was it the money?"

"That's exactly what it was. I wasn't sure at first, but as soon as they got me to the jail, I was questioned by two federal agents, and all they wanted to know about was my trip to Denver and the money."

"How did they know about it?"

"I'm not exactly sure, but I think they were watching the safe-deposit box in Denver. This is bigger than you could imagine, Patricia, and I'm pretty sure that your father was deceived into being a part of it."

"What are you talking about?"

"The best I can figure, your father was basically being used as a mule to carry money around for some kind of top-secret government organization. Whatever his client told him about his real estate business was just an elaborate cover story designed to keep him from getting too suspicious."

"Apparently it worked."

"I'm not so sure. I think he caught on while he was in Denver. Something must have happened out there that tipped him off."

"You said he was being used as a mule. What does that mean?"

"I just use that term to mean that he was carrying the money for other people. I don't know who those people were or what the money was for, but I'm certain that he didn't know what was actually going on. I'm also sure that the government was involved, but I don't know to what extent, or whether they were sending or receiving the money he was carrying."

"Who would they be sending the money to?"

"Like I said, I'm not sure about that yet. I don't even know what it was for, but there was a lot more money there than we thought."

"How much more?"

"A lot more. You know the abandoned mine at the cabin that you told me about?"

"Yes."

"I found a box, deep in one of the shafts, that was full of money. I counted eight million dollars." The line was suddenly silent. "Patricia. Are you there?"

"I'm here, Jack," she replied in a shocked tone. "Did you say eight million dollars?"

"Yep."

"Why would he have so much money?"

"I don't know yet, and someone obviously doesn't want me to find out. That's why they arrested me. They wanted to get me in custody so they could find out how I discovered the safe-deposit box and what I had done with the money."

"You didn't tell them anything, did you?" She was obviously worried that they might be coming after her next.

"Of course not. I didn't say anything about you or the money. I just played dumb for the most part. As far as I know, they don't know anything about you."

"Good," she said, sounding relieved.

"These feds, the one's that are after me, are bad news, Patricia. I was afraid they might be tempted to just get rid of me if I told them anything."

"I'm so sorry for getting you into this, Jack. If I'd have known—"

"Don't worry about that now," Jack replied, cutting her off. "I'm in deep, and I'm not going to stop until I know that we're all safe, or until they catch up to me."

"What are you going to do now?"

"I'm not exactly sure how I'm going to pull this off. I had some assistance getting out of the jail, and I was able to help myself to some files on the way out, including their file on your father, but I haven't had the chance to figure out what's going on. Once I figure out what I have, I'm going to try to cut a deal with them."

"What kind of deal?"

"Simple. I'll give them their files back if they'll leave us alone."

"Don't you think they'll come after you once you give their stuff back?"

"Not if I make and distribute copies of everything before I give it back to them. They'll think twice about coming after me if they think those copies will hit the six o'clock news."

"I want you to know, Jack, that I don't really care about the money. I only wanted to find something that would prove my father's innocence. I didn't mean for it to turn into all of this. You have to give the money back to them if it will help."

"No way, Patricia," Jack replied forcefully. "There's no way on God's green earth that I'm giving them the money. I nearly fell down a mine shaft and killed myself to find that money, and I'm not going to just hand it over without a fight. Besides, it's not that simple. These are bad men. They don't care about the money. They want to get rid of me and anyone else who might know something about it. I don't have a choice. Even if I were to give the money back, they would still have to shut me up. I've got to figure out what they were up to and turn it against them."

"You do what you want, Jack. You know what's best, but I don't need any of the money and I don't want you to get hurt. If they ask for it, I think you should just give it to them."

"We'll deal with that when we have to. For now, I just wanted to let you know that I was okay. I figured that my arrest would have been on the news."

"I hadn't heard a word about it."

"Thank God. Listen, I need to go, but I'll be back in touch. I don't want you to get pulled into this, and as far as I know, they have no idea that you're involved. I intend to keep it that way. When it's safe, I'm going to send you a package with copies of the files I took. If you don't hear from me within ninety days, or if you hear that something has happened to me, I want you to go straight to the CNN headquarters in Atlanta and hand-deliver them to someone who will take the story and run with it."

"I'll do it, Jack. Just…please be careful."

"I will. Don't worry. I'm alive and free right now, and I intend to keep it that way. Now, I need to go. Just hang tight, wait for my package, and I'll call you when I can."

"Okay, and good luck, Jack."

"Thanks," he replied. "I'll need it."

He needed to make one other phone call to Elizabeth before heading out to meet Sean. He didn't know exactly what he was going to tell her, but he would have to come up with something. He was sure that she would want to come and help him, but he didn't want her to get involved any more than she was already. He would have to figure out a way to put her off. He knew that the feds would not be any nicer to her because she was a girl. They would do what they had to do to get what they wanted, and he couldn't have that hanging over his head. He wouldn't be able to live with himself if anything were to happen to her. He couldn't just leave her hanging either. She was worried, and he had to talk to her and let her know that he was safe, and more than that, he wanted to hear her voice.

He dialed her cell phone, hoping that she had it with her. "Elizabeth. This is Jack," he said as soon as she picked up.

"Jack!" she said excitedly. "What's going on? I called the jail and they said you're not there. They said there was no record of you being there. I went by your house and it's been trashed. What's going on?"

"Calm down. I know. It's all screwed up. They never booked me at the jail, but I had a little help and was able to get out."

"You mean they let you out, or you escaped?"

"Let's just say I didn't have permission to leave."

"So they're after you?"

"You could say that."

"Well, what are you going to do?"

"I'm not exactly sure, but the first thing I need to do is to find out everything I can about the Four Horsemen."

"I looked it up, Jack, like you asked…the Four Horsemen, I mean. I found some stuff about it on the Internet. It's some old conspiracy theory from the seventies."

"It's not a theory, Elizabeth, and I think I can prove it."

"What? How are you going to do that?"

"I was able to pick up some files on my way out of jail, but that's all I can tell you right now. I'm pretty sure they will have all the information I need, but listen…I want you to stay out of this. I don't want you to get any more involved. These are very dangerous people, and they won't think twice about arranging an accident for you if they think you're in their way."

"I'm already involved, Jack, and I think they're already on to me. I'm pretty sure that someone's been following me."

"What do you mean?"

"I keep seeing this black car with tinted windows. It's everywhere I go. I'm scared, Jack."

"Me too, Elizabeth. I'm scared too, but I want you to promise me that you'll stay out of it. You need to get out of town for a few days if you can. Go visit a friend or something, but get out of here until this thing blows over."

"When will that be? When will this thing blow over?"

"I'm not sure, but I'm working on a plan. Just go. You can call the number that's on your caller ID and tell me how to get in touch with you, and I'll call and let you know when it's over."

"I'm not going anywhere, Jack," she said indignantly. "I'm going to stay here and help you."

"I don't want you to get hurt, Elizabeth."

"And I don't want to be hurt, Jack, but I can't leave you here alone to deal with this. Not by yourself. If what you're telling me is true…if the Four Horsemen are real, then you are in way over your head, and you're going to need all the help you can get."

He couldn't argue that point with her. He knew he was in over his head, and he was scared. But he just couldn't live with the guilt if she got hurt. "Elizabeth. You shouldn't get involved in this any more than you already have. I couldn't handle it…I mean…if you were to get hurt," he stammered.

"I feel the same way about you, Jack, and I'm not going anywhere. No matter what you say. I couldn't handle knowing that you were in danger, and I was doing nothing to help you. Now tell me where you are. I'm not getting off the phone until you tell me where you are."

"I can't. Someone might be listening to this conversation. I can't tell you where I am."

"Then meet me somewhere, Jack. You need to know what I found out about the Four Horsemen anyway."

"All right," he replied, finally giving in. If he couldn't make her leave, then he would have to keep her close.

"Okay. That sounds more like it. Where are we going to meet?"

"We can't meet at my house. I'm sure they're watching it. And we can't meet at your house if you think they're watching you too."

"Where are you now? I can come to you."

"I'd rather not say where I am right now. I'm on a cell phone and we can't be too careful about who's listening."

"You're right."

"I've got to go meet someone today to see if they can help. I can get a ride close to town, and you can meet me somewhere, but you'll have to make sure no one is following you. That means you don't take your car; you'll have to borrow someone else's, and you're going to have to find a way to get out of the building without anyone seeing you. Do you know where the service entrance is?"

"Yeah. I can take the service elevator down to the ground floor and there's a door down there that leads out into the alley where the dumpster is."

"That's right. When you're in the car and sure that no one is following you, call me at the number on your caller ID and we'll set up a place to meet. Did you get all that?"

"Got it. I'll leave here in a few minutes, and I'll call you when I'm sure everything's okay."

"All right. I'll be waiting on your call, and, most importantly, keep your eyes open and be careful. If you think someone might be watching, then just forget about meeting me. We can hook up later."

"I'll be careful, Jack."

They said good-bye, and then Jack discussed his plan with Tonya. She was understandably nervous but agreed to give him a ride into town to meet with Elizabeth. Jack sat on the couch waiting for her to call back and thinking about where they should meet. He wanted to pick a place that was outside of downtown and close to Sean's computer shop. After pondering the alternatives, he finally decided on a place. He would tell her to meet him in the main parking lot at one of the hospitals in town. It wasn't perfect, but he couldn't think of a place that was. At least it would be crowded, and they would have a chance to get away and hide among the crowd if the cops were to show up.

Nearly thirty minutes passed before his phone rang. He looked at the screen on the front of the phone and smiled when he recognized Elizabeth's number. "Hey," he said when he answered the phone.

"It's me," came her reply. "I'm out and I did some driving around, so I'm sure no one is behind me."

"You're positive?"

"I'm as sure as I can be. Did you think of a place to meet?"

"Yeah. Meet me in the main parking area of the hospital over by the Catholic high school."

"You mean Mem—"

"Don't say it," Jack said, cutting her off mid-sentence. "Someone might be listening. Just go there and I'll meet you as soon as I can. Just be in the main parking lot. If I can't find you, I'll call your cell phone again."

"Got it. I'm headed there now."

"Good. I'll see you in a few minutes." Jack hung up the phone and they jumped in Tonya's car heading for the hospital. The drive took about thirty minutes, and as they pulled into the parking lot, Jack saw Elizabeth sitting in a car that he didn't recognize. He thanked Tonya for the ride and told her that he would get a ride back to her place later that day. She said that would be fine and wished him luck, and he climbed out of her car and into Elizabeth's.

CHAPTER 14

▼

"Thank God!" Elizabeth said as he climbed into her car. "I was starting to worry about you."

"Yeah. Sorry about that. It was a pretty long drive for me to get here."

"Where have you been? And who was that you were riding with?"

He thought he detected a hint of jealousy in her voice. "That was Tonya."

"Who's Tonya?"

He definitely heard some jealousy that time. "I told you that I had some help getting out of the jail."

"How did she help?"

"Well, it wasn't her so much. It was her boyfriend. He was in the cell next to mine, and he and a couple of the guards helped me."

"How?"

"They led me up to the gate and just let me walk through it."

"They just let you walk out of the jail?" she said in disbelief.

"Yep. First they helped me grab some files and this laptop," he said, pointing to the computer he had brought with him, "then they let me walk out."

"That's crazy."

"I know, but they didn't like the way the feds were treating me. I guess they just believed the whole thing was a setup. I didn't ask a lot of questions, and the escape happened pretty fast. They told me to go and I did."

"You're a lucky man, Jack Hixson."

"I know, but I've still got a long way to go before this thing is over. What did you find out about the Four Horsemen?"

"I printed all of my research," she answered proudly, holding out a small stack of papers.

"That's great!" Jack exclaimed, taking them from her hand.

"The one on top is a newspaper article from 1971 that was published in the *El Centro Gazette*. It's a small town in southern California near the Mexican border. Apparently one of the reporters that worked for the newspaper back then uncovered the fact that an airfield somewhere in the desert outside of El Centro was being used to smuggle huge amounts of cocaine, heroin, and marijuana into the country. You can read the article yourself, but apparently he had an associate of some sort that was involved in the drug-trafficking business. Apparently his associate tipped him off about a major delivery that was scheduled to take place at that airstrip. When he went out to investigate, he found the stuff being off-loaded from a military transport plane into civilian pickup trucks."

"Does the article specifically refer to the Four Horsemen?"

"Yes. That's what the whole story is about. It says that the Four Horsemen is some kind of government organization that controls a large portion of the international drug trade. Apparently, they ship the drugs out of Third World countries and into the United States, where it is sold and distributed."

"Who does the distribution?"

"The article said that the Mafia was buying most, if not all, the drugs that were being brought into the country. They would turn it around and sell a lot of it to the street gangs in the inner cities around Los Angeles, Chicago, New York—all the major metropolitan areas across the country where there were active gangs. Those gangs were then selling the stuff on the streets."

"But why? It just doesn't make sense why our government would want to do that. I mean, they spend billions and billions of dollars every year to stop the drugs from coming into the country. Why would they turn around and bring the stuff in themselves?"

"The Four Horsemen don't exactly work with the same people that are trying to stop drugs from being brought into the country. The article makes it clear that this is top secret. Apparently, not even the president is aware. From what this reporter uncovered, there were elements in the CIA, the DEA, the NSA, and the Department of Defense that controlled the whole operation. That's where they got the name "The Four Horsemen"—from the four organizations involved in the project."

"But why are they doing it?"

"That's simple, Jack. It's the money. The Four Horsemen don't actually buy the drugs. They're just brokers who handle and provide protection for the transaction. Some of the money is used to cover the costs of the operation, but most of it goes back to the countries where the drugs originated."

"I'm confused. That makes even less sense," Jack said, rubbing his forehead. "They go through all of that trouble just to give the money away?"

"At the time this article was written, we were in the height of the Cold War, and our government's objective at that time was to stop the spread of Communism. The people who were producing the drugs in Asia and in South and Central America were fighting guerrilla wars against the Communists in their own countries. They used the money generated by the drug sales to buy weapons either from our government or on the black market."

"Weapons?" Jack asked in disbelief.

"That's the whole point. When this article was written, they were bringing in heroin and marijuana that was being cultivated in Vietnam, Laos, and Cambodia. It was all coming from groups that were trying to stop the spread of Communism in those countries."

"Like we were doing in Vietnam." It was starting to make sense.

"That's right. Vietnam and Cambodia and Laos. See, we were openly fighting in Vietnam, everyone knew about that, but we were also secretly fighting in Laos and Cambodia. We were helping the anti-Communist fighters in those countries. That much is pretty well documented by now. How do you think the Cambodians were able to pay for their weapons? Obviously, they weren't free."

"Uh huh," Jack said, nodding his head in agreement but still listening in shocked disbelief.

"Fighting a war isn't cheap, and these small Third World governments can't always afford the latest and greatest weaponry. What they do have readily available, though, are drugs. They can produce coca, marijuana, or poppies, and that translates into money. The Four Horsemen was formed in the late sixties, when the drug trade was really starting to boom, to broker the deals. Think about it. Americans, just like everybody else, are going to use drugs. You can't stop it. People have been looking for ways to get intoxicated since there were people, but more importantly, Americans can afford to, and do, pay incredible amounts of money to get high on these drugs. They are just tapping into that market. Think of the amount of money that is spent throughout the world on drugs in any given year."

Jack had never given it much thought but quickly realized the scale that they were talking about.

"I'm not sure how much it is, but it's a lot of money—hundreds of billions of dollars per year. You don't think that all that money changes hands without the people in power taking their cut, do you? And who is the most powerful country? We are."

It all made sense to him now. Agent Anderson had said something about the war that he was fighting. At the time he said it, Jack had no idea what he was talking about, but now it was clear.

"They've been doing it forever," he thought out loud.

"They've been doing it for a long time," Elizabeth said in agreement.

Jack had always wondered why whenever he saw news footage of rebel soldiers from some small, impoverished country, they always seemed to be carrying brand-new M-16 rifles or M-60 machine guns just like the American soldiers. "What else did the article say?"

"Not much. I called the newspaper that published the story to see if I could track down the reporter who wrote it."

"And what did he say?"

"Nothing helpful. I spoke to the editor of the paper. He told me that the reporter had died in a car crash shortly after publishing the story."

"A car crash?" he said skeptically.

"Apparently, he drove his car off a bridge. The man I talked to was working as a reporter at the same time as the person who wrote the story. He said they had been good friends. He always thought it was strange, because his friend had driven across that bridge hundreds of times and knew the road well."

"What happened? Why did his car go over the bridge?"

"Well, it was the middle of the night and no one saw the accident, but what was strange was that there were no skid marks in the road. He apparently didn't even try to stop or steer away from the edge of the bridge. It went off into a ravine and they didn't find the car for a couple of days."

"And the person you talked to was one of this reporter's friends?"

"That's right. He always wondered if his friend had opened the wrong can of worms, but he never really looked into it. He said that he didn't want to end up at the bottom of a ravine himself."

"So he was too scared to pursue it?"

"I think so."

"Were you able to find anything other than that newspaper story?"

"Of course. You know me. I'm the queen of research." She was right about that. All of the attorneys that Jack worked with at Cates & Stanley considered Elizabeth to be the best researcher at the firm. If you could tell her what you were looking for, she would read every case or article she could get her hands on that was related to your subject. If she couldn't find something, then it likely didn't exist, and he was glad to have her helping him now for that very reason. "I searched on the Internet for references to the Four Horsemen and was able to find several articles on Web sites that publish conspiracy theory—type stuff. Apparently, this was how our government funded the Contras in their conflicts against the Sandinistas in Nicaragua and Honduras. It also paid for the Stinger missiles that went to the Mujahadeen soldiers that were fighting the Soviets in Afghanistan back in the '80s. Now that I think about it, I remember having seen lots of news footage of rebel fighters all around the world that were carrying the same weapons that our soldiers use. I think I just saw a short article in *Time* magazine last month about how all these death squads in Columbia and Turkey are using American weapons to carry out their dirty work. I can't believe that nobody has ever asked questions about how these groups got their hands on those type weapons or who was paying for them."

"Yeah, well, that's because they are smart enough to cover their tracks. They use people like Jeff Patten, a small-town attorney, who they can trust and who no one would suspect to carry the money for them. Patricia said that he had met someone at his hotel for dinner the night before he died, and that was where the money came from. His contact must have been with the mob, and I'll bet the mysterious, disappearing client that asked him to go to Denver was part of the Four Horsemen. Supposedly, that guy…the client, I mean…was going to swing through Chattanooga to get the money from Jeff. Jeff Patten had no idea what he was getting himself into. And now we're knee-deep into it ourselves."

"I know, Jack. It's crazy. What are we going to do?"

"We're going to get ourselves out of it."

"How?"

"We're going to turn the tables on them. When I was leaving the jail, I was able to pick up some files and this laptop. They belonged to one of the federal agents that had me picked up, and I'm hoping that we'll be able to get all the information we need from them."

"What's on the laptop?"

"I'm not sure yet. That's where I need you to take me. I've got a friend who's going to try to crack the password. I've already gone through the files and they were pretty helpful, but I really want to see what's stored on this computer."

"What about the files? What did they say?"

"There were a couple of files that I was able to get. One of them had information about Jeff Patten and the other was stuff about me."

"You?" she said in a startled voice.

"Yeah. There were pictures of me coming out of the bank in Denver and some other personal information: address, phone number, employment records, credit report. It looked like someone had done a very thorough background check on me."

"What about the other file? The one about Jeff Patten?"

"Same kind of stuff: pictures, personal information. There was another file with some documents relating to the plane crash."

"Did they have anything to do with the crash? The Four Horsemen, I mean."

"No. They were surprised by that. In fact, there was a memo recommending that they not use civilian couriers for the money after that incident. Apparently, it was a hell of a lot of trouble to secure the crash site. More trouble than hiding an ordinary money transfer. The plane had crashed into the side of a small mountain, and they had to send people from the Air Force base in Tullahoma to guard the site while they looked for the money, which they obviously didn't find."

"But they found Jeff Patten's body?"

"No, he lived through the crash and was found half dead by a soldier in the woods near the base of the mountain. They got him to the hospital in Shelbyville, but he died in the emergency room. The soldier that took him to the hospital was the same one that sent the wallet to Patricia."

"That's right. I think you told me that before. At least, I know you said something about the soldier and the wallet."

Jack enjoyed talking to Elizabeth, but he didn't like sitting in one place for so long and was starting to get nervous. "We need to get going," he said. "Why don't we switch places so I can drive us over to my friend's place?"

Jack got out of the car and walked around to the driver's side and Elizabeth climbed across the seats. A minute later, they were on the road and headed to Sean's office.

They had driven less than a mile when Elizabeth suddenly blurted out, "There is a cop behind us."

Jack looked into the rearview mirror and saw a black-and-white patrol car directly behind them. He remembered the last time he had seen that and wanted to avoid a repeat. He had been so engaged in his conversation with Elizabeth that he hadn't been paying attention to his surroundings. For a moment, he had forgotten that he was a fugitive, but the sight of the police car behind him brought him quickly back to reality. His heart was pounding. "I see it," he said, trying not to sound too nervous.

"What should we do?" Elizabeth asked.

"Nothing. Just don't look back at them. I don't think they would be looking for us in this car." At least that's what he hoped, but he didn't even know whose car they were driving. He tried not to look back but couldn't help himself.

"We need to turn off this road," Elizabeth said in a shaky voice.

"I know. I know. I'm going to take this next turn right up here."

"What if they follow us?"

"We'll have to deal with that when it happens. They probably haven't even noticed us." Jack wasn't the most religious person, but he quickly found himself in the middle of a fervent prayer. He put on his turn signal and was relieved when he looked in his mirror and saw that the cop had not turned on his signal. The relief quickly faded, however, when he saw it make the turn right behind him. He made it about a hundred yards before he looked back again and noticed another patrol car in the distance behind him. It was coming up on them fast, and his heart sunk when the car behind him threw its light on. Jack had already made up his mind that he wasn't going to pull over. If they wanted him, they were going to have to catch him first. "Hold on tight," he said, glancing over at Elizabeth. "Here we go."

"Oh shit!" she screamed as Jack slammed on the brakes and spun around, doing a complete 180 in the middle of the road, barely missing a car in the oncoming lane. The cops had obviously not been expecting such a move, and by the time they got on their brakes, he'd already floored the accelerator and was speeding away from them.

Jack was driving like a maniac—flying down the road, dodging in and out of traffic, and blowing through intersections. He looked in his rearview mirror and saw that there were now at least four police cars behind him. "We've got to get off this road!" he exclaimed.

"There's a turn up here," Elizabeth said. She was holding on to the dashboard with both hands. "Turn!...Turn!...Turn!" she screamed as they came up on the next intersection.

Jack slammed the car into second gear, let the clutch out, and spun the steering wheel hard to the right, causing the car to slide sideways through the turn. As soon as he felt the tires regain their traction, he stomped on the gas again and the car shot forward. He looked down at his speedometer and saw that he was going nearly eighty miles per hour. The police cars were still close behind them and he could hear the wail of their sirens, letting him know that they were right on his tail. They needed to get out of the city and away from the traffic, but there was no clear way to do it. If they couldn't lose their pursuers, they would have to outrun them, and there was little chance of that.

Elizabeth turned around to look out of the back window. "They're still behind us!" she screamed.

"Not for long," Jack said as he jerked the wheel again, making a sharp right turn into an alley between two buildings. The car was bouncing up and down and as he sped through the alley. He slammed into a pile of trash cans that were in the middle of the road and sent them flying up over the hood of the car. He noticed several doors facing the alley on both sides of the car and prayed that no one tried to walk outside. He could hear the sirens of the police cars right behind him, and Elizabeth was screaming, "Go! Go!" from the passenger's seat. She had a terrified look on her face and couldn't seem to decide whether she should be looking in front of them or behind to see what the police cars were doing. After a few seconds, they shot out from behind the buildings onto the street and barely missed a car that was pulling up to the red light at the intersection to his right. He turned the wheel sharply to the left and kept the accelerator on the floor.

"Oh my God!" Elizabeth yelled as Jack heard the unmistakable sound of screeching tires and a forceful collision.

He looked behind them and saw the cars piled up in the middle of the road. The patrol car that had been right on his tail was on its top, perpendicular to the road with another patrol car against it. The lead officer had hit another car that was unfortunately driving past the alley at the same moment that the police car had come out. Had Jack and Elizabeth come out of the alley a second later, it would have been him lying upside down in the middle of the road. The wreckage completely blocked the alleyway, and the patrol cars that were left intact were forced to stop.

"I sure hope no one was hurt," he said as he looked over at Elizabeth, who was turned completely around in her seat, staring in amazement at the carnage they had left in their wake. He could see the shock in her eyes, and her face was ashen. It would be a miracle if everyone had walked away from the collision unscathed. He felt terrible about having caused such a terrible accident, but he had no other choice. At that point, in his mind, it was *kill or be killed.* If they caught him, he would have no chance to prove his innocence, and he had come so far. He had finally figured out what he had gotten himself involved in, and he had the evidence that he needed to prove it; if they caught him now, it would all be lost. In a way, it was their own fault, but Jack still felt sorry for them. They were just doing their jobs and had no idea that their bosses were more corrupt than the person they were chasing.

He went further down the road and checked his rearview mirror again to see if any of the police cars were still behind him. "That was close," he said, breathing a sigh of relief when he saw that they were no longer being chased.

"Too close," Elizabeth agreed as she turned back around and slid back into a sitting position. "I think I'm going to throw up."

The accident had completely blocked the alley, and there were no cars behind them. He glanced at the speedometer and saw that he was going seventy miles per hour down a city street. That would surely attract more attention, he thought, so he slowed down. He was still headed down the street that he had turned onto from the alley and knew that that it wouldn't be long before every cop in Chattanooga was looking for their car.

"We've got to ditch this car, Elizabeth."

"I know. They're going to be looking for us, aren't they?"

He wanted to tell her no, but he knew better. They had just jabbed a stick into a hornet's nest, and he knew that the most important thing they could do now was to run and find a safe place to hide. They needed to get out of the city and back to Tonya's place where they would be safe, or at least where they would be able to spot trouble coming up the driveway. But first, they needed to get rid of their transportation, and that made getting out to Tonya's difficult.

The phone rang as he was trying to figure out what his next move would be.

"Hello," he said nervously as he put the phone to his ear. He wasn't expecting anyone to call and hoped nothing had happened to Tonya.

"Hey, this is Sean. I thought you were coming by today."

"I'm trying," Jack said. He was relieved to hear Sean's voice on the other end of the line. Listen, man. I'm in real trouble here."

"I know." Sean sounded a little confused. "That's why you were bringing me the computer."

"I'm not talking about the computer right now. Elizabeth and I just barely got away from a fleet of cops that were chasing me up Third Street. I need to get rid of the car I'm in and get another ride."

"Oh…," Sean said after a moment of silence. "Who's Elizabeth?"

"She's a friend. Don't worry about that right now. Look, I don't mean to be short with you. I really appreciate your help, but I've got to deal with this car thing right now."

"I can come get you. Why don't you just ditch the car and meet me somewhere?"

"You are a lifesaver." Jack hated to ask him for more help than he'd already agreed to provide, but he felt as if he had little choice.

"Just tell me when and where, and I'll be there."

Jack thought about it for a minute and then decided on a place that was close by and easy to get to. "Meet me at the gas station there on the corner of Third and Holtzclaw. You know the one I'm talking about?"

"Yeah. The Texaco?"

"That's the one. We'll be inside waiting on you. Just pull up outside and we'll come out to your car."

"I know right where you're talking about. I'll be there in less than ten minutes."

"I really appreciate this."

"No problem," Sean replied. "Just hang in there."

Jack looked over at Elizabeth and smiled as he hung up the phone. She looked a little distressed.

"What are we doing with the car?" she asked.

Jack hadn't considered the fact that the car didn't belong to either of them, but they couldn't keep driving around in it. "I'm sorry, Elizabeth, but we've got to get rid of it," he said. "We can't keep driving around. They'll catch us for sure."

"I guess you're right," she said reluctantly, "but it isn't even mine. I borrowed it from one of the girls at work."

"Who did you get it from?"

"It's Linda's. You know, the secretary in the office next to mine."

"Oh yeah. I know her. We can leave the keys in it, and then you can call her once we get out of the area. She doesn't know what you were doing, does she?"

"No. She doesn't know that I was coming to meet you. I left her my keys just in case. She can just bring my car over here and switch."

"I hope she doesn't get pulled over," Jack said. "I'm sure the cops that were chasing us called in the license plate. You might want to tell her it was stolen."

"That'll go over real well."

"Well, we don't really have a choice. We've got to get rid of this thing, and the sooner the better." They were only about a mile away from the station where they needed to meet Sean and were already headed down Third Street in that direction. They drove another half-mile and turned right into a run-down neighborhood. They went a couple of blocks into the neighborhood and pulled over to the side of the road.

"Why are we stopping here?" Elizabeth asked. She was obviously nervous about the surroundings, but he was sure she would like the back of a police car even less.

"We're ditching the car."

"Oh. Here?" she asked. "I was afraid of that."

"We've got to get it off the road, and I don't want to take it to the gas station. They've probably got two-thirds of the police force out there looking for us right now."

"How are we going to get to the gas station?"

"We'll walk. It's only about a half-mile. We can stay off the main road on these neighborhood streets and be there in ten minutes if we walk fast."

"I guess I don't have much choice, do I?"

"Not that I can see," Jack replied. He hated to be putting her through this, but she had insisted on coming along. They got out of the car and started walking down the sidewalk toward the gas station. Jack had driven past the neighborhood many times during his life, but he had never really paid attention. Most of the houses on the street were in bad shape. The paint was peeling off, and most of the yards were bare dirt. Some were completely boarded up.

"This is a pretty rough neighborhood," Elizabeth said, reaching out to take Jack's hand. She looked around and then pulled him close to her. She was obviously frightened. *And she should be,* Jack thought to himself. She had picked up a fugitive, had been in a high-speed car chase, and was walking through a ghetto for the first time in her life. He felt terrible about it, but he had warned her.

"This is the product of the Four Horsemen," he said, trying to get her mind off her immediate surroundings.

"What do you mean?" she asked.

"I mean this ghetto. The Mafia channels all its drugs into low-income neighborhoods like this across the country, and it destroys the people and families that live here."

"Nobody makes them do drugs," Elizabeth responded defiantly.

"I realize that, but they do make sure they are available, and by keeping the drugs illegal, they keep the value inflated. That gives someone who would otherwise have to take a minimum-wage job a real incentive to get involved in the drug business. These people are the victims of a war that they're not even aware of. A war that you never see on the news or read about in the papers. A war that has no clear battlefields, but people are still dying. They're dying each and every day right here in our own country, some by their own hands and some at the hands of the people trying to force their hypocritical drug policy down their throats. The cops are going after the drugs and the drug users, but it's the people after us right now that perpetuate the whole nasty business; they are the real criminals. It's insane, but these people don't know any better."

"I never really gave it much thought, Jack, but you're right."

They continued walking toward the gas station and talking. They passed a group of young kids standing out in the street. One of them asked if they "needed anything" as they walked by. "No," Jack replied. "We're just passing through."

CHAPTER 15

▼

They came out of the neighborhood onto Holtzclaw Street about three blocks west of the gas station. They turned left, and a few minutes later, they were standing in the parking lot where they were supposed to meet Sean. Jack looked around but didn't see his car, so they walked inside to wait.

"Do you want anything?" he asked Elizabeth. "I'm going to get something to drink."

"Yeah, I would love to have a coke."

"What kind?" he asked.

"Whatever. It doesn't really matter, but something without caffeine please. I'm about as wired as I need to get right now."

Jack chuckled at her and went to the cooler in the back of the store to fetch their drinks. As he opened the door to the cooler, he looked outside and was relieved to see Sean pulling into the parking lot. He started to smile, but his heart suddenly dropped when he saw that a police car was pulling in right behind him. *Oh shit,* he thought nervously. *Surely Sean didn't turn us in.* His heart was racing as he walked slowly to the front of the store where Elizabeth was standing. She was already at the counter flipping through a magazine and trying to look inconspicuous.

"Don't look now," he said as he approached the counter, "but—"

"I know. I see them," she said before he could finish his sentence.

Sean had pulled up to the sidewalk right in front of the door, and the police car had pulled up to one of the gas pumps. Jack was happy to see that the patrol car hadn't followed Sean, but he was still nervous just being that close to a cop.

"That's Sean," he said to Elizabeth, glancing in the direction of the parking lot.

"Good. Let's just pay and get out of here."

He nodded in agreement and the two of them walked over to the counter. He set their drinks down in front of the cashier, and Elizabeth threw her magazine down next to them.

"I've got to have something to look at," she said matter-of-factly to Jack.

The cashier heard her comment and smiled at them. Jack smiled back at the cashier and handed him a five-dollar bill. He handed change to Jack, and they turned to walk out of the store. He and Sean made eye contact through the glass as they walked outside. Jack could see that he was nervous. So were Jack and Elizabeth, because the police officer who had pulled in behind Sean was now walking straight toward them. He walked in through one door as Jack and Elizabeth walked out through the other, nodding hello to them as they passed. Once they were outside, they looked at each other and quickly got into Sean's car and pulled away from the station.

"Holy shit, man!" Sean said as they left the parking lot. "That was intense."

"You're not kidding," Jack replied. "If you only knew…"

"It's been quite a day," Elizabeth said from the backseat in agreement.

Jack realized that the other two people in the car had never met each other. "I'm sorry," he said, feeling embarrassed at having lost his manners. "Elizabeth, this is Sean. Sean, this is Elizabeth."

"Nice to meet you," they both said at the same time.

"Man, I thought you guys were busted back there for sure. I heard 'em talking on the radio about a car chase on my way over here. Sounds like you barely made it."

"Just barely," Jack said, nodding his head. "We would've probably been caught if we hadn't gone through that alley when we did."

"They said on the radio that there was a big pileup."

"It was insane," Elizabeth chimed in. "The car right behind us T-boned a car that we barely missed. The car behind that one flipped over and blocked all the other cars that were chasing us in the alley. It was one of the craziest things I've ever seen."

"It sounds like a movie."

"Yeah…well, you don't get killed or hauled off to jail at the end of a movie," Jack said.

"I'm just glad you guys are okay."

"So are we," Elizabeth said.

"Okay, so where are we headed?"

"We need to get out to Middle Valley. I've got a friend out there. We need to drop Elizabeth off with her and then go back to your office to work on the computer."

"No need to do that. I brought the software I need with me."

"That's great," Jack said excitedly.

"Where is the computer now?"

Jack remembered the laptop he'd been carrying since they had ditched the car. He had handed it to Elizabeth when they had gotten in Sean's car. Elizabeth leaned over and slid her hand underneath Jack's seat and pulled out the computer. "This thing sure is light," she said as she handed it over the seat to Jack.

"Yeah," Sean said in agreement. "I'm sure it is. That looks like nice equipment."

"That's your tax dollars at work," Jack said, smiling. He looked back at Elizabeth and was happy to see her smiling too. "I need you to make copies of the hard drive for me if you can."

"Sure man. I can do that. I'll have to go back by my shop, but then I can just hook it up to my DVD burner and back up the whole hard drive. How many copies do you want?"

"As many as you can make. At least ten, maybe fifteen. The more copies I have, the safer I'll feel."

"What are you gonna do with the copies?"

"I'm going to send at least one of them to the feds that are after me. The rest I plan to distribute as insurance. If anything ever happens to me, the disks will start hitting news desks at CNN, CNBC, Fox News, you name it. If they know what I've got on them, they'll think twice about coming after me."

"Sounds like a plan. I'll make the copies, but I'll have to go back to my office to do it."

"That's fine. We can drop off Elizabeth when we get where we're going. We can sit there and get through the password, then we can head back to your office."

"So, you're just going to leave me alone with someone I've never met before?" Elizabeth asked.

"I wish there was another way to do it," Jack replied, "but it's not safe for both of us to be running all over town. I'm sure that they will figure out that it was you in the car with me, and don't think for a second that they'll not be out looking for you too. It's not safe for either of us now. I can handle myself, but I don't want anything to happen to you. If they catch me, I'll need someone on the outside to bargain with them."

"What am I going to bargain with?" she asked.

"The computer and the files that I'm going to show you when we get to Tonya's house. I hope it doesn't happen, but I may need you to play our cards. And you can't do that if you're in a jail cell."

"Oh...," Elizabeth said reluctantly. "I guess you're right. Someone needs to stay out of jail."

"And I'd rather it be you."

"Who is this Tonya person?" Sean asked.

"She's a friend of a friend, actually. I don't know her all that well, but she's already helped me a bunch. I know I can trust her, and no one would think to look for us at her place."

"How did you meet her?"

"I met her boyfriend while I was in jail. He was one of the people that got me out. He told me to look her up if I needed any help."

"How did you get out of there?"

"That's an interesting story. It was actually one of the guards at the jail that let me go."

"Are you kidding?" Sean asked incredulously.

"I swear. It was actually two of the cops and the person in the cell next to me that got me out. Dave, who is Tonya's boyfriend, was in the cell next to mine. He is an electrician who got hooked on crack and ended up in jail after trying to rob a liquor store. He flipped the main circuit breaker for the whole jail building, and I slipped out through the gate while the power was off."

"What were you doing in the parking lot?" Sean asked.

"Well, one of the guards had taken me from my cell up to the interrogation room several times while I was in there. He saw how they were treating me, and looked for my records. He saw that there was no arrest record and nothing to hold me on. I guess it just pissed him off that these federal agents were acting like they were above the law. He had another officer take me up to their office and watch the hallway while Dave and I grabbed the files and this laptop. Then I was escorted to the parking lot while Dave went down to the electrical room and threw the breaker. When the power went off, the guard opened the fence and told me to run. So, I did."

"That's a crazy story," Sean said.

"Yeah. You're just lucky that anyone was willing to help you."

"I know. The cops especially were risking their jobs, but I guess they believed me. Or maybe they just felt sorry for me, who knows, but if you could've seen the way these federal agents were acting. They basically treated the cops like children who didn't know what they were doing."

They talked the rest of the way to Tonya's, and Jack filled them both in on everything that had happened to him over the last few days. He also called Tonya to warn her that he had some friends with him and to ask her if it was okay if they came with him to her house. He didn't want to just show up with a crew of people that she wasn't expecting. She told him that it was fine but that there was nowhere for all of them to sleep.

"We're not all staying," he assured her. "Just Elizabeth and myself, if that's all right. She can have the bed and I'll just sleep out on the couch. My other friend, Sean, is just giving us a ride. We ran into some trouble earlier and had to ditch our car. Sean was nice enough to pick us up and give us a ride."

"Is everything okay?" she asked.

"Oh yeah, everything's fine now, but Sean and I need to go back into town for a little while. I was hoping that Elizabeth could stay with you while we are gone."

"That's fine."

"Great," Jack said.

*   *   *   *

They arrived at Tonya's trailer and headed inside. As soon as the introductions were complete, Sean followed Jack into the kitchen, where he set up the laptop. "Can you work from here?" Jack asked.

"Sure. This is fine. I brought the software that I need to crack the password. Just let me get it started and it'll automatically scan through the files looking for passwords."

"That's pretty cool."

"It's kind of ironic."

"What's that?"

"I've got this buddy that works for a large Internet service provider in Dallas. He copied this program from the FBI. Now we're using it against them."

"How did he get it?"

"They were doing some kind of surveillance on a suspect where they were watching all of his e-mails. I think it was some kind of Internet child pornography ring or something. They hacked into his computer using the ISP's server and were using this software to steal all of his passwords. I'll bet they never expected it to be used to crack one of their own computers."

"That sounds like some pretty powerful software. How did your friend get his copy?"

"He just made himself one. While no one was looking, I'm sure. I don't think they were giving away copies or anything. You could really do some damage to someone if you had all their passwords."

"That's what I was thinking. So how long will it take to get into this one?"

"It depends. You know how your computer will remember the passwords you enter so that you don't have to re-enter them every time you log on? Well, the software I'm using scans all of the files on the hard drive and pulls out all of the saved passwords and then plugs each one of them into the program you're trying to open. It'll just keep plugging away until it gets the right one and then you're in business."

"So how long does that take?"

"It depends. First of all, the software has to scan every file on the computer's hard drive, and there could easily be a hundred thousand files on there. So, it's got to go through each file and pull out the password embedded in that program. That's going to take a while by itself...maybe thirty minutes, maybe an hour. Once it pulls the passwords out, it will try each one of them until it finds the right one. If he uses the same password for just about everything, then it shouldn't take too long, but if he uses several different passwords, then it could take a little longer."

"So we're talking at least an hour?"

"An hour...maybe two or three hours, but once I get started, I can't stop it, or else I'll have to start it all over again. So it's cool if we're here for at least a couple of hours, right?"

"Yeah. Tonya said she doesn't mind, but we need to try to stay out of her way."

"I'm going to get this thing started, and then there's really nothing else I can do until it runs its course."

"How will we know when it's done?"

"We'll just have to keep checking it."

"Well, let's get started then."

"All right," Sean said as he plugged the laptop in and turned it on. Jack sat next to him, watching intently as he slid the disk into the computer and started the scan. Once it was running, they got up and walked into the den where Tonya and Elizabeth were talking. They seemed to be getting along pretty well, which made Jack feel better about leaving them alone together.

"I was filling her in on the day's events," Elizabeth said to Jack as he and Sean walked into the room.

"Sounds like you had an exciting morning."

"That's an understatement," he replied. "I thought we were busted for sure, but we were lucky."

"I'll say," Sean interjected. "And then, when I picked them up, there was a freakin' cop that pulled into the gas station right behind me. I couldn't believe it. I'm tellin' you, it scared the shit out of me. To be honest, I almost just kept driving right past the place."

"That would've been great," Elizabeth said sarcastically.

"But I didn't. I wouldn't have left you waiting on me like that."

"I'm just glad you called when you did," Jack said. "I don't know what we would've done.'

"I guess you would have been walking."

"I guess so," Jack replied. "And speaking of walking," he said turning toward Elizabeth, "did you call Linda about her car?"

"Yes. I called her while you were in there messing with the computer."

"What did she say?"

"She wasn't happy, but I explained the situation to her and told her that she needed to call and report that it was stolen."

"What did she say about that?"

"Like I said, she wasn't happy about it, but she said she'd do it. I told her she could just drive my car around until they found hers and returned it to her. I told where it was and told her not to try and get it herself, just to let the cops find it and return it to her. That way, she wouldn't be implicated as an accessory."

"And she was okay with that?"

"No. She was upset, but she'll be all right. We're pretty good friends, and I'm sure she won't tell them that she's talked to us."

"Good," Jack said, relieved. "That's one less thing for us to worry about."

"What's happening with the computer?" Elizabeth asked, changing the subject.

"It's working. Sean's got this program that will crack the password, but it might take a while. We just have to let it do its thing. Hopefully, when it's finished, we'll be able to find out what the Four Horsemen have been up to."

The four of them sat in the den, watching television, talking, and waiting. Sean got up every fifteen minutes or so and walked into the kitchen to check the progress. It took a little more than an hour for the software to work its magic. "We're in!" Sean exclaimed on his last trip to the kitchen. As soon as he said it, the rest of them rushed in to see what was going on.

When they got there, the image of the American bald eagle was just popping up on the screen, and there was a box underneath the image that said "PASS-WORD."

"Martha," Sean said as he typed. "Can you believe that's the password? I think that's Agent Anderson's wife or daughter or something. I don't know, but he uses that password for just about everything, so it must be somebody important to him."

Once the password was entered, the screen flashed, and then the familiar Windows operating system screen appeared. It then looked like every other computer Jack had ever used. There were vertical columns of icons on the screen, some of which Jack recognized, such as the virus scanner, the word processing and spreadsheet programs, and the Internet browser, but there were others that he had never seen before.

"Look at this," Sean said, clicking on an icon with the word "SAT-1" written below it. "I think it's satellite images."

"Of what?" Jack asked.

"I don't know. We're not logged in to their network, but it looks like you can download real-time satellite images from their network and see what's going on around the world."

"So they can watch the crops grow," Jack said in astonishment.

"Or they can check out airstrips like this." Sean opened a picture that had been recently saved showing what appeared to be a small airstrip in the middle of a jungle somewhere. They looked at several other pictures, each one showing a different location, none of which any of them recognized."

"Those look like poppies," Elizabeth said, pointing to one of the pictures that showed a field of pink flowers growing on a mountainside.

"Let's look at this," Sean said, clicking on the "E-mail" icon. Once again, the screen changed and showed a list of all the e-mails contained on the computer, some of which were new and hadn't even been read. He pointed at the screen and turned to Jack. "It looks like they're still coming. Look at the domain names on these e-mail accounts. Here's one from somebody at the CIA. Here's one from the NSA, one from the Department of Defense, and here's another from the DEA. Looks like some heavy players."

"Those are the Four Horsemen," Elizabeth interjected. "The DEA, the NSA, the DOD, and the FBI. That's where the project got its name. The Four Horsemen is basically a four-person committee made up of representatives from each of those four organizations. The actual Four Horsemen, the leaders of the operation, change over time, but they've got the same mission: to control the international flow of drugs and to use the profits to support proxy wars that are being fought to advance the interests of the United States government throughout the world."

Sean was nodding his head. "That's some heavy stuff. Let's see what this one says." He clicked on one of the e-mails from someone at *eagle88@dod.gov*. "This was sent three days ago from someone at the Department of Defense," he said as he read the message to Jack. "*Pickup successful. Delivery scheduled for 03:00 hours. Location: Airfield 12. Quantity: 2.43 tons.*" When he finished reading the message, he looked back over his shoulder. "I wonder where airfield 12 is and what they are delivering 2.43 tons of."

"I would say they're talking about heroin or opium," Elizabeth said. "I think there's lots of that coming out of Afghanistan right now. It's strange that we've got so many of our soldiers stationed there, but the drug supply has increased dramatically. The only way for that to happen is for our guys to look the other way."

"Look at this one!" Sean said excitedly. "It's from someone at the FBI a couple of days before you got arrested, and it's got your name on it." Jack looked down at the screen and saw his own name in the subject line of the e-mail that Sean had opened.

We've got the subject under surveillance. Background check showed one prior arrest on drug charges. That should be helpful in the event he finds the package. Bank was no joy. He came out empty-handed and went back to his motel. We will continue to follow subject and will advise if anything changes.

"That's you, man. They were following you—creepy."

"You're telling me," Jack said in agreement. "What does this one say?" he asked, pointing to one from *eagle24@cia.gov*.

"Let's see." Sean opened the e-mail and read it aloud. "*Airfield 92 secured. Approximate Coordinates: 67E and 37N. Awaiting further instructions.* It looks like this e-mail went to someone at the Department of Defense, and they just copied Agent Anderson."

"Let's see where those coordinates are." They looked at an atlas and found that the coordinates were located in Afghanistan—just to the west of the city of Mazar-I-Sharif.

"You were right," Sean said. "They're definitely shipping something out of Afghanistan, and it's probably opium and heroin just like Elizabeth said, but I don't understand why they are doing this. I mean…our government doesn't need the money. Are the Four Horsemen in business for themselves? Are they keeping the money?"

"No. They're using military transports and equipment to move the drugs around. That means they've got to have pilots, ground crews, fuel, and everything else that goes along with it. They'd get caught for sure if they tried to just keep the money for themselves. It's just too big an operation to keep completely secret."

"Then where is all the money going?"

"At this moment, I'm not exactly sure, but I'll bet most of it goes to the Afghan government."

"Why? I mean, why would we go to all the trouble to move drugs around and then give the money away? It doesn't make a whole lot of sense."

"Sure it does. Look, this isn't a moneymaking operation. I know that it makes a lot of money, but it's about worldwide stability and advancing our government's international political interests, and sometimes that can be expensive. The U.S. needs to keep the terrorists out of Afghanistan, and that requires a strong centralized government. We've seen what happens when there is no strong government in place, at least no government in place that doesn't actively support terrorists or allow their training camps to be located inside their borders."

"But why are they selling drugs to our government? Why not just give them money?"

"Simple. They need more money than we can give them—more than Congress is willing to appropriate, anyway. They need it to buy guns and tanks to protect themselves and to fight the terrorists and the remnants of the former Taliban government. They also need it to build schools and roads and all the other trappings of society that will keep their citizens pacified. Our government wants to make sure that they have all that, so that the government we installed will stay in power. But they also have a limited budget and don't want to wait for Congress to approve the funding. We've got our own domestic issues and can't afford to rebuild another country. The drugs are a way to make some quick cash."

"I never thought about all that."

"That's the deal. This organization, the Four Horsemen, brings drugs into the country from all over the world. The Mafia buys it and then turns around and sells it to the mid-level dealers, who distribute it throughout the country. The money is sent to wherever the drugs are coming from—in this case, Afghanistan—and then it's used to supply their armies or their infrastructure."

"How long has this been going on?"

"As far as we can tell it's been going on since the sixties. Elizabeth did some research and found an article about the Four Horsemen from 1971 that was published by a newspaper reporter from a small town in southern California, who, by the way, drove his car off a bridge shortly after his article was published."

Sean was staring at Jack with a bewildered look on his face. "What did it say?"

"Basically what I just told you, except at that time, the drugs were coming out of Cambodia and Laos, which are right next to Vietnam. The article accused the government of using the profits from the drugs to supply weapons to those governments, who, at the time, were trying to stop the spread of Communism into their countries. They were fighting Communism back then. Now, it's Muslim extremists that they're trying to stop. There's always somebody out there challenging the 'American' way of life, and the Four Horsemen consider themselves to be on the front lines of that war."

"So you're telling me that people have already published articles about this, and nobody did anything about it? Nobody has ever done anything about it?"

"Obviously not. Like I said, the reporter died shortly after the article came out, and you can bet that he didn't reveal his sources to anyone. If anybody was talking, I'm pretty sure that the reporter's untimely death shut them up."

"And now you've uncovered the whole thing again."

"I wasn't trying to, but it looks like that's exactly what I've done."

"And what makes you think they won't just get rid of you?"

"Unfortunately, I don't think that they would hesitate for a minute to get rid of me, as long as they were sure that that would be the end of it. Right now, they don't know what I know or who I've told. They do know that I have some of their money and some incriminating evidence, and I'm banking on the fact that they won't be stupid enough to get rid of me until they find out exactly what I'm up to."

"So what exactly is your plan?"

"Blackmail. Plain and simple. I'm going to give them back their files and this laptop once I am assured that no harm will come to me or anyone close to me. If anything does happen, they know that all the information I have will hit the press, and then they're going to have lots of explaining to do."

"I hope it all works out for you."

"Me too, Sean…me too. Now let's see what else we can find on this computer."

They spent the next hour combing through the files stored on the hard drive. They found many more e-mails, from each of the four organizations that were involved in the project, that had incriminating statements like the ones they had just read. The address book read like a who's who in the American government, the international drug cartels, and Third World governments. There were schedules and delivery manifests and records of wire transfers to foreign bank accounts. They found lists of the people who were involved in the operation, as well as detailed maps showing pickup and drop-off locations around the world. There were also pictures of various people and places, including the pictures of Jack that Agent Anderson showed him while he was being questioned.

Before they had gone through a third of the files, it was obvious to Jack that he had hit the jackpot. He had all the information he would need to blow the lid off this conspiracy and expose it to the world. He now represented a serious threat to the Four Horsemen, and they would have to deal with him accordingly. Once he had made copies of the information on the computer, it would be time to call Agent Anderson to see what he could work out.

They continued reading e-mails and looking through the files for a few more hours. By the time they had seen most of what was on the computer, it was getting late. Jack and Elizabeth were both exhausted, so they decided to call it a day and get some rest. Sean left the laptop and Tonya agreed to take Jack to Sean's office the next day so that they could make copies of the hard drive. He wanted to send out the copies as soon as he could, and he needed to put together the list of the people he would send it to.

CHAPTER 16

▼

"I'm beat," Jack said, yawning and looking up at the clock. "And it's only eight o'clock." He looked out one of the windows and saw that it was starting to get dark.

"Me too," Elizabeth said, nodding her head in agreement.

"You can have the bedroom, Elizabeth," Jack said. "I'll just sleep out here on the couch."

"That's okay, Jack. You sleep in the bedroom too," she said, looking him straight in the eyes. "I'd really rather not be alone tonight."

Jack hoped that she wouldn't notice the devilish smile that was suddenly plastered across his face. "Are you sure?" he asked, trying to sound sincere. "I don't want you to be uncomfortable and don't mind sleeping on the couch."

"Yes, Jack. It's fine. You can keep your hands to yourself, can't you?" He was glad to see that she too had a big smile on her face as she said it.

"I'll try, but I'm not making any promises."

"I guess that's good enough for me."

"Okay, you two," Tonya butted in. "Sleep wherever you want, but I'm gonna stay up and watch a little TV. There's a dresser in the bedroom back there, and I'm pretty sure that I've got some pajamas Elizabeth can wear in the top right-hand drawer. Jack, you can wear something of Dave's. There should be some T-shirts in that dresser too. Check the bottom drawers."

Jack had only known Tonya for forty-eight hours, but he could see what Dave must have loved about her. She was really quite attractive, although she was not Jack's type. She was quiet and had a very warm personality; it hadn't taken long for them to feel completely comfortable around her. He felt sorry for her, living way out in the middle of nowhere in a trailer, all by herself with her boyfriend in jail. He couldn't believe how she was so willing to help someone that she didn't even know. And she wasn't just helping him. She was letting him and Elizabeth, fugitives as they were, use her home as their base of operations even though she barely knew either of them. He would have to make sure that her part in all of this didn't go unrewarded.

"Thanks, Tonya," Elizabeth said, breaking Jack's concentration. "I'm going to go ahead and turn in."

"Okay," Tonya replied. "I guess I'll see you guys in the morning. I usually get up around six o'clock, but I'll try to keep it quiet. I know you've had a big day and are probably exhausted. Tell me what time you want to get out of bed, and I'll make us a pot of coffee. If anybody wants some, I'll make breakfast too."

"You're too kind, Tonya," Elizabeth said. Her tone of voice made it clear that she felt somewhat guilty about everything Tonya was doing for them. She shot Jack a quick look and then turned back to Tonya. "Jack and I will get up in the morning and help you with that."

"You don't have to. Seriously, I'm not talking about anything fancy. Just some scrambled eggs, bacon, and toast. I make it almost every morning. It'll be nice to have some company for breakfast. I haven't had any real visitors since Dave started getting into trouble."

"Thanks again for everything, Tonya," Jack said. "You know we couldn't do this without your help."

"Yes, Tonya," Elizabeth said in agreement. "Thanks a lot. I can't tell you how wonderful it is to have met you, and there aren't words to tell you how much I appreciate all of your help."

"Okay…okay. That's enough," Tonya replied meekly. "You're making me blush. You're both very welcome. Now go to bed, and I'll see you in the morning."

As they walked down the hallway toward the bedroom, Jack started to get nervous. The fact that he was getting ready to spend the night with Elizabeth was starting to sink in, and he felt a familiar stirring of emotion. He wished the circumstances were better, but he would take the chance to be with her any way he could get it. He had certainly been attracted to her before, but now he was sure that he was falling in love. She was the silver lining that surrounded the dark clouds he had been living under. He only hoped that she felt the same way.

"Which side do you want?" she asked as they walked into the room.

Jack looked down at the double bed in the middle of the room. "I'll sleep on either side. Whatever makes you more comfortable."

"Why don't you take that side by the window and I'll sleep closer to the door. How's that?"

"That'll be just fine."

"Good. That's settled. Now I'm going to put on some pajamas," she said, opening one of the dresser drawers and pulling out a short, silky nightgown, "so you turn around and close your eyes."

Jack could feel his face turning red with embarrassment as he turned around to face the wall and put his hands up to cover his eyes. His face, however, wasn't the only sensation he was feeling.

"Okay," she said, as something soft hit him in the back of the head. She had pulled a pair of gym shorts and a T-shirt out of one of the other drawers and thrown them at him while he wasn't looking. "Now, put those on and I'll cover my eyes."

He quickly slid his clothes off and put on what she had just picked out. They weren't sexy like what she was wearing, but it was all he had to work with, and he wasn't going to worry about it. When he finished getting dressed and turned around, he found that Elizabeth had already crawled into the bed. Not that he would have minded too much if she would have snuck a peek. He wasn't exactly a bodybuilder, but he wasn't scrawny either. He went to the gym three times a week and had a slim, muscular body that he felt pretty good about.

He walked over to the bed and pulled the covers back so that he could slide under them. The nightgown Elizabeth was wearing had thin straps that went up over her shoulders, and it came about halfway down her thigh. It was tight at the waist and really complemented her slender figure but was loose enough at the top so that the side of one breast was exposed. She was truly a magnificent sight to behold, and Jack was trying hard not to exhibit any signs of his excitement as he slipped into the bed next to her and pulled the covers over them.

"Are you going to turn off the light?" she asked.

"Oh…yeah," Jack said in an embarrassed tone. He had been so excited about getting into the bed with her that he hadn't even noticed that it was on. "I'm sorry. I was…I forgot…" Once again, in Elizabeth's presence, Jack had lost the ability to speak.

"Don't try to fool me, Jack. I know you just wanted to get a look at me in this skimpy little thing I've got on."

"No. I wasn't…I just forgot to…" Jack knew his cheeks were red and he felt so embarrassed.

"It's okay, Jack. I'm just kidding," she said softly, trying to put him at ease. "You sure are cute when you get all flustered like that. And you can leave the light on for all I care."

Jack was mesmerized by her smile and quickly got up to turn the light off. He slipped through the darkness, back into the bed, and crawled under the covers. As he turned toward Elizabeth, their legs brushed and he felt her smooth, shaven skin against his own. It was just about more than he could stand, and his arousal was becoming evident.

She turned to face him and then took hold of his hand. "You know, Jack," she said in a soft and sexy voice, "it would be nice if you would kiss me now."

Jack lay there for a brief moment. He knew what to do but wasn't sure exactly how to do it. He wanted this to be the best kiss she'd ever received, or, at the very least, one she wouldn't soon forget. He closed his eyes, placed his hand gently on the side of her face, and then leaned forward to oblige her request. As their lips met, everything else in the world faded into obscurity. He wasn't thinking about Smith or Anderson or the money or jail or anything other than how soft and sweet her lips felt pressed against his. He wanted that moment to last forever and hated for it to end, but he knew that all things, even the good ones, had to end. He pulled back from her, and they looked into each other's eyes. She smiled, sending his heartbeat racing, and he leaned forward again. This time the kiss was more passionate and was followed by several more.

Eventually, their hands started to wander and their bodies closed in on each other. He was completely absorbed in the moment and the feel of her silky clothing against his hands. After several minutes of long, slow kisses, she reached up and pulled his shirt off over his head. They continued to kiss, but Jack didn't know whether he should try to take her nightgown off. Without question, he wanted to, but he was satisfied with what he had, and he didn't want her to think that he was being too aggressive. His question was answered, however, when she sat up and pulled it off herself. The moonlight trickled into the bedroom through the window, casting shadows across her body and allowing Jack to get a glimpse of her beautiful breasts. He was truly, and without a doubt, falling madly in love.

They made love with incredible passion, and for Jack, it was unlike any other experience he'd had. When she touched him, it sent shivers up and down his spine. Their embrace seemed to last an eternity and their climax was simultaneous. He felt an emotional attachment with Elizabeth that had never been there with any girl before her. While they held each other, nothing else mattered, and for a short while, he truly felt as though they were the only two people in the world.

*　　*　　*　　*

The next morning came too early. They had gotten plenty of sleep, but Jack hated to get out of the bed. It felt so good to be lying next to Elizabeth. He didn't want the closeness to end, but he knew that he had important things to do. He needed to get to Sean's to make the copies of Anderson's hard drive. He also wanted to see if Sean would take him by his house to get the money. He was worried that if he didn't get it soon, someone else might find it. It was hidden well, but Elizabeth and his mother had both told him that they had gone by his house and that it had been ransacked, presumably by Anderson and his goons. It wasn't likely that anyone had found the money, but if they looked long enough and hard enough, they would eventually find it.

He rolled over onto his side and put his arm around Elizabeth. She was warm and he could feel her chest expanding and contracting with each breath. It felt so right to have her there next to him, and he hated that their first night together had to come to an end. He lay there watching her breathe and hoping that he would have many more opportunities to be with her, but first he needed to "take care of business." It wasn't long before her eyes cracked open, and she looked up at Jack with a big smile.

"Good morning," she said in a soft, crackly voice as she turned to face him.

"Good morning to you," Jack replied, staring into her big brown eyes.

She lifted her head from the pillow and kissed him on the lips. "I hate to get out of this bed," she said, stretching her arms back over her head and letting out a big yawn. "It feels so nice being here next to you."

He was so glad to hear her say what he was thinking. He had been afraid that she would wake up thinking that they had made a mistake. They were both under a lot of pressure, but he knew that his feelings for her were real. "I know what you mean. I feel like I could just stay here wrapped up in these covers with you forever." She smiled and leaned forward and kissed him again. And again, he was all to happy to oblige her.

"I want you to know how much it means to me to be with you right now," he said earnestly. "I wish that things weren't so crazy, but…"

"I know, Jack. I wish things were more normal too, but I believe that everything happens for a reason. I mean…well…" She was blushing and Jack could tell that she was trying to get her thoughts into words. It was kind of nice to see that she occasionally got tongue-tied too. "I've been attracted to you for a long time, ever since I came to work at the firm, but I was afraid to say anything to you about it."

"Afraid?" Jack said in disbelief. "I didn't think you were afraid of anything."

"I was afraid you wouldn't feel the same way. Especially after our little tryst at the firm Christmas party. I had the feeling that you…well…I was worried that you thought it had been a mistake."

"I'm sorry…I should've…"

"No, don't be sorry. I'm just glad we finally got the chance to spend some time together. If things hadn't happened the way they did, and we hadn't gotten ourselves into this mess, then last night might have never happened."

"I'm just glad that last night did happen. I want you to know that I've been interested in you for a long time too. To be honest, I was worried that you thought the whole Christmas party thing was a mistake too. That's why I backed off, but I've been thinking a lot about you since that night. I'd like to think that I would have eventually done something about it, but if this is what it took to get us together, then I'm glad it happened. I didn't think I'd be saying that, and I wish it was over, but I am glad that it happened."

"Me too, Jack."

They lay together for a few more minutes, just holding each other and enjoying each other's embrace. They finally decided to get up when the smell of coffee started to filter into the room. They walked into the kitchen and found Tonya sitting on the couch sipping on a cup of the coffee she had just made and watching television.

"Good morning," she said as they walked into the room. "Did you guys sleep okay?"

"Yeah, we sure did." Jack looked over and saw that Elizabeth was blushing again.

"Good. I was just getting ready to make some breakfast if ya'll are still interested."

"I am," Elizabeth said. "Let me go brush my teeth and I'll help you with it."

"Okay. I'm going to finish my coffee and then we'll get started. Do you guys want a cup?"

"I do," Elizabeth replied. "How 'bout you, Jack?"

"That sounds great. I'll be happy to help with the breakfast too."

"Don't worry about it, Jack. Elizabeth and I can handle it. Why don't you take your shower while we get the food together. I know you've got places to be this morning, so we ought to get moving."

"That's fine with me," Jack said. "Elizabeth can brush her teeth, and then I'll go ahead and get in the shower."

"There's towels in the closet back there. You know where they are. Just make yourself at home."

"Thanks." Jack turned and headed back down the hallway toward the bathroom.

*   *   *   *

They ate their breakfast, and Elizabeth got showered while Jack and Tonya cleaned up the kitchen. She finally came out to join them and, within a few minutes, Tonya was ready to go too.

He looked at the clock in Tonya's dashboard as they were pulling out of the driveway and saw that it was just a few minutes before nine o'clock. It took them about thirty minutes to get to Sean's store, and Jack was glad to see his car parked outside all by itself when they pulled up. He had given one of the cell phones he had bought the day before to Elizabeth in case anything happened while he and Sean were together. "You're going to stay with Tonya, right?" he asked as he was getting out of the car. "Sean and I have to take care of a few things, and then he'll bring me back out there this afternoon. If that's all right with Tonya, I mean."

"Yes, of course. That's fine, Jack. I don't have to work today. She can run some errands with me, and then we'll head back to the house." She looked over to Elizabeth to see if she objected. "Is that okay with you, Elizabeth?"

"Sure. That's fine, but promise me, Jack, that you'll be careful."

"You know I will," he said, smiling and winking at her.

"You better," she said, smiling back.

"I'm going to go inside and make sure Sean's all right with everything. He said yesterday that he didn't mind helping me out today, but I'm gonna check to make sure that's still the case. If you'll wait just a minute, I'll come back out to tell you what's going on."

He went inside and found Sean sitting behind a computer that was set up on a large table at the back of the sales area. "Hey," he said as Sean looked up from the screen.

"I was wondering when you'd get here."

"I've got the girls waiting out in the parking lot. Are you going to be able to run me around a little bit today and then take me back out to Tonya's?"

"Sure man. I was already planning on it. If you brought the computer, I'll start making your copies right now. It shouldn't take too long to make them. I've got a customer coming in to drop off a tower and monitor around 10:30, but I'm free after that."

Jack walked back out to Tonya's truck and Elizabeth rolled her window down. "Okay girls. He's going to take care of running me around today, and we'll be back out to the house later this afternoon."

"Be careful and we'll see you there."

"I will," Jack said, leaning through the window to kiss her.

Jack walked back into the store as if he was floating on a cloud.

"You look happy," Sean said.

"Yep. I'm feeling pretty good right now."

"What's up with that?"

"Well, I finally got—"

"Elizabeth, huh?" Sean said before he could finish his sentence.

"Yeah…Elizabeth." Jack could feel his face turning red as he thought about their night together.

"Way to go, dude. She's hot."

"No doubt about that," Jack replied, his cheeks still glowing red. He handed Agent Anderson's laptop to Sean, who connected it to his computer with a thick cable.

"I'm making the first copy now," Sean said after a minute or so, looking back at the computer in front of him. "I can make the rest of them from the disk I'm making right now. You can take the laptop after that and look through the files some more while we wait on my customer."

"I'd love to have a look at some more of the e-mails."

"They're pretty interesting?"

"You're not kidding. I need to make a list of all the people he contacted. It ought to shake him up good if I can run down the list for him."

"I'd say so, but be careful. You don't want to piss them off too bad. I'd say that most of the people he's dealing with are very powerful, and I hate to say it, but I'm afraid that if they put all of their resources on it, they're gonna be able to find you."

"They haven't found Bin Laden yet," Jack said smartly, "and they've been looking for him for years.

"Yeah, well, Bin Laden's got millions of dollars. That'll buy a lot of friends, and you don't have that going for you."

"Actually," Jack said with an impish grin on his face, "I do."

"What? You're telling me that you've got that kind of money?"

"That's exactly what I'm telling you. That's what got me involved in this whole ordeal in the first place. You know I told you that I went out to Denver."

"I heard you talking about it, and I saw those pictures yesterday of you coming out of some bank."

"I went out there to try and find some money that Jeff Patten had been carrying for the Four Horsemen when he died."

"So I guess you found it."

"I did, but not at the bank. It was in an abandoned mine shaft on some property that Jeff Patten's family owned just outside of Denver."

"You never did tell me how you got involved in any of this anyway."

"I guess I've been so wound up, I didn't even think about it."

"So how did you get involved?"

"You remember Clark Patten, don't you?"

"Yeah, the guy we used to hang out with back in high school. I always wondered what happened to him."

"Right. That's him, and his mother is Jeff Patten's daughter. She came to me and asked me to look into her father's probate file at the courthouse to see if we could find anything to answer some questions she had about her father's death. Well, I pulled the file from the courthouse and discovered that my firm had been the one that handled his estate."

"Okay…," Sean said, listening intently and nodding his head.

"So, I pulled the firm's old file out of storage, and I found this key to a safe-deposit box that he had rented in Denver on the day he died. Apparently, he had told his secretary and wife that he was going out there to pick up cash that he was supposed to deliver to one of his clients, who we now know to be part of the Four Horsemen, but his plane crashed on the way back."

"And no one ever found the money?"

"We weren't exactly sure about that, but when we found the key, I had to go out there and look for myself."

"But you said you found it in a mine shaft or something, didn't you?"

"Yeah, that's right. I went out there and looked in the box but didn't find anything except for some old paperwork, which turned out to be the clue that led me to where the money was actually hidden."

"So where is it now?"

"Unfortunately, it's at my house. That's one of the things I wanted to talk to you about. I wanted to go by there and get it today, and I'm gonna need you to drive me."

"Are you kidding me? Don't you think they'll be watching your house?"

"No. I'm not kidding at all, and yes, I'm sure they are watching the house. But the money is hidden in my bedroom."

"In your bedroom, huh?

"Yep."

"At your house? How in the hell are we supposed to go into your house, get the money, and get back out without getting caught?"

"We'll distract them."

"How?"

"Well, we're not actually sure that anyone is watching my house. I know they went through the place because Elizabeth stopped by there and said it was trashed. So did my mom, but we don't know if anyone is there now."

"I think we should assume that they are watching the place," Sean said emphatically. "How are we going to get in without being seen?"

"They don't know who you are, do they?"

"No. I sure as hell hope not." Sean had a look of hesitation on his face.

"Well. I say we go over there. You drop me off on the street behind the house, and I'll walk through the woods to the back door…"

"And what do I do?"

"You're going to park in the driveway and walk up to the door like you're coming over to see if I'm home. If anyone is watching, they'll be watching you, and I should be able to slip in and out through the back. If anyone tries to stop you or ask you any questions, just tell them that you're a friend and that you haven't heard from me in a while. Tell them that you heard that I had been arrested and were just stopping by to see if I'm all right."

"And what if they see you?"

"If they see me, I plan to run like hell. I'd suggest that you do the same."

"That sounds…uh…"

"Yeah, I know, but I've got to get in there. If you don't want to be involved, I'll understand."

"How much money are we talking about?"

"Several million dollars."

Sean didn't think about it for very long before saying, "I guess I'm in. You're sure you got millions of dollars in there, right?"

"Yeah, assuming they haven't already found it, but I hid it in a good place where I doubt anyone would think to look."

"Okay. I'll take you over there, but we better not get caught."

"We'll just have to be real slick."

"Real slick. You can say that again. Anyway, it looks like the first copy is done. I guess I need to make the rest of these copies. Here's the computer. It's plugged in and running. You can look through some more of those e-mails while I'm getting these copies ready."

Jack sat down at the table in front of Anderson's computer and opened the e-mail program. He read through each one carefully, making notes of the sender. When he had gone through all of the incoming messages, he opened the file containing all of the e-mails that had been sent out by Anderson. "This guy doesn't delete anything," Jack said amusedly as the file opened.

"What do you mean?"

"I've got every e-mail he's ever sent or received from this computer. He never cleaned out the history files."

"How far back do they go?"

"Over a year."

"That's good, isn't it?"

"It sure is, but I need to go through them."

"You've got some time. My customer won't be here for another thirty minutes or so."

"That should be plenty of time to get started on them. There's probably two or three hundred e-mails here."

Sean made more copies of the hard drive, and Jack went through the e-mails. His customer showed up shortly after 10:30, and Sean helped him bring his computer in and talked to him for a few minutes about his problem. After they were done talking, the man left, and Sean turned back to Jack. "All right," he said as the door closed behind him. "Are you ready to go?"

"Yeah. I'm ready, but give me a second. I need to call this son of a bitch and let him know that I'm alive and wanting to make a deal."

"Who's that?"

"Anderson," Jack replied.

"Are you gonna call him now?" Sean asked in a surprised voice.

"Yeah. Here's his phone number," Jack said, pointing to the screen in front of him. "He put his mobile number in this e-mail to a Colonel Jackson at the Pentagon. At least I'm pretty sure this is his number. He's asking this colonel to call him, and they've e-mailed each other quite a few times. There must be twenty e-mails to this one person and even more from him."

"I guess I'll just sit here and listen while you make the call."

"Wish me luck," Jack said nervously as he picked up the phone and began to slowly dial the number. His hands were noticeably shaking as he held the phone up to his ear to listen. After the third ring, a man's voice appeared on the other end of the line and said hello.

"Hello. Is this Agent Anderson of the Drug Enforcement Agency?"

"Yes," the voice replied gruffly. "Who's this?"

"This is Jack Hixson. I think you've been looking for me."

"Hello, Jack. As a matter of fact, we have been looking for you. I wasn't expecting you to call, but it's good to hear your voice."

"I'll bet it is." As soon as he heard the familiar voice, his nervousness subsided and was replaced with anger.

"Where are you? And how did you get this number?"

"Well, I'm happy to report that I'm not where you are, and I plan to keep it that way."

"Well then, what can I do for you, Jack?"

"I think you know what I want. I want you to give it up. I want you to leave me alone and stop looking for me."

"Now, you and I both know that that is not an option I can live with. Why don't you save us both a whole lot of trouble and tell me where you are."

"You know I can't do that, Agent Anderson, but I would like to send you something."

"What's that?"

"I wonder if you've noticed anything missing. You know, the files you had in the file cabinet at the police station. The ones relating to the Four Horsemen. Oh, and maybe a laptop computer."

"I don't know what you're talking about, Jack."

"I think you do, but if you say you don't, then maybe we don't have anything to talk about. Oh...and by the way, using your wife's name as the password on your laptop wasn't the smartest move you could have made. I thought they trained you guys better than that."

"You little son of bitch," he responded angrily. "What do you want?" Jack could hear a mix of frustration and anger in his voice.

"I told you. I want you to leave me alone. I want you to go away, and I want this to end. Now!"

"I'll bet you do. You'd like that a whole lot, wouldn't you?"

"Not any more than you would like to have your files and computer back."

"All right, smart-ass...what exactly are you proposing?"

"I propose a swap. Your files and your laptop for my freedom and the money."

"I'm listening."

"I hope so."

"How do I know you haven't made copies?"

"I'm not stupid, Agent Anderson. I have made several copies of both the files and the hard drive of your computer. In fact, I was going to send a copy to Colonel Jackson at the Pentagon. You seemed to e-mail him an awful lot, and I'm sure he'd be happy to see what I have in my possession."

"Listen, you little shit. You don't know what you're up against. This isn't some little game we're playing here."

"I have no doubt about that. In fact, you're probably the biggest drug smuggler in the world. I see where you just brought in a new shipment from Afghanistan, and you're expecting another this week. That's a lot of heroin hitting the streets. I wonder how many Americans will die from that shipment?"

"Like I told you before, Jack, there is a war on, and people die in war."

"Even people that don't know or care about your war?"

"Even those people, Jack. Do you know how many people died on September eleventh? Do you have any idea? It all could have been prevented, Jack. It all could have been prevented if that hellhole of a place called Afghanistan had been under control. There wouldn't have been a place to train the scum that flew those airplanes if one of our people had been running the show over there. Instead, you've got a bunch of extremists that hate us…that hate America and everything it stands for, and they provided the ground support for those goddamn terrorists. But it won't happen again, not from Afghanistan, and do you know why, Jack?"

"Tell me why."

"Because our people run the show there now."

"But will they always be your people? Americans are dying here every day from the drugs you are bringing into the country, so you better be sure of what you're doing."

"One thing I know about people is that they're greedy. If you keep the money rolling in, you keep their loyalty. Before Afghanistan and Muslim terrorists, it was Nicaragua and Honduras and the Communists. Before that, it was Cambodia and Laos. There is always someone trying to destroy our way of life, Jack, and unlike you, who sits oblivious on the sidelines, I am on the front lines fighting to protect what you hold dear."

"And freedom's not cheap, I guess."

"That's right, Jack. It's not cheap. It never is. War is a messy business. It's messy and expensive, but I'm here to fight for you and all the bleeding-heart pacifists like you."

"I appreciate that, Agent Anderson, but forgive me if I decide that it is you, not me, who is the problem. You're no better than the people you try to destroy.

You make drugs illegal and fight to keep them that way so that you can turn a bigger profit. And people aren't just dying of overdoses. Mothers and fathers are going to jail over the very drugs that you bring into this country. They leave their children to be raised by the corrupt system you and your kind create."

"All right, Jack. I'm not going to have an ethics debate with you. Just tell me what you want, and I'll run it up the flagpole."

"You know what I want. You see what you can do, and I'll call you back at this number. And remember, if I go missing, or if anyone I'm associated with goes missing, you'll be in a world of hurt. I've got enough evidence here to blow the lid off your whole operation, and don't think for a second that I won't do it. In fact, it's already done. Let me put this in terms that you will be able to understand. The gun is loaded and the hammer is cocked and it's pointed directly at your head. Whether or not the trigger is pulled is up to you. Is that clear?"

"It's clear. But what do I get in return for your freedom?"

"You get my assurance that I will not turn you in."

"Your assurance. What does that mean?"

"Not a whole hell of a lot, but it's all you're going to get right now. And you need to make your decision quickly, because I'm tempted to just go ahead and turn all of this information over to the press right now. Like you, I get very upset when I don't get what I want."

"You do that, and you're a dead man. You're a dead man and so is your precious little girlfriend."

"I figured as much," Jack said, trying not to sound intimidated. "I'll hold off for now, and I'll give you a couple of days to think about my proposition. You do whatever you need to do to get this thing figured out, and I'll call you back at this number." With that, Jack hung up the phone. His palms were sweating, and he was trembling from head to toe, but he had pulled it off. Now all he had to do was to lay low and wait for a couple of days until he called Agent Anderson back.

There was no way, in Jack's mind, that Anderson could refuse. He had no choice. Jack had the goods on his entire organization, and now Anderson knew it. After all, it was his laptop that Jack had taken. He had to know what was on it.

*   *   *   *

"That sounded pretty good, man," Sean said as Jack put the phone down.

"You think so?" Jack replied.

"Yeah, man. You actually sounded pretty tough. Let's just hope they go for it."

"I don't see how they can't. I mean, I've got them by the balls. The information on this laptop will destroy their organization and send a bunch of people to jail for a long time. Right now, these guys think that they are above the law, and I don't think many people have ever tried to stand up to them. The few that did probably found themselves at the bottom of a lake or ravine somewhere like the reporter that tried to break the story back in the seventies."

"I hope we don't end up there," Sean said in a dire tone.

"Well, we've got a better position than most. We've got evidence that is absolutely damning, and it's something that can't be made up. They know that now, and I don't think they'll try anything stupid."

"Let's hope not."

"All right then. Are you ready to head over to my place?"

"I guess I'm as ready as I'll ever be."

"Okay then," Jack said. "Let's go."

CHAPTER 17

▼

They got into Sean's car and headed over to Jack's house, first circling the block to make sure they didn't see any suspicious characters hanging around. It didn't appear that anyone was inside the house, but they noticed a white delivery van that Jack didn't recognize parked just up the road and across the street. Jack ducked down in the seat as they drove by, and Sean tried to get a look inside, but the windows were tinted too dark for him to see if anyone was there. They were nervous, but it was now or never, and they decided to go for it.

"Okay, Sean," Jack said anxiously. "Let me out at the bottom of the hill behind my house; then you can go ahead and pull in the driveway. If there's anyone in that van, that ought to get their attention. I'll come up through the woods in the backyard and go in through the back door."

"Just be quick about it."

"I will. I'm just going to run in, get the money, and then run back through the woods to the bottom of the hill. It'll only take a couple of minutes, and I'll wait in the bushes down there at the bottom of the hill until you come back to get me."

"All right, man," Sean said. This wasn't the kind of activity he did every day, and Jack could tell that he was nervous. "Are you sure you want to do this?" he asked.

"Yes, I'm sure. There's several million dollars there that belongs to me, and I'm going in there to get it. Now, let's do it."

"Okay. What exactly do you want me to do?"

"You just go up to the door and knock."

"That's all? Just knock on the door?"

"Knock on the door, ring the doorbell, look in the windows, or whatever. It needs to look like you're actually hoping that I am home. Just be sure to take your time, and if anyone tries to talk to you, tell them you're a friend of mine, that you haven't heard from me for several days. Tell them that you were worried and that you were just stopping by to check on me."

"All right then," Sean said as they turned onto the street behind the house. "Here we go."

They pulled up to some bushes that lined the street directly behind the house, and Sean slowed down just enough for Jack to jump out and hit the ground running. He quickly slid into the bushes, and Sean drove back around the block and pulled slowly into the driveway. He sat in his car for a moment as if he was getting something together and then got out, walked up to the front door, and started knocking.

By the time he got to the door, Jack had already made it up to the back of his house. He wanted to peek around the corner to see if anything was going on in the van up the street, but he knew better. He needed to go straight in, get the money, and get out of there as quickly as possible.

He crouched down and made his way carefully and quietly to the back door. As he slid his key into the lock, he peered inside through a window and saw for himself that the place had been trashed. Most of the furniture had been turned over and was lying on the floor; the drawers had been pulled out and their contents dumped on the floor. It looked like a tornado had ripped the place apart, but he needed to get in and out quickly and would have to worry about the mess later.

He ran back to his bedroom and pulled the molding away from the wall by the closet, revealing his hiding place. The blinds in his bedroom were closed, making it too dark for him to see into the opening or tell whether the money was still there, but he reached his hand in and was happy to feel the bundles that he had put there just days before. He ran quickly into the kitchen and grabbed a trash bag from underneath the sink, then went back to his room and pulled the money out, quickly stuffing it into the bag. When he had put the last one in the bag, he stuck his hand into the hole and felt around to make sure he had it all. When he was sure that he had retrieved all the money, he tucked the bag under his arm and made his way back toward the door he had just come through. As he reached the end of the hallway leading from his bedroom, he heard a nearby voice and froze like a stone statue. He couldn't make out what they were saying, but there were definitely two voices. One of them belonged to Sean, and he didn't recognize the other.

Jack stood still, listening intently and trying to understand what they were saying, but the voices were too muffled, and he didn't have time to try to figure it out. He had what he had come for, and it was time to get the hell out of there. He made his way back to the door as quickly and as quietly as possible. When he got through it and was standing outside, he broke into a dead sprint, running down the hill and through the woods carrying the heavy plastic bag. He quickly made his way into the woods to the bushes where he told Sean he would be waiting and sat on the ground with the garbage bag in his lap.

Within minutes, he heard a car coming down the street. As the sound got closer, he got ready to jump out, but he stopped when he realized that it didn't sound as if it was slowing. The car drove past his hiding spot in the bushes, and his heart nearly stopped when he saw the familiar black-and-white paint scheme and realized that it was a police car. *That would have been unbelievable,* he thought to himself. To have come this far, gotten the money back in his possession, and then to have jumped out of the bushes carrying a big bag full of money, right in front of a cop, who was undoubtedly eager to take the money and throw him in jail. Again, he froze like a statue and sat silently until he was sure the patrol car had passed. He decided that he wouldn't even think about coming out of those bushes until he was sure that it was Sean on the other side.

After what seemed like an eternity, he heard another car coming up the road. This time, he heard the squeak of brake pads as it pulled up in front of him. He poked his head up so that he could see out of the bushes and breathed a heavy sigh of relief when he saw Sean's car sitting at the curb less than twenty feet away. He looked closely to be sure that Sean was alone and then jumped out from behind the bushes and quickly made his way over to the car.

"That was close," Sean said as Jack got in and closed the door behind him. They quickly pulled away from the curb and headed down the road.

"I heard some voices. What was going on up there?"

"You were right about them watching your house. As soon as I pulled up in the driveway, someone got out of that van that was parked up the street."

"Who was it?"

"I didn't exactly get his name, and he wasn't wearing any kind of uniform."

"What did he say?"

"He asked me what I was doing there."

"And what did you tell him?"

"I did just like we talked about. I told him that I was a friend of yours and that I had heard from your mom that you had been arrested."

"What did he say?"

"Hold on, I'm not finished. I told him that I hadn't heard from you in several days, and I wanted to stop by and see if you were okay. Then I asked him who he was and what he was doing there. He said that it was a known drug house and that they were just watching it to see who came around while you were in jail."

"They didn't ask you where I was or say anything about me not being in jail anymore?"

"Not a word. I told him that I had never known you to use drugs, and I think it made the guy nervous when I started to ask him questions. He wasn't expecting that."

"What else did he say?"

"That's about it. I mean, once he was satisfied that I wasn't you, he seemed to lose interest in me. He wasn't about to let me go in the house or anything. In fact, I looked in the window while he was standing there and commented on the fact that the place was trashed, and then he told me that you weren't home and that I just needed to move along. I stood there talking to him for a few minutes, so you'd have enough time to get in and out."

"Which I did, by the way," Jack said, smiling and rubbing the outside of the large plastic bag that sat in his lap.

Sean looked down at the bag that was sitting in Jack's lap. "Is that it?" he asked smiling. "Is that the money?"

"Yes it is," Jack replied. He looked down at the bag and slowly opened it so that Sean could see inside.

"Holy shit," Sean said in an astonished voice. He wasn't paying attention to the road, and when he took his eyes off the money, he had to jerk the wheel to keep from hitting a car that was parked on the curb. "You weren't kidding, were you?"

"I told you."

"How much is there?"

"This is just a little under eight million dollars. Well…it's eight million less a couple hundred I spent on hotels and car rentals on the way home from Colorado."

Sean could barely keep his eyes on the road. "I've never seen anything like it."

"I hadn't either," Jack replied. "Now let's get out of here."

"All right, man. All that money makes me nervous."

"I know," Jack said. "It makes me nervous too."

They drove slowly and carefully back to Tonya's house, with Sean being careful not to exceed the speed limit or run any yellow lights. It was obvious to Jack that he was more than a little scared. It was apparently starting to sink in to him that this wasn't just fun and games. If looking at the files on a stolen government computer hadn't made it real enough for him, then driving down the road with eight million dollars stuffed in a trash bag apparently did.

"Take it easy," Jack said to him when he nearly ran off the road.

"Sorry man. I'm just...I mean...I'm just thinking about..."

"Well, don't think about it right now. Whatever it is...don't think about it. Just concentrate on the road," Jack replied. "Just focus on getting us back to base and then you can do all the thinking you want."

"What are you gonna do with all that money?"

"I plan to keep part of it."

"Part of it?" Sean said curiously.

"Yeah. It doesn't all belong to me, actually. I plan to give a big chunk of it to the person who got the whole thing started, and then I'm gonna give a nice little piece to you, Elizabeth, and Tonya for all your help. The rest I'll keep for myself, but I've got to make sure that I have a deal with Anderson first. All the money in the world does me no good if I have to spend the rest of my life in hiding."

"And I don't know if there's really anywhere you can hide if these people want to find you."

"Thanks for the encouragement," Jack said with a smirk on his face. "That's why I've got to cut this deal. If they think for a second that they can just eliminate me and that their problem will go away, then we both know that's what they'll do. I don't have any doubt about it."

"I sure hope it all works out Jack...for everybody's sake."

They were pulling into Tonya's driveway as their conversation ended. Her truck was parked outside, and Jack was glad to see that they were back from running errands. He thought about the night before and was excited about seeing Elizabeth.

As they pulled up and got out of Sean's car, Tonya came running out the door, and Jack knew instantly that something was wrong.

"They took her," Tonya said in a shaky voice. "They took her. I tried to stop them, but..."

"Slow down," Jack said. She was obviously very excited by whatever had happened. "Slow down and tell me what happened. Where's Elizabeth?"

"They took her, Jack."

"Who took her?" Jack looked over at Sean, who stood silently by his car.

"The cops. They were waiting for her at her house, and..."

"Her house? What were you doing at her house?"

"I knew it was a bad idea, but she just wanted to stop by and get herself some clothes and her toothbrush. As soon as we pulled in, they swarmed around the car and put handcuffs on both of us. Then they took her away." Tonya was obviously very shaken up.

"Just slow down and tell me exactly what happened." Jack appeared calm, but his stomach had turned to knots, and he could feel the rage starting to build up inside. If those bastards harmed one hair on her head, there would be hell to pay.

"Okay," Tonya said, starting to tell her story, "we left Sean's store and stopped by the drugstore to pick up some things that I needed around the house. She didn't have much money on her and didn't want to spend what she had, so she asked me if I would take her by her house so she could pick up some things. I told her I didn't think it was a good idea, but she wanted to do it anyway. She insisted that we do it, and I gave in. I told her that I would buy her a damn toothbrush, but she wouldn't let me. She wanted her own."

"Okay. So you took her by her house."

"That's right. We went to her house, and it didn't look like anyone was around, so we got out of the car and ran inside. We were just going to be a minute or two and then we were going to leave. When we came back out, they were everywhere. There must have been ten cops."

"Were any federal agents there?"

"Well...I'm not sure. I wouldn't know the difference. It all happened so fast, and it was so confusing. There was one man there in a suit. His name was Agent something. One of the cops called him Agent...oh, I can't remember. I'm sorry, Jack. I'm sorry."

"It's okay. It wasn't your fault." Jack was trying to sound as calm and sympathetic as he could. "What did they say?"

"They wanted to know where you were."

"What did you tell them?"

"Nothing. We didn't tell them anything."

"Did they ask who you were?"

"Yeah, but we told them I was a friend of hers and that I didn't even know who you were."

"That's good."

"They must have believed me because they let me go. They said she had driven a car used in a chase yesterday and that the car had been found abandoned. They said they knew she had been in the car with you."

"Shit," Jack said, balling his fists and shaking his head. He knew that it had been a bad idea to get her involved. "What did she tell them?"

"She said that it wasn't her in the car. She told them that you and her worked together and that you had called her from the jail and that was the last time she'd heard from you. They didn't believe her. She told them that you two barely knew each other." Tonya was still shaking and almost in tears at that point. "They took her anyway."

There was a moment of silence and then Sean spoke up. "I hate to butt in, guys, but if they took down your license plate number, Tonya, they might have let you go just so they could follow you home. They could be here any minute."

Jack hadn't thought about that and suddenly became very nervous.

"No. I watched to make sure no one was following me."

"What about the license plate?"

"It's registered at my parents' house still. They won't be able to track it back here."

That put Jack's mind somewhat at ease, but it was another close call. Actually, it was more than close, they had taken Elizabeth, but he was still free and he still had all of his bargaining chips. Only now the stakes were much higher. He thought about it for a minute and decided that it was time to call Anderson again. He was going to make a deal now or there was no deal to be made. If Anderson didn't work something out right then, he would drive himself to the CNN headquarters in Atlanta, less than two hours away, where he would turn over everything he had found on the Four Horsemen. He would not allow Elizabeth to sit in their custody for one second more than she had to. "Looks like it's time to call Anderson again. We're going to get her back, and we're going to do it right now."

"What can we do?" Tonya asked. The look on her face told Jack that she felt terrible about what had happened, but he knew that it wasn't her fault, and he didn't blame her. In fact, he felt sorry for her.

"I don't know right now."

"You know we'll do whatever we can to help," Sean chimed in.

"I know you will, and I really appreciate that. We couldn't have made it this far without your help. But now I just need to call this son of a bitch and set up an exchange. The laptop and his files for Elizabeth and our freedom. There's nothing you can do to help with that, really, but I'm sure that I'm going to need help from both of you to set up the swap."

"Just tell us what you need," Sean said as Tonya nodded her head. "I've got all kinds of gadgets that might be helpful: video equipment, two-way radios. You name it, I've probably got it."

"All right. That'll probably come in handy when I'm ready to meet him, but let's go inside first so I can make the call. We'll figure out our game plan after I arrange a meeting. I'm going to insist that we meet in a public place where there will be lots of people. If I could get you and Tonya to stay back and film it all with your video camera…"

"I've got some small radio transmitting devices that you can wear, and I can make an audio recording of the whole thing too."

"That sounds great. Where'd you get equipment like that?"

"I don't know," Sean replied. "I'm a gadget freak. I've just picked it up over the years."

"How about meeting him down by the aquarium on the river, where I picked you up the other day?" Tonya said, changing the subject. "There's always lots of people walking around down there, and it's also wide-open in every direction."

"That's a good idea," Jack said, smiling at both of them. "I'll tell Anderson to meet me outside the aquarium tomorrow morning."

"I've got some digital cameras, and one of them has a telephoto lens. Tonya and I will have to get down there early to work out where we can shoot from, but we'll each videotape from different perspectives and I can dub in the audio from the voice recorder I'll give you. We need to get as much on these guys as we can, in case they try to double-cross you."

"That's good…real good. Now keep it down while I make this call, so they don't know I've got anyone with me. I want them to think that I'm on my own."

"Good luck, Jack," Tonya and Sean said at the same time.

Jack dialed the number he had called earlier that day and immediately recognized Anderson's voice when he answered. "Agent Anderson. This is Jack Hixson."

"Well there, Jack, I didn't expect to hear from you so soon. To what do I owe the honor of your phone call?"

"Cut the shit, Anderson. I know you've got Elizabeth and I want her back."

"I figured as much. Once we had the girlfriend, it was only a matter of time."

"I'll tell you what's a matter of time. It's a matter of time before I personally deliver a copy of your computer hard drive to every news reporter in North America. I think it's only a matter of time before you are the one looking for a place to hide. You need to remember who and what you're dealing with. I'm not just some schmuck that thinks I've got you figured out. I'm the schmuck that has enough evidence to put you and all of your cronies behind bars for the rest of your lives."

"Really, Jack?"

"Yeah. Just let me read you a few of the names that I was able to get out of just your e-mail program." Jack stuck his hand into his pocket and pulled out the list he had made earlier that day.

"That won't be necessary, Jack."

"Listen to me, Anderson, and listen good. I'm only going to tell you this one time, so you need to pay attention. I want Elizabeth back and I want you to leave us alone...for good."

"And what do I get?"

"You get nothing, you son of a bitch. You get to stay out of jail." Jack was becoming furious at the fact that Anderson was still trying to negotiate with him. "I don't think you understand what's going on here, Anderson. I'm sure you're not used to it, but I'm the one in charge now. You don't get to play hardball with me anymore. The game is over, dumb ass, and I have all the marbles. You will do what I tell you or I go public, and I mean right now. This is not a joke and you better believe I'm not bluffing."

"And what exactly do you want me to do?"

"I want to meet you somewhere of my choosing to make a trade. Just like we talked about this morning. Only now I've got some additional demands because you kidnapped Elizabeth."

"What additional demands?"

"You're going to take Elizabeth to the hotel of her choice, and it better be a nice one. I mean, she better not tell me that you put her up in some seedy motel. You're going to get her a room where she is comfortable, and then you're going to bring her to me in the morning."

"Are you kidding me?"

"Does it sound like I'm kidding? Listen to me. If you harm her in any way, it's over. It's all over. Is that clear?"

"Yes, Jack, it's clear. Now where do you want to meet?"

"I'll call you in the morning and let you know, but you better be ready to go when I call, and all you need to bring is Elizabeth. If I see too many police cars around, or even too many cars period, whether they are cops or not, I'm going public."

"You're not being reasonable, Jack."

"Well, you've pissed me off now, and I don't have to be reasonable. This is going to go my way, and that's the only way it will happen."

"What about the money?"

"Oh, you can rest assured that I'm keeping that too. That's my fee for having to deal with scum like you." Jack was feeling supremely confident at that moment.

"And when are you going to call?"

"I'll call when I call, and not a moment sooner. You just better be ready to go at a moment's notice. I mean that. And Elizabeth better have a smile on her face when I see her. And she better be telling me about the hotel minibar that she emptied on your account. Do you understand me?"

"I got you, Jack, but let me tell you something. This isn't the Boy Scouts you're dealing with, and you would do well to remember that. Whatever you've got on us, however big you think you are, you need to remember who you're dealing with."

"Well, it sounds like we both got some things to think about then, doesn't it. Now you go find out where she wants to stay tonight and I'll call you in the morning." With that, he hung up the phone. His hands were trembling as he pushed the button to end the call, but unlike that morning, he was trembling more out of anger than fear. They had truly pissed him off by going after Elizabeth, and he didn't care what happened now as long as he got her back safe and sound.

"Wow. I sure would hate to make you mad," Tonya said. He had been so focused on the telephone call that he had nearly forgotten that anyone was listening to the conversation.

"He just makes me so damn mad," he said, shaking his fists in the air.

"Obviously."

Jack sat the phone down and looked at the ground as if he were thinking about something. "I've got to make one more call," he said after a moment.

"Who are you calling this time?" Sean asked.

"I'm calling the person that got this whole thing started."

"What do you mean? Who's that?"

"She is a client of mine that I told you about this morning. She is the one who asked me to look into her father's death, and that request is what got all of this started. Her father was Jeff Patten. You know…the one that had been used back in the seventies by the Four Horsemen to carry the money."

"Oh, yeah," Sean said, nodding his head. "I remember seeing his name in those files that we were looking at."

"That's right. He hid the money and then died in the plane crash."

"Why did she ask you to look into it? Did she know about the money?" Tonya asked.

"Well, sort of. At least, she thought there might be some money," Jack responded, remembering that Tonya hadn't really heard the story of how this all got started. "But she really contacted me just to check his probate file to see if I could find anything relating to his business dealings prior to his death. What I found was a key to a safe-deposit box in Denver, and when I went and checked it out, I found some documents that had clues that led me to the money."

"Wait. Wait. I don't get it," Tonya said in a bewildered voice. "Why were you looking into his business dealings?"

"He had taken some money from friends and family just before he died. It was supposed to be invested in a business venture that his client was working on, but he died before he could deliver the money to the client. This 'client' of his made up this elaborate story to get him to carry the money for them. They said that they were setting up a real estate development business and that they needed investors. They told him that he was to meet with an investor in Denver, and he thought the money that he was to pick up was an investment in that business, but, of course, we know it was actually a mobster that he was meeting with, and the money he was carrying was actually drug money. He didn't know that, though; thinking that it sounded like a good investment, he had put together some other money that he was going to give to his client, but he died before he got the chance."

"So he had collected other money that he was going to invest himself?"

"That's right. Unfortunately, his client disappeared after he died in the plane crash, so there was nowhere to invest the money."

"What happened to the money he had collected?"

"Nothing. Everyone got their money back, but they thought that he had been trying to take it for other reasons and just happened to die before he could spend it."

"So she came to you to see if you could find out what had happened to the mysterious client?"

"Basically, yes. She just wanted to get a clearer picture of what was going on in the weeks leading up to his death so that she could prove he wasn't a crook. It was mostly for her own benefit. I think most of the people that he had taken money from have probably already passed away, and besides, it was so long ago and they had all gotten their money back anyway. She just hated knowing that people thought that her father was trying to steal from them, and she wanted to know for her own benefit whether or not it was true."

"Okay," Tonya said. "That makes more sense. So, you found the key in an old file and…"

"And one thing led to another, and here we are."

"So that's how all this got started?"

"That's how I got involved. I feel bad because I haven't been keeping in contact with her very well throughout all this, but I didn't want her to get dragged into it. I'm running around with all this money, a big chunk of which is rightfully hers, and I haven't been able to call her to let her know what has been going on. Anyway, I'm gonna walk outside and give her a call right now to let her know that I'm alive." Jack picked the phone up off the table in front of him and went outside, dialing as he walked.

"Patricia," he said as soon as she picked up the phone.

"Jack. Is that you?"

"It's me."

"Well, thank God. I've been worried sick about you. Where on earth have you been?"

Jack could hear the desperation in her voice and felt bad that he hadn't talked to her more often, but things had been happening so fast. "I'm sorry I haven't called you, but I've been so involved. I really couldn't..."

"It's okay, Jack. I understand. I've just been worried about you. Are you all right?" she asked. "Is everything all right?"

"Almost. I've got a few things I still need to get done, but it appears that everything's going to work itself out." He didn't want to go into too much detail about what was going on. If she knew the full truth, she would be paralyzed with guilt over having gotten him involved in all of this.

"Are you all right?"

"Yes. I'm okay, and I've got the money with me."

"Jack. I feel so bad for having gotten you involved. I just wanted to clear my father's name, and I ruined yours in the process."

"Don't worry about that. I've got the evidence to clear your father's name and mine too. I don't want to explain it to you over the phone, but I'm sending you a package with copies of everything I've got. I don't want to talk about it right now; once you read what I'm sending you, you'll know exactly what your father was doing in Denver, who asked him to go there, who he was meeting, and why he was selected. It definitely shows that he was being manipulated. He was very cleverly deceived, and the evidence I have shows that he really had no idea what he was involved in."

"I don't know how to repay you, Jack."

"You don't have to. Believe me, assuming everything goes according to plan, I'll be very well compensated for my efforts."

"Let's hope that it does."

"You can say that again, Patricia."

"What will you do after this?"

"Who knows? It all depends on what happens over the next few days."

"What does that mean?"

"Like I said, I've still got a few things I need to do, but if all goes according to plan, and I expect that it will, then I'll probably be on my way out of the country."

"Yes. I think that sounds like a good idea."

"Patricia, I need to get going. I just wanted to check in with you to let you know that everything was all right and that I had it all worked out."

"I certainly do appreciate your calling me."

"No problem, but it's probably the last time I'll be able to talk to you for a while. I'll be back in touch, but it may be a few weeks, so don't worry if you don't hear from me for a while. Now, if you don't hear from me within the next six weeks, then I want you to follow the instructions in the package I'm sending you."

"Okay. I will, but it won't do you any good asking me not to worry," she said.

"I know. Just try to keep it to a minimum, and I'll be back in touch with you as soon as I can."

"Be careful, Jack. Be so careful."

"I will. And don't worry. You'll hear from me soon."

"I hope so."

They hung up the phone and Jack walked back inside. It would be getting dark soon and he was already exhausted from the events of the day. He hated the thought of Elizabeth spending the night in Anderson's custody, but he didn't know how else to handle it, and there was just no other way to accomplish what he wanted to get done that day. He needed some time to set up his meeting with Anderson, and he wanted to make the exchange while plenty of people would be around. That way, Anderson would be much less likely to make a scene or do anything stupid, like trying to capture him.

He still needed to get the copies they'd made of the files and the hard drive sent out in case something happened to him, and he planned to put the packages together that evening and put them in the mail on his way to the meeting. He wanted to send a copy to his parents and one to the colonel at the Pentagon that Anderson had traded so many e-mails with. Sean could hold a copy and Tonya could hold one too. He would also send a copy to Patricia and to Scott Hall at his law firm. He would figure out what to do with the other copies once he had Elizabeth back. He also wanted to go ahead and give some of the money to Sean and Tonya. He wasn't sure exactly how much was appropriate, but thought two hundred and fifty thousand each sounded like a nice round figure.

"I need to get some packages together."

"What kind of packages?" Tonya asked.

"I want to go ahead and get the copies of the hard drive and the other files together and ready to send out to some people. I also need to put an instruction letter together to go with them."

"You can use my computer for your letter," Tonya said. "What can we do to help you?"

"Will one of you run down to the store and get some of those big brown mailing envelopes?"

"I'll do it," Sean said. "How many do we need?"

"Just a handful. Maybe five or six. Just make sure they're big enough."

"I got it," Sean said. "I'll run down to the store and pick them up, and I'll be right back."

"Good. I'll work on the letter."

"And I'll make something to eat," Tonya added.

Jack hadn't thought about food until she said something, but once she did, he realized that he was starving. He hadn't eaten anything since breakfast. "That sounds great."

"Okay. I'm gonna hit the road. I'll be right back," Sean said as he turned and walked out the door, leaving Jack and Tonya alone in the den. Tonya started heading to the kitchen and Jack walked over to the table where the files and the bag of money were sitting. He picked up the bag, walked over to the couch, and sat down, setting the bag on the coffee table in front of him.

He looked over at Tonya just in time to see her eyeballs popping out of her head. "Holy...is that it?"

"That's it," Jack replied. He started pulling out ten-thousand-dollar bundles and put them on the table in two equal stacks until each of the stacks had twenty-five bundles.

Tonya couldn't stop staring. "You mean that's been sitting there on the table since you got back this afternoon?"

"Yep."

"What are you doing now? What are those piles for?"

"You mean who are they for."

"Okay. Who are they for?"

"One is for you and the other is for Sean."

"Oh my God!" she said excitedly. "Are you serious? That money is for me?"

"That's right. There's two hundred and fifty thousand dollars in each of your piles." He thought for a second and then pulled out two more ten-thousand-dollar bundles and put it next to one of the stacks. "Here is an extra twenty thousand to cover Dave's legal bills. I know his court date is coming up soon, and this ought to get him the best criminal defense attorney in town. You can also go down there and bail him out until his court date. He told me that you couldn't afford it, and I'm sure he'd like to spend some time at home. I can tell you first-hand that jail is not a comfortable place to be."

"I'd love for him to come home," Tonya said with an enormous and gracious smile on her face.

"I'm sure you would."

"Who do you think we should use as his lawyer?"

"I never really did any criminal defense work, so I'm not really up on who the best ones are, but I know some attorneys that do that kind of work. I'm gonna write a few names down here for you and you can talk to them. If you like one of them, hire him. If not, you can surely find one that you do like, and this should be more than enough to cover the fees."

"Thank you, Jack," she said, nearly crying. "I thank you, and I know if Dave was here right now, he would thank you too."

"It's the least I can do for you. Hell, if it weren't for the two of you, I'd most likely still be sitting in a jail cell right now."

"Well, whatever...I just can't thank you enough."

"Really. It's the least I can do." Jack walked over and handed the money to Tonya. "Now put it somewhere safe."

"I will," she said. "I just can't thank you enough. This will make such a difference for us. I'm gonna go put this away right now." She took the money and walked down the hallway toward her bedroom.

While she was in the bedroom, Jack walked over to the computer that was set up on a small desk in the den and turned it on. He sat and typed the letter that would accompany the package that he was sending out to Colonel Jackson at the Pentagon. That one would be a little different from the others. He would hand-write the note that would go to his parents, and Tonya and Sean didn't need a note to go with theirs. By the time he was finished typing, Tonya had walked back into the room and he read it aloud:

Dear Colonel Jackson:

Enclosed you will find copies of documents that I removed from the files of one of your affiliates by the name of Special Agent Anderson. I am not sure of his first name;

however, I believe he is employed by the Drug Enforcement Agency. Also enclosed is a CD-ROM containing a copy of Agent Anderson's computer hard drive from which I took your name and address. You will note upon reviewing the enclosed files that they relate to an organization known as the "Four Horsemen" and that they describe the current and past operations of that organization in detail.

I am writing this letter and sending the enclosed files so that you will know the significance of the information that I possess. As I am sure Agent Anderson has informed you, he and I have struck an arrangement whereby my silence will be maintained in return for my freedom.

Please note that I have sent more than ten copies of the enclosed files to various people around the country to ensure my continued safety. Should anything happen to me, the files will immediately be distributed to the media.

Sincerely,

Jack Hixson, Esq.

"That sounds pretty good," she said when he finished reading it.

"You think so? It's not my best work, but I think it gets the point across: Back off or I'm going public."

"I think that's very clear," she said, nodding her head in agreement.

Sean returned from the store as they were discussing the letter, and Jack read it to him as well. He agreed that it conveyed the relevant points. "When are you going to send it out?"

"I'm planning to drop it in the mail on the way to meet Anderson tomorrow. You got the envelopes, didn't you?"

"Yeah, they're right here," he replied, pulling them out of the bag he was holding and setting them on the table. "You know, we ought to make some photographs of you with the files and the laptop before you give them back. You'll probably never need them, but it's just one more piece of evidence you'll have to prove that the copies are real."

"That's a good point, Sean."

"I've got a Polaroid camera here somewhere," Tonya said.

"While you're looking for that…," Jack said as he walked across the room and picked up the stack of money that was still sitting on the coffee table. He held it out to Sean, who reached out and took it.

"What's this?" Sean asked.

"This is for all your help. There's two hundred and fifty thousand dollars there."

"Wow, man!" Sean said in a surprised tone. "Thanks! I don't know what to say. I wasn't expecting this."

"And I wasn't expecting to need all this help. Both you and Tonya have really stuck your necks out for me on this, and I wanted to make sure you knew how much I appreciated it. Like I told her, I wouldn't be here right now if it weren't for you. I'd probably still be sitting in a jail cell or at the bottom of a lake somewhere."

"Look, Jack. I appreciate the money, but I'd have helped you anyway. I want you to know that."

"I know, Sean, and I appreciate it, but you took a real risk helping me, and I just want to make sure you get some kind of reward."

Tonya had already come back in the room and was snapping pictures of the files and the laptop that she had arranged on the table. "Now...Jack you come over here and sit down in front of this stuff and let me get a picture of you sitting with the files."

Jack walked over and posed while she took the pictures. "Be sure to get a close-up of the computer screen in some of them," he said.

They took nearly twenty photographs showing the computer, the money, and the paper files—some with Jack and some without. When they were done, Jack put the pictures in the envelope that he was sending to his parents. He sat down and handwrote a short note telling them to put the package somewhere safe and also telling them that if they had not heard from him by the end of the sixth week after they received the package, they should take it to a reporter and tell them that they had gotten it from their son who was now missing.

He prepared similar letters for Patricia and the attorney at his firm and made sure that Sean and Tonya each had their copies as well and that they knew what to do with them. He told them that he was planning on leaving the country for a while after his meeting with Anderson tomorrow and added that he would contact them as soon as he was able.

They sat around and talked a little more, and before long, Jack found himself yawning and decided to turn in for the evening. After gathering his stuff, he went into the bedroom that he had slept in the night before, turned out the lights, and crawled into the bed. It felt empty without Elizabeth.

He set the alarm clock for six and then tried to sleep. As he laid his head on the pillow, he caught a faint wisp of Elizabeth's perfume that was left from the previous night. He was so worried about her that he couldn't get comfortable, and spent most of the night tossing and turning. He hoped that Anderson had taken his warnings to heart and that she was being taken care of, but he wouldn't truly rest until he had her back.

CHAPTER 18

▼

Jack couldn't wait for the morning to come. Unable to sleep, he got out of bed just before six and went to the kitchen to make some coffee. Before long, he was joined by Tonya and then Sean, who had decided to stay the night on the couch so they could get an early start. They each had a cup of coffee and finalized their plans for Jack's meeting with Anderson that would take place later that morning.

Sean would drive them downtown and drop Jack off by the aquarium. He would park on the street across from the meeting spot and walk into one of the nearby parking garages so that he would have a good vantage point from which to videotape the exchange between Jack and Anderson. Tonya would do the same from another location.

"We'll have to stop by my office on the way down there," Sean said, "so that we can pick up the cameras."

They continued talking until they had their general plan straight, but there was no way that they could get every aspect of the plan resolved. There were so many what-ifs to consider, and they easily could have sat there discussing them until the day was gone, but they had work to do. They decided to go ahead and make their way downtown to do a little reconnaissance. If something unexpected came up, they would have to deal with it, and if something went wrong, they decided it would be every man for himself.

They got in Sean's car and headed toward downtown, stopping on the way to drop the packages they had prepared the night before in the mail. Once the packages were on their way, they headed on to Sean's office to pick up the equipment.

"Here's the cameras," Sean said, standing at the door to his office.

"Did you say you had some other gadgets that we could use too?" Jack asked.

"Yeah. I've got some two-way radios that we can use to talk to each other. They're pretty small. Small enough to fit in your pocket. You'll have to remember to turn it off before Anderson arrives. Tonya and I might need to talk, and we don't want the thing going off in your pocket and giving us away."

"That's right," Jack agreed. "We don't want him to know that we're making a video of this. There's no telling what could happen if he got spooked."

"Let's try not to find out," Tonya interjected.

"Okay," Jack said. "Got anything else we could use? You said something last night about a radio transmitter."

"Yeah. I saved the best for last. I got this little transmitter that you can wear in your shirt pocket. It looks just like a ballpoint pen, but it's actually a microphone and transmitter that'll send a good signal up to five hundred yards. I've also got a receiver that I can hook up to a tape recorder, and we can record everything you say to each other. Just be sure to speak clearly."

"Man, that's awesome!" Jack said enthusiastically. "Where did you get this equipment?"

"eBay. Where else?"

They got their gear together and headed out the door. It was not yet nine o'clock, but they were eager to get down to the riverfront to check it out. Once there, they got set up and Jack made the call.

"Anderson. This is Jack. Are you ready?"

"We're ready."

"Good. Now listen carefully. I will be downtown in front of the Tennessee Aquarium in twenty minutes. That's on Market Street next to the river. I will be alone, and I'll have your computer and your files with me."

"Okay."

"I expect that you and Elizabeth will come alone as well. If I see too many cops down there, or any suspicious-looking people walking around, then the deal is off."

"And what about your girlfriend?"

"I'm sure I'd get her back when the story of the Four Horsemen hits the news, but that doesn't matter because you're going to do this exactly as I say. We're not going to have any problems, are we?"

"Not from this end, Jack."

"Good. I'll be there in twenty minutes. I'll wait only five minutes for you to show—five minutes. If you don't show, then the deal is off. Got it?

"I got it."

"Good. I'll see you in twenty minutes."

As he hung up the phone, Jack looked up at the third floor of the parking garage across the street, where Sean was standing by with his camera. "Are we ready?" he said into the radio he was holding.

"I'm ready," came Sean's reply, followed quickly by the same from Tonya, who had taken up her position on a nearby street corner.

"Tonya. How's your location? Can you see from there?"

"Oh yeah. I can see fine from here. I should be able to get some good video. Just stay close to where you are now and try not to get behind the fountain on your left."

"Will do. I'll try to keep a clean line of sight for you."

"Good. As long as you stay close to where you are now, we'll be fine."

"I'll try, but if I've got to move around, you'll have to do the same. Just try to keep the view focused tightly on us."

It didn't seem that twenty minutes had passed when a familiar-looking black sedan pulled up to a nearby curb and parked in front of one of the meters. The occupants of the car got out, and he immediately recognized both Elizabeth and Agent Anderson as they started walking toward him through the crowd. His heart started racing as they approached, and it was obvious that neither of them had seen him yet. He watched them closely as they approached and looked around to make sure that no one else was with them. "I see them," he said into the radio.

"I see 'em too," Sean replied.

"Where are they?" Tonya asked. "I don't see them."

"Do you see that turnaround area where the horse and buggy are sitting next to that black car with the tinted windows?"

"Yeah," she replied.

"Look about a hundred yards from Jack in that direction and you'll see them."

"I got them. I see them."

"Okay, keep it down," Jack said. "Here they come." He turned his radio off and quickly slid it into his pocket. As they approached Jack, he and Elizabeth made eye contact, and she picked up her pace. Anderson saw Jack too and stayed right on her heels the whole way. He didn't want her slipping away before he could get what he had come for. When they got within several feet, he reached out and took hold of her arm.

"Hello, Jack," he said gruffly.

"Hello, Agent Anderson," Jack replied, nodding his head and glaring at him. "Are you okay?" he asked, turning his attention to Elizabeth.

"Yes, I'm fine, Jack."

"Good," he said and then quickly turned his attention back to Anderson. "Now, let's get this over with. Here's your computer and here's your files."

Anderson reached out and took them from Jack's hands. "You're a lucky man, Jack Hixson. It doesn't always end this well for the hero."

"I know that. Don't forget, I've read your files."

"How can I forget?"

"You shouldn't," Jack said sternly. "And you should also remember that I meant what I said. If anything ever happens to me or Elizabeth, or any of my friends or family for that matter, your little club will be in the news so fast, it'll make your head spin."

"And what are you going to do now, Jack? Now that you're a rich and free man."

"I'm going to leave the country for a while. At least till things cool off here."

"Well, at least we agree on something. That's exactly what I was going to suggest to you. And just so we're clear, our little arrangement works both ways. If any word of what you know leaks into the public, there will be nowhere you can hide. This thing is bigger than you can imagine, and while I and my accomplices may go to jail, there are others out there who are not subject to the laws of our country that would not think twice before tracking you down and slitting your throat. The information you possess is very dangerous, Jack, and you would do well to respect that fact. Do you understand what I'm telling you?"

"Yeah, I understand."

"You played your cards well. Better than anyone before you. Now take your girlfriend and your money and get the hell out of my face. I don't ever want to see you again."

"The feeling is mutual," Jack said, taking Elizabeth's hand and turning to walk away. He felt as though the weight of the world had been lifted from his shoulders. He didn't look back to see what Anderson was doing. He didn't care. It was finally over, and he had won!

EPILOGUE

▼

"Patricia, this is Jack."

"Jack!" she said excitedly after recognizing his voice. "I'm so glad to hear from you. Is everything okay? Where are you?"

"Everything is just fine, Patricia. Did you get the package I sent you?"

"Yes, I did, and I wanted to thank you."

"Did you read the file on your father?"

"Yes, Jack. I knew he was innocent. I just knew it."

"I think it's clear from the files that he was fooled into believing that he was doing legitimate work for legitimate clients."

"They handpicked him, Jack."

"Yes, they did, and now you have the proof."

"I just can't thank you enough, Jack."

"You don't have to, Patricia. I want you to know that everything worked out for me. It was scary there for a while, but it all worked out as well as I could have ever hoped for."

"Do you still have the money?"

"Yes, I do, and I'm sitting here with my lovely new wife, Elizabeth. We're sitting outside a café in Budapest, sipping on a cup of espresso, and enjoying our honeymoon."

"Your honeymoon? What are you talking about?"

"Well, you haven't met her yet, but Elizabeth was the paralegal at my office who helped me pull the whole thing off. She is the one who found the files from your father's estate. She was with me when I found the key to the safe-deposit box, and she stayed with me throughout the whole ordeal. We decided to fly to Vegas and tie the knot before heading over to Europe."

"That's wonderful."

"I thought you'd be happy for me. I've got some other good news for you too. Do you have something to write with? I've got a number for you to write down."

"Okay. Go ahead and give me the number."

"5-3-4-7-8-8-9-2-1. Did you get that?"

"Yes, but what is it? It doesn't sound like a phone number."

"It isn't. It's the account number at the First Bank of Switzerland where your money is."

"What money? I told you that I didn't care about the money, Jack."

"You don't have to care about it, but there's two million dollars there that might come in handy someday. If you don't want it, give it to Clark and tell him it's from me. I'm sure he could find a use for it. I've got the rest of it in an account of my own. If you ever need any more…"

"When will I see you again?"

"You'll see me. It'll be a while, but you'll see me. I think we're just going to hang and see the sights for a while. Travel around for a year or so. Who knows," he said as he lifted his cup to his lips and took a sip.

"Well, what about your job?"

"Elizabeth and I both turned in our notice. We've got plenty of money for the time being, and if we're conservative, it'll last us the rest of our lives."

"And no one is looking for you?"

"Nope. No one is after us, and I'm pretty sure they're going to leave us alone as long as we leave them alone."

"I'm so happy for you, Jack."

"Thanks Patricia. I owe it all to you."

"I don't know about that, Jack. I think you did all the work."

"Well, I appreciate it all the same."

"So you're just going to hang around Europe?"

"Until we get bored or homesick."

"And then what?"

"Who knows."

VISIT THE AUTHOR'S WEBSITE

WWW.MICHAELWILLIAMSBOOKS.COM

978-0-595-34488-8
0-595-34488-7

Printed in the United States
34629LVS00005B/63